OFF
THE GRID

OFF
THE GRID

To Catch a Thief
Book 3

Kay Marie

All Works By Kay Marie

To Catch a Thief
Hot Pursuit
Stolen Goods
Off the Grid

The Love Match
The Love Rematch
The Love Lie

Confessions
Confessions of a Virgin Sex Columnist!
Confessions of an Undercover Girlfriend!

To my family for their unconditional love,
my friends for their overwhelming support,
and my fans for their incredible enthusiasm.
Thank you from the bottom of my heart.

\- 1 -

Leo

Agent Leo Alvarez stared out the window and across the tarmac at the sinister gray clouds looming on the horizon.

I will not allow a little rain to ruin my first vacation in months, he decided, refusing to let any worry or anger bubble to the surface.

Instead, he leaned back in his cushy chair and took another sip of the red wine he'd grabbed for free at the bar a few feet away. Business class was great—well worth the splurge. He hadn't flown anything besides coach, well, ever, but this lounge thing? He could get used to this. There was free booze, free food, and free newspapers, not that he'd read the one draped across his lap too carefully. He *was* on vacation, after all. But he'd wanted to skim the headlines.

Fifty-Seven Arrested in Second-Largest Mob Roundup in History.

Famed Art Thief Robert Carter Finally Brought to Justice.

Wanted Felon Thaddeus Ryder on the Loose with a Twenty-Million-Dollar Degas.

Yada, yada, yada. Leo knew the details by heart—heck, he'd lived them. He and his partner, Nate Parker, were agents in the Organized Crime Unit of the FBI, and they'd been working on infiltrating the Russian mob for nearly four years. Two years ago, they'd caught their big break on the case that would eventually lead to all these arrests. One of their undercover agents sent word of stolen art being used as collateral in an arms deal their team had been tracking. The painting led them to Robert Carter, an infamous art thief who'd been evading the Feds for nearly half a century. Two weeks ago, Nate had managed to turn Carter's daughter, Jolene, into an informant in exchange for a plea deal. The Russians had somehow gotten word, which sent him and Nate racing down to the Caribbean to save their lead. After a high-speed boat chase, a shoot-out on a private island, and a massive explosion, they'd finally gotten what they'd been after all these years—evidence to use against the Russian mafia in court. Jo gave them access to all her father's files, and though it wasn't airtight, it was more than enough to begin making arrests.

Fifty-seven arrests, to be exact.

During the shoot-out, Nate had taken a bullet to the calf, and was off on medical leave for a few weeks. Despite his partner's absence, Leo had tried to stick around the office to help with the paperwork, but his boss practically shooed him out the door with a pat on the back. *You deserve a vacation, Alvarez. And I don't say that lightly. Now get the hell out of my office before I change my mind.*

Leo had done just that, booking a flight to Hawaii before he had time to second-guess. Because, well, the boss was right—he damn well did deserve a break. The beach, the surf, and a Mai Tai or two sounded as close to heaven as a guy like him could possibly get. His little brother, Manuel, agreed to meet him out there for a few days. Manny lived in San Francisco, so a hop over to Hawaii was practically nothing for him, and he was headed to Hong Kong for business next week, so the timing was sort of perfect. Leo couldn't wait to greet him with a forearm around the neck and a knuckle scrub to the top of his head. Little Manny Alvarez may be a hotshot tech executive now, but before he'd founded the start-up that made him millions, he was a scrawny street kid. To Leo, he'd always be the little brother who needed protecting, no matter how old or how rich he got.

The phone in Leo's pocket vibrated, pulling his thoughts from the past and the ever-darkening sky outside. He jolted, then slid the phone out to read the name across the screen. With a sigh, he answered.

"Don't even think about it, Parker."

"Leo," his partner said slowly, apology already heavy in his voice.

I'm not going to like this. Not one little bit. "Do you know where I am?"

"The airport."

"Do you know where I'm going?"

"That's what I'm calling you about."

"I'm going to Honolulu, Parker. It's six thirty in the morning, my flight leaves in half an hour, and I didn't sleep at all last night so I could finalize all my reports before I left."

"I know, but—"

"Vacation, Parker. A much-needed vacation. I've already bought a packet of Twizzlers and a bag of chocolate-covered almonds for the trip. I spent twenty minutes reading through the in-flight entertainment, picking out the movies I want to watch. Do you know you get a personal TV in business class? And free liquor? And food? And a seat that goes completely flat? Don't take this away from me, Parker. Not now. Not after I saved your ass on that Caribbean island, and helped you get Jo a plea deal, and convinced the guys that your relationship with her was completely legal and not at all a violation of the code of ethics."

"I know." A heavy sigh came through the line.

Leo knew that sigh. He loathed that sigh.

Suddenly, the storm clouds on the horizon weren't what had his heart plummeting. He downed the little bit of red wine he had left and rubbed his palm over his face. *I'm going to regret this. I already do.* He sighed. "All right. What is it?"

"It's Jo."

Of course it's Jo, Leo thought, shaking his head.

For the past month, every aspect of their lives had been about Jo. First, she'd been their target during their stakeout in the Caribbean to get information about the heist she, her father, and her partner, Thad Ryder, were planning. Then, she'd been their lead as they spent a week following her around New York City, trying to uncover her plan and turn her loyalties. Now, she was their informant, giving them everything she could against the Russians and helping them answer the only question left—where exactly Ryder and the twenty-million-dollar Degas she'd helped him steal had gone.

It wasn't that Leo didn't like Jo—he did. She was bubbly and fun, smart and savvy, and watching her turn his buttoned-up partner into a lovesick puppy had been entertaining as hell, but...

Hawaii, he thought longingly. *And Mai Tais. And a few days with my little bro, who I haven't seen in, God, I don't even know how long.*

Leo squeezed the phone in his hand and sighed as the dream slipped away. Nate was his partner and his best friend. They'd saved each other's lives on more than one occasion. If he was calling, it meant something serious was going down, and Leo needed to hear him out.

"What about Jo?"

"Not Jo, so much as her friend."

He scrunched his brows together in surprise. "Her friend? Who? How is she connected?"

"Her name is McKenzie Harper. Age twenty-five. Professional pastry chef. Lives on the Upper East Side of Manhattan, blonde and about five—"

"Yeah, yeah, you can skip the rundown. What's going on?"

"This morning, Jo told me someone hacked into her personal computer. She ran a trace on the IP address but it was scattered. There's no way to know for sure, but she thinks it was the Russians hacking into her messages, looking for contact from Ryder. We both know they're trying to permanently silence the asshole before we can find him."

Leo frowned and nodded. Jo's partner, Thad Ryder, was the only person left who could positively ID the Russians her father had been working with and who could provide eyewitness testimony to their crimes in a court of law. The Feds were after him to offer a plea.

The Russians were after him to offer a bullet to the head. It was a race against time to see who found him first. But Leo and Nate had been taken off the case due to Nate's less-than-professional relationship with Jo, which was fine with Leo. Because…Hawaii.

"Anyway, they were nosing around her chat with two of her online friends, McKenzie and a girl named Addison. Jo tried calling them both, but no answer. I called the local precincts and there's been a missing person's report filed for Addison. Apparently, her boss arrived at her place of work this morning to find a dead body, bullet casings, and a whole lot of blood. We think she was possibly approached by Ryder as a way to contact Jo, but the Russians got wind and interfered. As of right now, we're working on two theories—Ryder kidnapped her to get to Jo, or she was taken by the Russians to use as collateral."

"And McKenzie?" Leo asked, though he had a sneaking suspicion of what was coming next.

"No word."

There was a pause. The silence stretched, full of hesitation on one end and stubborn denial on the other.

Leo caved first. "You want me to go to New York?"

"I wouldn't ask if it weren't important," Nate pushed forward, taking the opening. "I tried the boss first, but he doesn't want to waste an agent on a hunch, not when this police report about Addison down in South Carolina might be a lead on Ryder. He told me to call the NYPD. They're on their way to stake out her apartment. And they're good. I know they're good. They're one of the best police forces in the country, but—"

"They're not me," Leo finished, not bragging, just being honest. Before joining the Feds, he'd been a marine. And before that, the streets in the less-than-desirable neighborhood where he'd grown up had done their part to train him. More importantly, Nate trusted him. Which meant Jo trusted him. Which meant he was the only one either of them would trust with one of her dearest friends.

"They're not you," Nate echoed.

"Okay." Leo hardly believed his ears as the word slipped through his lips. Then again, he did. He'd always had a hard time saying no to the people he cared about, especially when they needed his help. It had never seemed like a character flaw until right now, with the sands from those Hawaiian beaches slipping through his fingers. *Why, why, why did I answer the phone?*

"I'd go myself, but I'm still on crutches dealing with this damn leg injury, and— Okay?"

"You heard me."

"Thank you, Leo," Nate rushed to say, gratitude heavy in his Boy Scout voice. "Really, thank you. I know how much this trip with your brother meant to you, how much you need a vacation—"

"I said okay, Parker," Leo cut in, shaking his head as his partner laid it on thick. "I never said I was happy about it."

Nate snorted over the line. "I owe you for this, Leo. Anything you want, just tell me."

"Oh, anything I want? How generous." Leo grinned. He didn't need anything. This was what partners did for each other, what friends did, but he couldn't help pushing when Nate left him such an easy opening.

"Anything, Leo. Name it."

"How about a new partner?"

"Very funny."

"I've been eying a new Harley…"

"Leo."

"Okay, okay. I'll settle for a business-class seat to Hawaii, leaving from JFK tomorrow night, assuming all goes well."

Nate sighed. "I'll see what I can do."

Leo turned and scanned the board over his shoulder. "So will I. There's a shuttle to New York that's boarding now. I'd better go if I want to catch it."

"Thank you."

"Enough, or you'll give me an even bigger ego than I already have. Don't worry about the flights—that was a joke. I'll figure it out later, after I have McKenzie secure. Just tell Jo I expect some cupcakes or brownies, anything gooey and chocolatey really, when I get back to DC."

"Th—"

Leo hung up and shoved the phone back into his pocket. He hated being thanked for things he felt were common decency to do.

Given the choice between a vacation and saving an innocent life, well, there was no contest. If he chose Hawaii only to find out that something serious had happened to Jo's friend, he'd never forgive himself. Leo had waited months for a break. He could wait a few days more. Manny would understand. It was hardly the first time his job had come between him and his family, and it wouldn't be the last. Life as a Fed was unpredictable, to say the least.

Leo slung his bag over his shoulder and ran across the business-class lounge, ignoring the not-so-subtle looks from the people around him. He burst through the doors and kept going, not pausing until he reached the gate he'd seen on the board, the one flashing *final call* to New York.

"I need to get on this flight, now," he said as he barreled into the information desk.

The attendant kept a pleasant smile on her face, unfazed. She probably dealt with more crazy in a day than most people did in a lifetime. "Of course, sir. If you give me your ticket, I'd be happy to scan it."

Leo flashed her a grin and held up his finger. "About that…"

"You don't have a ticket, sir?" The attendant's lips twitched, but she kept that slightly dead-in-the-eyes yet accommodating expression plastered to her face. *Oh, she's good*, he thought. *I'm going to have to be better.*

"I do have *a* ticket," he answered smoothly, and forced the frustration down as he brought his most debonair expression to his face. "It just happens to be to Honolulu. But there's been a change of plans, and I need to get to New York as soon as possible. Please."

"I'm sorry, sir," she replied calmly. "This flight is full, but I'd be happy to get you on the next available one leaving in…" She looked down and quickly clicked a few buttons on her keyboard. "About two hours."

"That's wonderful of you. Thank you so much for the help. Really, I mean it," he said, holding her gaze.

The edges of her lips twitched appreciatively. He'd learned in his life a little kindness could go a long way, especially when mixed with flirtation—hell, he could only imagine the amount of mistreatment she experienced on a daily basis from stressed travelers. But sometimes, he had no choice but to play the federal-agent trump card. Abuse of power wasn't his typical modus operandi, but if those storm clouds he'd been watching from the business-class lounge were any indication, this airport wouldn't be functioning in two hours. If McKenzie's life was really on the line, he couldn't afford to wait.

"But I'm afraid I have to get on *this* flight, right now. It's a matter of national security."

Her eyes popped wide.

Leo leaned in before she got too alarmed and darted his gaze left, then right, as though what he was about to say were some incredible secret. Then he slipped his badge out from his backpack and casually slid it across the desk. By the time he met her gaze again, curiosity lit those dark brown eyes. She leaned closer, lured by his voice and his words.

He almost had her.

"I'm Special Agent Leo Alvarez with the FBI, and I'm needed in New York as soon as possible. There's been an incident. It hasn't hit the news yet, but I need to be there before it does." Not a lie, technically, just a very, very exaggerated version of the truth. "And I need you to help me. Please."

The attendant glanced around before she spoke to make sure no one else was listening, as though the two of them were in cahoots. "What happened?"

He shook his head slightly and grabbed his badge, then stuffed it back into his bag. "I'm not at liberty to say, but trust me, you want me in New York."

"Well..." She stood straight, looking down at her screen, then up at him, then down again. "I could call my manager, quickly. Maybe there's something she can do..."

"That's all I'm asking," he said, letting gratitude give weight to his words. "Thank you. And your country thanks you too."

He was laying it on thick, but hey—it worked. Ten minutes later, someone offered up their seat for a five-hundred-dollar credit, and Leo took the man's place. While the flight attendants prepared the cabin for boarding, he pulled out his cell phone and dialed. There was one more call he had to make.

"Leo?" A muffled, sleepy voice crackled over the line.

He sighed. "Hey, Manny."

"You do know it's like four o'clock in the morning on the West Coast, right?"

"I know. Sorry, little bro." *No turning back now.* He scrubbed the sleep from his eyes and pressed on. *Goodbye, Hawaii. Goodbye, vacation. Hello, frigging New York.* "There's been a change of plans…"

- 2 -

McKenzie

McKenzie Harper woke up the same way she did every morning—to the beep of her 6 a.m. alarm. She didn't press the snooze button. She didn't grumble or groan. She simply reached over to her nightstand, pressed the *off* button, and sat up, ready to begin the day.

Though she'd been born in Connecticut, New York City was her soul mate—it never slowed, never stopped. It was always go, go, go. Yet there was an order to the chaos, meticulous planning that went on behind the scenes to make sure each detail ran smoothly. The trains worked on a strict schedule. The architecture followed a specific scheme. The natives moved to a set of unwritten rules. And McKenzie liked to think she was the same— structured, precise, and constantly moving forward. Which was why she always began her day the exact same way, like clockwork. First, she eased out from underneath her covers and slid her feet into the slippers waiting on the floor. Second, she made her bed and fluffed her pillows, using an old design trick her mother had taught her to give them extra volume. Third, she brushed her teeth, allocating twenty seconds for her top left molars, twenty for her front teeth, twenty for the top right molars, then repeating on the bottom. As a pastry chef, she could never be too careful. Fourth, she changed into her workout clothes and neatly folded her hair into a braided high ponytail. Fifth, she repositioned her slippers by her bed for that evening. And sixth, she ate breakfast before her daily five-mile circuit through Central Park. Since it was the beginning of summer and the sky was a beautiful clear blue, she stepped out onto her private balcony with her morning meal—overnight oats she'd prepped the day before and a single-serving carton of orange juice.

Her true one-bedroom apartment would be considered a luxury size and location to most New York City residents, but this little four-by-ten sliver of paradise with a table for one was her favorite part. Even at six fifteen, the streets were alive with beeping taxis and barking dogs, with bicyclists and early morning risers. The gentle rustle of leaves provided a subtle background and a reminder that Central Park was only one avenue west of her building. She took a deep breath, pulling the energy into her lungs and letting it linger as a smile rose to her lips. A lot of people came to New York to be discovered, but McKenzie didn't mind staying hidden. In a smaller town, her isolation might've been suffocating, but not here. New York was too alive, too bustling, too vivacious. Here, she never truly felt alone.

Her phone vibrated against the wrought-iron tabletop.

McKenzie pulled her gaze from the street and glanced at the screen. Her grin widened as soon as she saw the message flashing across it, even as her brows scrunched together in confusion.

Addy? At this hour?

@Sprinkle-Ella: HELP!!!

Addison was one side of what McKenzie liked to think of as her little baking trio, a threesome that was completed by their other friend, Jo. Addison was a cake designer in the south, and though her fixation on flowers, the color pink, and all things frilly made McKenzie roll her eyes on a somewhat daily basis, her heart was pure gold. And Jo, well, Jo was the entertainment. She was an at-home baker longing to turn her hobby into a profession, and though McKenzie was at the complete other end of the spectrum—a French-trained pastry chef with a bachelor's degree from the Culinary Institute of America—Jo's drive and enthusiasm were nothing if not admirable, and completely infectious.

They'd met about two years ago in an online forum for fans of a baking competition. Even though they only chatted online, McKenzie still thought of them as her best friends. In some ways, her only friends. The food industry in Manhattan, like every other industry in this city, was cutthroat. She regarded her coworkers as competition instead of as colleagues, and the backwards hours of working in the evenings instead of the mornings didn't exactly make socializing outside of her job easy. She didn't mind being alone though. McKenzie was fine by herself. She was used to it. An only child with two absent parents didn't have the luxury of acknowledging loneliness.

Her phone vibrated again.

One more time.

Whatever was going on, McKenzie was sure it could wait a few more seconds while she finished her oatmeal. Addy and Jo were both prone to dramatics, while she was more practical—she liked completing one task before moving on to the next.

But her curiosity got the best of her, because McKenzie honestly couldn't for the life of her remember the last time either of her friends had texted before noon. She liked to keep to her morning-run routine, Jo was perpetually sleeping in, and Addy never liked to text while she was at work. The afternoons and the evenings were usually their sweet spot.

Okay. What the hell is so important?

Putting her spoon down, she lifted her phone and opened the group chat.

@Sprinkle-Ella: Baking emergency!

@Sprinkle-Ella: This chocolate-obsessed bride is driving me crazy. She wants some sort of soufflé style cake, with a gooey exploding center, covered in a rich, melty ganache...on her wedding day!! Does she not understand she'll be wearing white??

@Sprinkle-Ella: It's a total code brown situation!

Oh, come on! I'm eating. McKenzie nearly spit out the bite of oatmeal she'd been chewing. This conversation was wrong on so many levels. Was Addy serious right now? The last things she wanted to start the day thinking about were code brown situations—of any variety. Not the chocolate kind (that bride was deranged), and especially not the other kind.

Before she had time to respond, a message from Jo came through.

@TheBakingBandit: Code brown?

@Sprinkle-Ella: Code brown.

McKenzie shook her head, unable to quite believe what she was reading. Her friends were…unique. But this was special, even for them.

She opted to give them the benefit of the doubt.

@TheGourmetGoddess: Do either of you actually know what code brown means?

@TheGourmetGoddess: I really don't think you do…

After a moment, a response from Addy came through.

@Sprinkle-Ella: Chocolate emergency…?

McKenzie barked out a laugh, unable to hold it back. The sound gave way to a sigh. *Typical, so typical.* She took a sip of orange juice and another bite of oatmeal before she sank into her seat, eagerly typing into her phone.

@TheGourmetGoddess: You're too pure for this world.

@TheBakingBandit: Email me your recipe for the melty ganache and I'll see if I can think of a way to make it less messy!

@TheGourmetGoddess: You? Help make something cleaner? Am I in an alternate universe?

@TheBakingBandit: I'm a whole new Jo! ;)

@TheBakingBandit: Send me the recipe…

@Sprinkle-Ella: Will do!

@TheGourmetGoddess: Do you actually need my advice? Or do you just enjoy putting me through mental torture?

@TheBakingBandit: The second one!

@TheBakingBandit: Definitely the second one :P

McKenzie snorted under her breath and shook her head. If being neat and orderly and not wanting to discuss code-brown situations at the crack of dawn was a sin, she'd be going straight to hell. But she was pretty sure her friends would be right there with her—for other reasons, of course.

@TheBakingBandit: I'll help Addy out! Don't you worry! Good luck with that presentation today, I know you're going to kill it!

@TheGourmetGoddess: Thanks! If either of you need help with that ganache, just holler. If any other code brown situations come up, leave me out of it.

McKenzie turned her screen off and gathered the trash. It was already six thirty, and she needed to be at the restaurant by 8 a.m. to start preparations. The head pastry chef had gone off on a rant last week and quit. He'd done it before—like she'd said, the food industry in this city was enough to drive anyone insane, and the

French seemed predisposed to dramatics, at least the ones she'd met. This time, however, his dismissal had stuck. The head chef and the owner were done putting up with his bull, and now there was a job opening she intended to fill. Given that she was only twenty-five and a woman, the odds were definitely stacked against her. But she could do it. She'd been the pastry sous-chef in this kitchen for three years, she knew the menu inside and out, and the rest of the kitchen staff loved her—well, tolerated her, anyway. This job was hers to lose. All she had to do was knock her presentation out of the park.

The head chef had been interviewing candidates all week, and today at noon, it was her turn—her do-or-die moment. She had to prep six brand-new desserts for a taste-testing with the head chef, his chief sous, the owner, and two investors. The menu was one she'd been working on for a year, just in case an opportunity like this presented itself, and it was good. French-inspired, but with a creative twist, which was exactly what she did best. Her favorite dish was probably her high-end take on the classic s'more—marshmallow crème brûlée with a caramel-chocolate drizzle served flaming with a cinnamon biscotti on the side. The owner would probably like her traditional croquembouche the best— an impossibly high tower of profiteroles held together by a butterscotch drizzle, stuffed with chocolate buttercream, decorated with spun-sugar poufs and gold-leaf accents. He liked to display one at the front of the house every Christmas season, and McKenzie had never found the prior head pastry chef's to be particularly inspired. Along with those two was a peanut-butter-cup-inspired soufflé, an assortment of éclairs (her absolute favorite dessert—to make and to eat), a berry torte perfect for the summer, and a colorful selection of elegant macarons to complete the set. McKenzie had prepared as much as she could earlier in the week, but the few remaining hours in the kitchen this morning were when the magic would happen.

She'd considered forgoing her run altogether for the extra hour in the kitchen, but in the end, McKenzie knew she needed the time to think. Which was exactly what she did as she laced up her sneakers, turned her phone to airplane mode, and took off toward the park. For forty-five minutes, as her feet pounded down a trail her body knew by heart, McKenzie went over every meticulous detail of the day—a down-to-the-minute schedule, from the time it would take her to shower and travel to the restaurant, to how long she would need to bake each aspect of each dessert, to the exact minute she'd need to take them out of the oven before presenting them to the chef. Her focus was acute. On her run, in the shower, as she dried off, got dressed, and gathered her hair into a tightly coiled bun, she thought of nothing but the details spinning in her head.

McKenzie was a pastry machine and today, not a single thing in the world would get in her way. At least, that was the goal, until the doorbell to her apartment rang.

What the hell? McKenzie looked at the clock on her microwave. It was 7:34, which meant she had exactly ten minutes to catch the subway downtown if she wanted to roll into the kitchen on time. The walk to the station would take two of those minutes, the wait for the train anywhere from two to five more, which left her three minutes to answer the door. Her mysterious caller would be lucky to get even that.

McKenzie took five seconds to glance through the peephole. A man wearing jeans and a plain black T-shirt stood before her door with what appeared to be a backpack slung over his shoulder. He was attractive, there was no denying it, with his bronze skin, hazel eyes, and scruffy black hair, but he was also a complete stranger, which meant she simply didn't have time to deal with him right now.

"Please go away," McKenzie called through the door.

"Miss Harper?"

At the sound of her name, an odd spike of fear flared in her chest. McKenzie was used to New York. There were stalkers, criminals, harassers, and plain-old crazy people, and she'd seen them all, but none of them had ever called her by name.

Whoever this guy was, she wanted him gone—now.

"I'm—"

He stopped talking and widened his eyes as soon as she opened the door, which suited McKenzie just fine. It gave her the opening to fill the silence. "Hi. Whatever you're selling, I'm not interested. I don't know how you know my name, and I don't know how you got past the doorman downstairs. If you come here again, I'll report you. Have a nice day. Goodbye."

Then she closed the door in his face and looked down at her wrist. She still had two minutes spare. *If he's not gone in one, I'm calling the cops. Nothing—and I mean, nothing—is getting in my way today.*

- 3 -

Leo

Leo stared at the closed door with his mouth agape. When she'd first opened it, he'd been struck dumb by her sheer beauty. Reading stats on a screen—blonde, five-foot-nine, blue eyes, slim—and seeing them in person were two very different things. Her features were striking, and they'd slapped him good. But the second she opened her mouth, that smooth skin gained sharp edges, and now he suffered from a very different problem—verbal whiplash. It wasn't that he was used to having women fall at his feet—okay, it was partially that he was used to having women fall at his feet—but the abrupt dismissal stung.

It's the jeans, he reasoned as he lifted his arm to knock again. Normally when he was on the job, he wore a suit, which automatically gave him an air of authority.

The plain clothes were working against him. Leo straightened his shoulders and plastered a suave smile across his lips before he gently rapped his knuckles against the wood a second time.

"Miss Harper, please open the door. My name is—"

"I'm sorry," she cut him off. "I'm not interested."

He ground his teeth. Leo wasn't used to people getting under his skin. He knew how to keep his cool. He was the smooth, good cop to Nate's grumpy stickler. *Be charming. You catch more bees with honey. Don't get annoyed.*

"My name is Leo Alvarez." He finished his previous thought, making his voice a touch louder. "I'm a special agent with the FBI, and I was sent here for your protection."

Let's see what you think of that. He stared at the door, expectant.

Nothing.

Oh, come on! he grumbled silently. This girl was something else.

Leo glanced around the hall, taking note of the marble trim around the doorways, the smooth tile along the floor, the gilded sconces. There'd been a doorman, this was the Upper East Side, and Central Park was less than a football field away. This was a posh building, in a posh neighborhood, with a posh occupant. If there was one thing he'd learned about rich people in his limited time spent with them, it was that they didn't have time for anyone deemed lesser. Right now, to her, he had the sense he was just an unnamed Hispanic guy in a hallway where he didn't belong. Out of place and unworthy. The very thought made his blood boil.

Typical. Fucking typical.

Leo pounded—ahem, knocked—on the door again.

I could be on my way to Hawaii right now. I could be getting drunk for the first time in months with my free business-class booze. I could be tearing up to a sappy drama in the privacy of my overly large, expensive seat with my team none the wiser. I could be—

"If you don't leave, I'm calling the cops."

I am the cops, he wanted to snarl, but he took a deep breath and pulled out his badge instead, then held it up to the peephole indignantly. "There are half a dozen NYPD in the foyer of the building. I'm sure one of them would be happy to assist you."

The door swung open.

That crystalline gaze flicked from his face, to the badge in his hand, back to his face. Her lips pursed and she closed the door behind her, presenting him with her back as she clicked the lock into place. She jiggled the knob three times, as though out of a force of habit, before brushing by him on her way toward the elevator.

"Miss Harper," he said again, tone a little sharper than intended.

"You have the wrong person."

"Are you McKenzie Harper?"

She continued marching down the hall. The rubber soles of her loafers squeaked against the tile floor. The gold bands around her wrist jingled with each step. Her lips, however, were silent.

"I'll take that as a yes," he said and chased after, not used to so much hostility from someone he was trying to protect. A suspect, sure, they gave attitude for days. But everyone else usually treated the Feds with awe and respect. *With a little common freaking decency.*

Not McKenzie Harper.

She lifted her hand with the elegance of a ballet dancer and pressed the button down. Then, and only then, did she finally grace him with her attention and release a heavy sigh.

"Is this about my father?"

"What?" The word blurted out before Leo could stop it. *Her father? What does he have to do with anything?* He made a mental note to look into that later, but cleared the question from his mind. "No. As I was trying to explain before, my name is Agent Leo Alvarez and I work in the Organized Crime Division of the FBI. We have reason to believe you've become a person of interest to some very dangerous people, and I've been assigned to your protection for the next few days, until the threat has passed."

She blinked twice, expression still as stone, and then shook her head curtly. "No, I'm sorry. You must have the wrong person."

Leo sighed, but the sound was covered as the elevator *ding*ed. She stepped on, then turned, extending her hand. For a moment, Leo thought her tune had changed a bit and that maybe, just maybe, she was going to hold the door for him. But no, her fingers turned to the side and pressed a button he couldn't see five times in quick succession.

The elevator door started sliding closed.

For God's sake, he silently growled and jumped forward, catching the metal as it passed the halfway mark. He forced his way inside.

McKenzie lifted her hand to her shoulder and clutched her purse strap, using her elbow to clamp the leather bag against her side. Leo had seen the move plenty of times before.

Relax, lady. I'm not going to rob you.

She kept her eyes glued to the little screen above the door as the fingers of her other hand went to her bracelets and rubbed them in a way that seemed habitual. Her lips moved. It took him a moment to realized she was quietly murmuring the floor numbers as they made their descent.

"Miss Harper," Leo said again, softening his tone, trying a new tactic. "I know this must be a lot for you to take in. You must be overwhelmed—I know I would be. But you are the person I'm looking for, and you need to listen to me. Do you know a woman by the name Jolene Carter?"

McKenzie's head turned sharply and her acute gaze latched onto his, alight for the first time with a flicker of interest. "Jo?"

"Jo, whom I believe you know only as an at-home baker, is in reality an internationally renowned hacker and art thief—"

"Wait—Jo?" McKenzie interrupted.

"Jo."

"My Jo?"

"Your Jo."

"Is a…criminal?"

"*Was*," Leo corrected. "She's reformed. Two weeks ago she handed herself over to the FBI in exchange for an immunity deal, and she's been helping us ever since. Are you aware of the situation that's been in the news recently? The mafia roundups? And a man named Thaddeus Ryder who is on the run from police?"

"I…" She trailed off, blinking slowly, then shook her head. "I watch the news every morning after I run. I know exactly what you're talking about, but Jo? She bakes cookies. And she's a slob. And she was talking to me about code browns an hour and a half ago. There's no way your Jo is my Jo. I'm sorry, there's just not."

"They're the same person," Leo cut in, ignoring that code-brown comment—because, *what?* Finally, this stubborn woman was having a normal reaction, one he knew how to handle with a relentless assault of facts, until denial was no longer possible. Sparing a second, he glanced up. They were four floors from the lobby.

"Jo was partners with Thad Ryder, and when she turned herself in, he went on the lam. The Feds are looking for him, but so is the Russian mob, because if we catch him first and manage to talk him into a deal, Ryder will provide invaluable eyewitness testimony we can use against the mafia in court. Which is what brings me here, to you. Roughly an hour and a half ago, Jo informed the bureau that someone had been hacking into her private files. We believe it was the Russians, looking for communication between Jo and Ryder. Instead, they found her communications with you and your other friend, Addison. We believe they suspected that Ryder was planning to use you or your friend as a way to get to Jo, and they wanted to cut him off at the source. Local police in Riverbend, South Carolina, received a call early this morning, a missing person's report, filed on behalf of your friend Addison. No one has seen her since eight o'clock last night, and the bakery where she worked has been ransacked. At this point in time, it's unknown if she was taken by Ryder or by the Russians, but we have reason to believe someone may be coming for you next."

The elevator *ding*ed and the door slid open.

McKenzie jolted and jerked her head to the side, darting her gaze toward the cops waiting idly in the lobby. Leo was impressed by her awareness. He recognized the look in her eyes—it was the same one he'd seen on any number of the agents he'd worked with over the years. She was in shock, and yet, her mind was shrewd, calmly assessing the situation, cataloguing every detail of what she saw.

Leo didn't like it.

He didn't like it at all.

Hysteria was much easier to deal with, as surprising as that might sound. When a person was falling apart, all they wanted was someone who could hold them together. Leo knew how to deal with that. How to wrap his arm around a victim and subtly guide them to a patrol car. How to hand them a glass of water and get them to open up. How to become their savior. People who could compartmentalize were difficult. They didn't automatically listen. Instead, for better or worse, they questioned.

Worse, he thought with a sigh. *Definitely worse.*

"I believe it's in your best interest to please come with us." Leo tried to pounce before all her mental capabilities returned, but the second he spoke, he already knew it was too late. Those icy eyes turned toward him, cool and calculating. He pressed on. "We'd like to escort you to a safe location—a hotel room we have secured for the next few days. The bureau will pay for all of your expenses, room service included." That wasn't exactly true. Nate was the one who would be hefting the bill, at least until he got formal approval from the boss, but she didn't need to know that. "Think of it as a vacation."

The word stung rolling through his lips. *A vacation.* Black sand beaches and crashing waves flashed before his eyes as he blinked—there and gone, exactly like his moment of victory.

"I can't," McKenzie said, turning toward the front door of her building and hastily stepping away. "Thank you very much for your concern, but I'll be fine. I don't have time to be kidnapped today. I don't have time for a vacation. I don't have time, period. I have to go."

"That's not how this works." Leo chased after her, shaking his head. "They're not going to call you to pencil in a time for your abduction. They'll just grab you."

"Again, thank you for the offer, but I have the most important presentation of my life in a few hours, and I can't waste another minute talking to you." She had a way of making the words *thank you* sound more like *F-U* as they passed through her lips. Leo rolled his eyes. *Frigging New Yorkers.* "I'm sure this is all just a big mistake. Goodbye."

Good Lord, this woman was exasperating, and she'd almost reached the door.

That's it, Leo thought, *no more Mr. Nice Cop. This is for your own good.*

He reached out and grabbed her hand, stopping her where she stood. "I'm sorry, Miss Harper, but it wasn't a request. You're coming with me."

She froze, going still in a way that made the hairs on the back of his neck stand on end, as though she were a predator hiding in the bush one second before launching into attack.

He winced. *I shouldn't have grabbed her.*

"Excuse me?"

Leo dropped her arm in the same second she yanked it free. He gulped as she turned to glance over her shoulder. Death himself would have had a less menacing stare.

"Am I being arrested?"

"No."

"Am I being detained?"

His shoulders writhed. "No, but—"

"Then, like I said, thank you, but no thank you."

Leo glanced around, quickly making eye contact with some of the NYPD watching this interaction go down, hoping someone might step in. They were the best cops in the world, but they stayed quiet. Because he was in their jurisdiction, stepping on their toes in their turf where he didn't belong. He was a Fed, and the Feds never got very warm welcomes from the local authorities.

Before he could think of anything to say, McKenzie shoved the front door of her building open and strode out onto the busy street.

Thanks, guys.

He ran after her.

"Miss Harper!"

She didn't slow.

"Miss Harper!"

She disappeared around the bend.

"McKenzie!"

Not even a pause.

Goddamn, she's fast.

Leo kept his eyes glued on her platinum-blonde bun as he chased her across Eighty-Sixth Street and down a set of stairs to the underground subway platform. Clearly a native, McKenzie didn't miss a beat as she scanned her MetroCard and slid through the turnstile, never glancing back. The screech of a slowing train echoed across the cavernous tunnel, loud enough to make Leo wince as he ran thigh-first into the locked turnstile, no card in hand. He cursed—at his luck and at the bruise he'd no doubt have later.

The first car slid into view. McKenzie took a step forward. Leo put his palm on top of the scanner, shifting his weight. *Now or never.*

He jumped, vaulting over the bars and onto the platform as the doors to the train rolled open. McKenzie followed the herd inside and turned, eyes widening in surprise as she made eye contact with him.

"Miss—"

"Not so fast," a deep voice growled and a hand clamped around his forearm, jerking him painfully back. Cold steel circled his wrist, then cinched into place with a resounding clink. "I saw you jump."

Now, this is a first. Leo sighed. He hadn't seen the cop standing watch on the platform. His gaze had been too locked on the target, but it wasn't his fault. He was used to working as a pair, and Nate usually handled the surroundings.

"Let me go. I'm a Fed."

"Oh, like I haven't heard that one before."

"No." Leo used his other hand to grab his badge and shoved it into the cop's face indignantly. *Three times in one day—that's got to be a record or something.* First the flight attendant. Then McKenzie. Now this. *I'm never going out in casual clothes again. I'll sleep in my damn suits if I have to.* "I really am a Fed, and I have to get on that train."

The cop's jaw dropped and he let go.

Leo turned.

But it was too late. The doors slid closed. McKenzie lifted her palm, offering a small wave as the train lurched into motion and sped away.

- 4 -

McKenzie

The last thing McKenzie saw before the platform disappeared from sight was the fiery glare burning to life in the agent's eyes.

She dropped her hand with a sigh. *That wave might have been a mistake…*

A spark of guilt flickered in her gut. The agent had seemed like a nice enough guy, and he was clearly trying to do what he believed was best. It wasn't his fault he'd been misinformed. Jo and Addy—McKenzie's Jo and Addy—were fine. She'd spoken to them this morning. No one was kidnapped last night. No one was a criminal. They'd been their normal bubbly and entertaining selves, discussing code browns and chocolate ganache without a lick of stress in sight. Even the cops made mistakes, and McKenzie knew that better than most. Any other day maybe she would've tried to explain her apprehension, but not today. Her schedule was too tight. There was no time to waste, especially not for a Fed.

At least, that was what she told herself. But as McKenzie continued to stare into the impenetrable black on the other side of the train window, a memory seeped through the cracks, oozing to the forefront of her thoughts—the real reason she'd simply had to get away. She could blame work as much as she wanted, and it was probably mostly true, but there was something lurking beneath all that ambition. The agent had no way of knowing what his sudden appearance at her front door would unlock, but the little bit of guilt she might have otherwise felt was quickly smothered by the weight of her past.

"McKenzie, honey, would you get that?" her mother called from the dining room, where she sat with two other ladies discussing their upcoming charity auction.

Her father was upstairs in his study, but McKenzie was by the front door, in the middle of untying her cleats. Her mother hated when she dragged mud through the house, so she always sat on the cold stone floor of the foyer the second she got back from soccer practice to tug them off. She stood, one foot bare and the other in a half-undone cleat, and yanked open the door.

Two men in suits stood on the other side, tall and imposing.

She'd never seen them before.

"Is your father home?" one asked. His voice was deep and kind, but overly so, with the subtle hint of suggestion. No one recognized fake in another person's tone better than a middle school girl.

McKenzie crossed her arms. "Why?"

The men shared a look. "We need to speak with him."

"Who's there, honey?" her mother called, a strain of annoyance in her tone. She hated to be interrupted when she had guests—there was nothing more important than maintaining her mirage of perfection.

"Two men," McKenzie shouted back.

"Mrs. Harper?" The man who'd been talking loudened his voice. "Are you home? Could you please come to the door? We need to speak with your husband."

"Excuse me," her mother murmured to her friends. The words were faint, but McKenzie heard the fear laced through them. She turned in time to see her mother freeze as she stepped around the door. Her face fell. A sudden dread raced through McKenzie's nerves, tying them into a bundle of knots.

"Mom?"

"Go upstairs," her mother ordered, voice dark. She kept her eyes on the men.

"Mom?"

"Upstairs, now!" That time her tone was shrill. "Yolanda, take McKenzie to her room, please."

"Yes, ma'am," her nanny answered, appearing out of nowhere. "Come, mija."

A loving hand pressed against the small of her back, guiding her up the stairs as her mother shouted, "Charles!"

McKenzie reached her bedroom door, but before she followed Yolanda inside, she heard her father's study door open. The look in his eyes froze the air in her lungs. She couldn't breathe. He lifted the corner of his lip, seemingly calm, but McKenzie knew exactly what it was—the face of a man trying and failing to be brave.

Her father walked closer and knelt before her, then put his finger beneath her chin. "It'll be okay, Mac. I promise."

Then he hastened downstairs. McKenzie watched him, ignoring Yolanda's attempts to guide her into her room until her father disappeared from view. She spun toward her nanny the instant he was gone.

"Yoyo, what's going on?"

"It's okay, mija," her nanny whispered, using a soothing voice as she guided her into her room.

McKenzie raced for the bay window on the far side of her room, then dropped to the cushions and pressed her nose to the glass. She had a perfect view of the front yard. Two black cars she didn't recognize were parked in the circular drive. On the street, there were three more cars, but they had a word she recognized written on the side—police.

Muffled voices traveled up the stairs like thunder, growing louder, quicker, an oncoming storm. Suddenly, the two men appeared below her window. Her father stood between them, his head hanging low and his wrists bound by gleaming metal. Before McKenzie could process, they shoved him into the car. Her mother ran out, screaming and yelling, chasing after the cars as they slid undeterred down the drive. McKenzie didn't move until two arms came around her, pulling her into a warm chest.

"Estara bien," Yolanda murmured, holding her close and running a soothing hand through her hair. "Estara bien."

It was only then she realized she was crying.

The Feds came back a few more times after that. Once to ransack the house. Once to drop her father off on bail. Once to drag him off to jail. The experience had given McKenzie a knee-jerk reaction to police officers showing up at her front door—hide.

Don't think about that.

Not today.

Bright lights pierced her eyes, painful. McKenzie blinked, clearing her vision and her mind. They'd arrived at the next platform just in time. She gripped a pole to keep her balance as the train slowed, a gut reaction after living in this city for so long. As soon as the doors opened, she strode off. Usually, she waited until the next stop to get off, but she needed to get out of these tunnels. She needed to move. She needed the distraction.

Think about your menu.

Think about your plan.

As McKenzie shuffled with the masses, her focus returned to her food, her one constant. She reviewed the numbers—each perfect measurement, each precise minute—finding solace in their consistency. Baking, at least, would never fail her.

When she finally yanked open the door to the restaurant and stepped into the kitchen, McKenzie was ready. First things first, she pulled out her chef coat, shrugged it on, and double-checked the bun on top of her head to make sure it was still tight. Loose hairs were the death of any great dish. Then she pulled her recipes from her bag—all handwritten and color-coded by time. She had them memorized by now, but it was helpful to have the pages set out along the prep table just in case. Many of the steps had been crossed out—she'd made nearly all the decorations and doughs earlier in the week—but there was still plenty left to do.

McKenzie folded her fingers together and stretched her arms high overhead, taking a deep breath.

You can do this.

You will kill this.

These desserts are your—

The door to the kitchen swung open.

"You're early," McKenzie groaned, trying and failing to stifle her sigh. How many times had she asked the line chefs to give her a few hours alone to prep? "I'm supposed to have the kitchen to myself until— Oh. It's you."

The federal agent she'd ditched in the subway leaned against the wall with his arms folded and a single dark eyebrow raised. "It's me."

McKenzie frowned. "What are you doing here? Who let you in?"

"Someone who respects authority."

Must've been one of the waiters. McKenzie shrugged and returned her gaze to her papers. "I thought I made myself abundantly clear before. Thank you, but no thank you."

"So did I," he said. Out of the corner of her eye, she saw him use his foot to push off the wall. When he reached the prep area, he put his palms against the table and leaned forward, gaze so piercing McKenzie couldn't help but look up. "When I make a promise to protect someone, I honor it. So, I'm here. And I'll be here. Whether you want me to be or not."

The golden highlights in his eyes flared with unspoken challenge. McKenzie was more than happy to oblige. This was her kitchen, her safe place, and she wouldn't be intimidated here. He didn't seem more than an inch or two taller than her, so she put her hands on the table and leaned in, meeting him at eye level. "Some people might call that harassment."

The muscles in his arms flexed, drawing her attention. His bronze skin was contoured and hard in all the right places. "Some people might call it admirable."

"Some people understand how to take a hint."

"Some people understand how to show some gratitude."

"For what?" She scoffed. "Barging into my place of work and promising to stalk me?"

"No," he clapped back, shaking his head. "For sacrificing my time and energy in order to keep you safe."

"I'm not in danger!"

"Yes. You are."

Somehow, their faces had moved closer, a little too close. McKenzie could feel the warm brush of his breath on her skin. The muscles in his square jaw were clenched. A layer of scruff covered his cheeks. His hair swept over his eyes, steeping them in shadow, so only the barest hint of glittering green was visible. She felt that stare in every part of her, as though it were a physical caress. The heat in the kitchen spiked, even though she hadn't had a chance to turn the ovens on yet.

The ovens!

Crap!

McKenzie tore her gaze away, finding the clock on the wall. She was ten minutes behind. She needed to preheat all the ovens, and she needed to start baking, dammit! With a sigh, she slumped her shoulders and relented, if only for the sake of her rapidly disintegrating schedule.

"Fine," she murmured, using her palms to push back off the table and break away from this Fed who had seemingly made it his life mission to babysit her. "Fine, if you're so hell-bent on protecting me, do it. I don't care. But I am not leaving this kitchen and there's nothing you can do to make me. So, go stand in the corner or something, and don't under any circumstances get in my way. Got it?"

"Got it." He stood and stepped back, one foot behind the other, holding her gaze the entire time, until his spine hit the wall. Then he held his hands to either side and arched his brows, as though asking if that was satisfactory.

McKenzie nodded and returned to her work.

Okay, time to croquembouche. She had a hundred profiteroles that needed to be baked, filled with cream, and stacked into a dazzling tower all in under three and a half hours while she finished five other desserts.

"Excuse me," the agent murmured, breaking her concentration yet again. McKenzie slowly slid her gaze across the room to meet his eyes. At least he had the courtesy to appear chagrinned. "It just occurred to me that I have no idea how long I'm going to be standing here. Do you by any chance have a chair?"

Without a word, she marched over to the closet, pulled out a folding chair, and handed it to him before returning to her spot at the prep table.

Okay, now—

"Oh," he interrupted again. And again, McKenzie pulled her gaze across the room to meet his eyes. "Do you know the Wi-Fi password?"

She closed her eyes and held them like that for a moment as she took a breath. "Give me your phone."

He did.

She typed in the password, handed it back, then resumed her spot at the table, hesitating for a second. He didn't say anything, so she turned around to pull her raw profiteroles and cream from the fridge. The dough was cool but no longer frozen. She'd pop them into the oven as soon as the preheat was done. McKenzie squeezed the edge of the piping bag she'd filled yesterday night, forcing a dollop of cream onto her finger to taste. The consistency was nice, thick yet smooth. The chocolate and hazelnut came through nicely.

So far, so good.

When she turned back around, Agent Alvarez was out cold. The back of his head leaned against the wall, tilting to the side. His legs were outstretched and his ankles crossed. One hand held his cell phone flat against his chest, while the other had dropped from his lap to dangle over the floor, lifeless.

My knight in shining armor.

A smile came unbidden to her lips, and McKenzie shook her head ruefully.

She didn't look away, even though she knew she should. The cut angles of his face were softer in sleep. His lips weren't pursed, but plump and slightly opened. His chest rose and fell with deep, peaceful breaths. Her walls lowered, just an inch, as she watched him sleep so soundly, seemingly exhausted by her, or maybe by this city—it had a way of eating people alive.

Just as she was on the verge of finding him somewhat endearing, an offensive snarl erupted from his lips, like a dying lion roaring in its sleep.

What the hell?

McKenzie flinched back. The sound came again, a gravelly engine sputtering and rasping as it hung on for dear life.

You have got to be kidding me. That's not a snore. That's—that's a crime against humanity. My humanity.

The agent didn't seem to care. He snored again, louder this time.

Oh, for the love of God, McKenzie silently growled as she marched across the room and grabbed her bag. She stuffed her earbuds in, then turned her music on. Another snore pierced the air, muffled this time, but there. She slid the volume up to ten and returned to the prep table. *No more, and I mean* no more, *distractions.*

- 5 -

Leo

Leo woke with a start, hand going to the gun at his waist before he remembered where he was—in a kitchen, in New York, no longer stuck in the deserts that haunted his dreams. He took a deep breath and called on the techniques he'd learned to cope. The first step was using logic to calm the panic in his mind.

You're not in the Middle East anymore.

You're in the USA.

You're safe.

His heartbeat slowed. His pulse returned to normal. When the ache in his chest subsided, he focused on the next step—confrontation. He needed to remember the traumatic moment and expose his fear in order to counter its power over him. At least, that was what the self-help books said.

We were infiltrating a suspected terrorist hideout, Leo recalled, forcing the memory to the forefront of his thoughts so he could face it head-on, wide awake and ready this time. *Bullets flew everywhere. I was at the rear providing cover with my M16A4. We were slowly gaining ground.* Through his night-vision goggles, the world had been nothing but shadows and chartreuse light. Until suddenly, everything flashed the most brilliant white, so bright it blinded. He was thrown back with the blast. *I couldn't see. My leg was on fire. There was so much screaming.* When he came to, the house was engulfed in flames and half the team was down. The walls groaned, caving in on themselves. He ignored the pain in his calf and scrambled across the floor to check for survivors. The first three bodies he came upon had no pulses. The fourth one did. It was faint but there, and that was all he needed. *I hefted him over my shoulders and ran. I went back in and saved as many as I could. I did everything I could. I didn't leave anyone behind. Then I got out. I left. I came home.*

The scars hidden beneath Leo's pant leg itched with the memory, but he pushed the feeling down. Rubbing a palm over his face, he wiped the sleep and the nightmares away. He blinked a few times to clear the visions, then scanned the kitchen, dragging his mind forcefully back into the present.

His eyes bulged.

The quiet, industrial kitchen he'd fallen asleep in now bustled with activity. The once-empty prep table in the center of the room was covered in desserts. Three more chefs worked the stovetops, oblivious to his presence. Two waitresses chatted quietly in the corner, not so oblivious, if their quick peeks in his direction and embarrassed smiles were any indication. McKenzie worked in the center of the storm, a white bud in each ear blocking out the rest of the world. Her focus was unbreakable. Every movement was calculated and precise. The look in her eyes was fierce. She was a machine as she drizzled a caramel-like sauce over what looked like a stack of doughnut holes piled two feet tall, though Leo couldn't imagine that was right.

How long was I out?

He glanced down at his wrist—it was almost noon, so about four hours.

Wow…way to go, dumbass.

He sighed and shook his head, disappointed in himself. Contrary to what the woman in front of him believed, Leo had come to New York to protect her, and passing out hadn't been a part of the plan. Apparently, the complete lack of sleep the night before and the free wine in the business-class lounge had proven too strong a combination to ignore. Leo didn't even remember falling asleep. He'd pulled out his phone to text Nate and—*bam!*—he was out like he'd hit a frigging wall.

Crap—Nate! I really am dropping the ball today.

He never sent Nate an update. For all his partner knew, McKenzie was kidnapped and Leo was dead on the side of the street. The thought made him wake faster than anything else possibly could. Leo sat up straight, hand going to his pocket, but it was empty.

Phone. Phone. If I were my phone, where would I be?

He ran a hand over his chest.

I'd been texting Nate when I fell asleep, so…

Leo winced, anticipating the sight before he managed to look down at the floor. There it was, his new phone, in pieces across the industrial tiles. He reached down, snatched the shattered bits off the floor, and tried to press the *on* button. Nothing. The display was black as midnight, blacker even, because at least the night sky still had stars. His screen was a complete abyss.

It must've fallen off while I was sleeping.

Or maybe it slipped when I woke up.

Leo blew a frustrated breath through his lips, letting them vibrate against each other as he pushed the annoyance down. Emotions did nothing in a situation like this. If being a Fed had taught him anything, it was focus on the task ahead, and right now that task was updating his partner. He needed to let Nate know he'd found McKenzie, that she was safe, and that he was watching her. Well, would be watching her—with both eyes open, this time.

"Excuse me," he said, making eye contact with one of the waitresses glancing in his direction. "Could you—"

"Okay, people," a familiar voice interrupted him. "It's go time."

Leo's nostrils flared. *She has* got *to stop doing that.*

He spun in his chair.

"Amy, I need you to take the macarons and the éclairs first." McKenzie kept talking, paying Leo absolutely no mind. She pointed to the right side of the prep table, and Leo couldn't help it as his gaze followed. A tray with five little metal Ferris wheels sat along the edge, decorated with macarons, bright pops of color amid so much stainless steel. Next to that were five chalkboard trays with three éclairs each. The sight made his mouth water. His empty stomach may or may not have gurgled. "Sarah, the soufflés come out of the oven in two minutes and thirty-three seconds, and then I need them served immediately. When you come back, Amy, the berry torte is in the fridge chilling. Then I'll need you both for the crème brûlée. I'm serving it flaming so you need to be careful. And when all that is done, I'll bring out the showstopper. Are we good?"

"Good," one of the waitresses said.

"You got it," the other replied.

"Great." McKenzie nodded, then turned her attention back to the mound of doughnut holes sitting on the table before her. She grabbed a set of tweezers and a flat sheet of gold. Leo watched, confused, as she peeled flakes of gold from the sheet and carefully attached them with studied precision to the display.

"Excuse me," he said cautiously. Her gaze flicked in his direction for the barest instant before returning to her work. The only way he could think to describe the motion was *tired*.

"Welcome back to the world of the living," she commented as her lips twitched.

Leo chose not to acknowledge the remark—hell, he deserved it for falling asleep on the job. "Can I ask..." He watched her apply a few more flecks of gold. Though his mind knew the words that should've completed the question—*can I ask where there's a phone I could use?*—his mouth came up with something else. "What the hell is that thing?"

She didn't pause. "It's called a croquembouche."

"Are those..." Leo took a step closer, letting the words drag out because he knew they were so wrong, and yet, he couldn't stop himself. "Are those doughnut holes?"

One of the chefs near the stovetop started choking.

"No." A sneer passed over her face as though the question were offensive. She glanced over her shoulder at the chef having a fit in the corner, and then looked at Leo. "They're profiteroles."

He stared at her blankly.

"Cream puffs?" she said, trying to explain.

Leo nodded, trying to play it off as though he understood, but the confusion must've been written all over his face. With a sigh, she grabbed one of the little balls from a tray to the side, what appeared to be extras, and tossed it in his direction. Leo caught the pastry smoothly in his fist, then took a bite. Pure buttery, sugary bliss exploded in his mouth.

"Holy shit, these are good."

A smile danced across her lips. For the first time since he'd met her, those blue eyes twinkled with a little bit of warmth. The ice queen dissolved, and in her place was someone definitively human and infinitely more beautiful. Leo much preferred laugh lines and wrinkles to stony perfection.

She inclined her head toward a pot near her elbow. "Use the spoon to drizzle on some butterscotch and then get back to me."

Leo did just that, groaning as he chewed his next bite. She watched, a note of pride in her expression, but not an ounce of surprise. Clearly, McKenzie knew these things were little bites of heaven, and she wasn't ashamed to admit it. Leo blinked as he licked the butterscotch from his lips, looking at McKenzie anew. There was nothing sexier than a confident woman. She held his gaze in unspoken challenge, as though she'd be damned to be the first to look away.

A timer *ding*ed. They both jolted.

McKenzie spun and reached for an oven while Leo finished the pastry in his hand, topping it with another spoonful of butterscotch. By the time she turned around with a baking dish in each hand, she was the machine again—hard eyes and lips pursed in concentration. He could practically see the calculations in her gaze.

Leo turned to the waitress still waiting by the door, taking an educated guess on her name. "Sarah?"

She turned to him with brows raised in question.

Leo pulled the edges of his lips into a wide smile, sinking back into the role he knew how to play—kind, flirtatious stranger. "Could you please point me in the direction of a phone?"

"Sure." She smiled back. "There's an office through this door, down the hallway, and on your left. If you can't find it, there's almost always someone floating around who'll be able to help."

"Thank you."

"And can I just add," she whispered as he pushed open the door, "my boyfriend has a snoring condition, and those little nose-strips did wonders with him. You should give it a try."

"What?" Leo froze, letting the door smack him in the ass as he met her encouraging stare.

She lifted her fingers to her face, gesturing to the arch of her nose. "Those little strips. You wear them at night. I don't really know how they work, but after a few nights, they shut my boyfriend right up."

Leo didn't miss the under-the-breath snicker coming from McKenzie's side of the kitchen, but he pointedly kept his gaze from swerving in that direction. "It can't be that bad."

Sarah winced and dropped her hand as her eyes went wide. "Of course it isn't."

"It can't be."

She nodded and pulled her lips into her mouth, biting them shut.

Leo frowned. "Can it?"

Her eyes narrowed in apology.

Leo stepped into the hallway, letting the door close as his life flashed before his eyes. That girlfriend in college who broke up with him after the first time she spent the night in his dorm. The guys giving him the nickname Buzz at training because they said he sounded like a buzz saw when he slept. His brother sleeping on the living room couch because he didn't want to share a room. He knew he snored…but that bad? Really?

Leo walked down the hallway, keeping an eye out for an office on the left. A waiter approached from the other end, eying him strangely.

"Can I help you?" he asked, but the way the words rolled slowly out made the question sound more like, *Who the hell are you?*

Was suspicion the go-to emotion in this city?

Leo sighed. "Hi, I'm Agent Alvarez—"

The waiter's eyes popped wide with understanding. "Oh, the narcoleptic Fed from the kitchen. What's up?"

Leo growled under his breath. "I need a phone."

"The office phone is back here."

The waiter reached back and pushed open a door. Leo marched through it, located the phone, and dialed. His partner picked up on the second ring.

"Parker, do I snore?"

"Does a bear shit in the woods?"

"No, I'm serious," Leo said, gripping the phone tight as he leaned against the edge of the desk, turning his back to the door. "My snoring, on a scale of one to ten, how bad is it?"

"Leo, what does this have to do with anything? Did you find McKenzie? Are you in New York?"

"Yes and yes. Just humor me."

His partner sighed over the line. "Leo, on a scale from one to ten, where one is a pleasant purr and ten is a jackhammer against the skull, you're an eleven. How's McKenzie?"

He ignored the question. "Why didn't you tell me?"

"I thought you knew."

"How the hell would I know? I don't hear myself when I'm sleeping."

"I guess I figured someone else already told you."

"Is that why you sleep with earplugs when we're on assignment?"

"Obviously. Why else?"

"I don't know, I just assumed you were weird like that."

Nate snorted. "Are you done having an existential crisis?"

"I don't know." Leo shrugged, rubbing a palm over his scruff. "This is a lot of information to take in all at once."

"Buy some nasal strips and get a grip," Nate retorted. Leo scoffed. His partner ignored it and plowed on, getting back to the topic at hand. "McKenzie?"

"The ice queen is fine. I found her at her apartment, and she refused my help. So I chased her down the subway, hopped the barrier, and nearly got arrested, no thanks to you—"

"Well, fare beating *is* against the law."

Leo heard the barely contained laughter in his partner's voice. "And now I'm stalking her at her place of work. If I get arrested for police harassment, I'm taking you down with me."

"It can't be that bad. She's a pastry chef. Ask her if she makes your favorite—cronuts."

Leo rolled his eyes, yet inside he paused. *That's actually not a bad idea.* "Any update on the other friend, Addison?"

"Forensics is still working on a crime-scene report, but we pulled some footage from an ATM across the street. A man matching Ryder's description showed up at her bakery after hours last night, and then two Russian henchmen started shooting shortly after. Based on the tire tracks in the back, my guess is Ryder took off with Addison. Motive is unclear, but Jo thinks he did it in a misguided attempt to save her friend's life."

They both snorted at the same time. A few years as a Fed could turn any kindhearted soul into a cynic.

"Any leads?" Leo asked hopefully. The sooner they caught Ryder, the sooner McKenzie would be safe, and the sooner he could hop on a plane to Hawaii.

"None."

He sighed. "Okay. My phone broke, so I'll call again in a few hours for an update. I'll swing by the field office for a backup after I escort McKenzie home tonight."

"Sounds good." Nate paused. Knowing someone for so long made it easy to anticipate when they weren't quite finished speaking, so Leo waited patiently, even though he already knew the words that were brewing. "And thank you, Leo. I mean it. Thank you."

"Don't sweat it, Parker. What are friends for?"

Not partners. Friends.

"Oh!" he cut in quickly before Nate could hang up, remembering McKenzie's words from before. "There is something you could help me with. McKenzie mentioned her father before, as though he might have been the reason I showed up outside her door. What's the story there?"

"Her father?" Confusion colored his partner's words. "No clue."

"Something in her tone made it sound important. I was going to run a background check before my phone broke. Could you run one for me? Let me know what you find when I call back in a few hours."

"Already done."

"Great. Thanks, man. Oh, and tell Jo I have a new dessert for her. Profiteroles."

"Profiteroles?"

"Go with it. She'll know what I'm talking about."

Leo didn't need to see his partner to know he was currently shaking his head in incredulity. "Bye, Leo."

"Bye, Parker."

They hung up. In the following silence, the creak of the door was unmistakable.

Leo froze.

"If you wanted to know about my father, you should've just asked."

The wince started before he even heard her voice and deepened as that sharp sound sliced through him. Of course it was McKenzie standing behind him, with the way his frigging luck was going today. Who else would it be?

Leo turned slowly, holding back a sigh as he met her frigid eyes. She leaned against the frame with one arm wrapped around her waist and the other holding a plate of desserts, staring at him as though willpower alone could put him in an early grave.

Well…shit.

- 6 -

McKenzie

Pure, unbridled loathing blossomed like a flower in her chest, sending a wave of furious heat down her limbs. To think she'd actually walked over here to apologize!

McKenzie's fingers tightened around the plate of desserts in her right hand, the peace offering she'd so naively decided to prepare now that her presentation was over. Well, the momentary lapse in judgment had passed. Any inkling of pity left in her system was thoroughly flushed away by the words that had just come out of his mouth.

Now, she was pissed.

Which was really a shame, because not even five minutes ago she'd been feeling on top of the world, fully aware she'd hit her tasting menu out of the park.

"I'm not sure what you overheard—"

"Us ice queens aren't known for our hearing," she drawled, cutting him off. The Fed had the decency to wince.

"I'm sorry," he continued, stepping closer. He held his hand aloft as though begging for a moment to explain. "I shouldn't have called you that."

"Why not? It fits." *And I've been called much worse. Sticks and stones, buddy. Sticks and stones.* "My father, since you're so interested, was convicted of embezzlement and fraud, and was sentenced to twenty-five years in federal prison."

McKenzie had been thirteen when her father was arrested, and kids at that age were vicious. Hell, their parents had been vicious too. There was no crime so offensive to rich people as white-collar crime. Her family probably would've been pitied, maybe even forgiven, if her father had murdered someone—but steal their money? There was no coming back from that. McKenzie and her mother had been kicked out of their country club, excommunicated from the social scene, and black-listed from every town function. She eventually dropped out of her private school due to the bullying, not that the public-school kids were much better. Her mother sank into equal parts depression and denial, putting on a brave face and burying all the hurt deep inside, too deep for her daughter to penetrate. If they didn't talk about it, maybe it wasn't happening. If they didn't share their pain, maybe it wasn't real. If they pretended everything was fine, maybe it would be. With that avenue closed, McKenzie retreated to the kitchen. It became her safe space, the only place she could go to release all the emotions she kept pent up inside. After a childhood like that, words had lost their power to hurt her.

Agent Alvarez's jaw dropped.

"He's innocent," McKenzie added as she gave him the good old Manhattan once-over, trying to make him feel smaller than flattened gum on the bottom of a shoe. "In case you were wondering, though I doubt it. Most of the Feds I know never really cared about the truth, only the win. It didn't matter who they put away as long as someone got blamed."

He licked his lips as his brows twitched and a hint of sympathy sparked to life in his eyes. She'd seen that look before—that pitying stare from a cop convinced he was right, and that she was just the grieving daughter steeped in denial. But her father *was* innocent. There was no witness or piece of evidence in the world that would convince her otherwise.

"That must have been difficult," the agent said slowly, each word carefully selected and measured. "I'm sorry you had to go through that."

"Don't be," McKenzie commented, voice clipped— she'd played this game before. *I'd rather be an ice queen than a sucker, Agent Alvarez. Thanks ever so much for reminding me of that fact.* She had half a mind to chuck this tray of desserts at his head. It took all her self-control to instead place it on the desk by his side—after all, it wasn't her food's fault he was an asshole. "I thought you might be hungry after your *strenuous* morning."

The agent's jaw clenched at the dig, but he nodded graciously and kept his mouth shut.

"The rest of the staff is here to start preparations for dinner service, so there's no room in the kitchen for extra bodies. If you insist on staying, I'm sure the owner would be more than happy to set up a table for you in the main dining room. My shift won't end for another twelve hours, so don't expect to see me before then."

"Thank you, Miss Harper," he murmured. "I'll be waiting."

McKenzie held his stare for a moment, hoping the fire in her eyes made him burn, and then she turned on her heels. Before the door clicked closed, she heard a heavy sigh fill the room behind her, but she paid it and him no mind.

Instead, she marched back to the kitchen, redirecting the ire churning deep in her chest. Fury was the best kind of fuel, and McKenzie poured every ounce of frustration into her food, her focus as acute as ever. She was acting as head pastry chef until a new one was officially hired, so even though her presentation was over, the job interview still continued. Could she handle it? Would she fail? Would she flourish? The hours flew as she pumped out dessert after dessert, determined to prove to the head chef exactly what she could do. The chaos of the kitchen was like a warm embrace. Banging pans and hectic shouts drowned out her thoughts. There was no time to think beyond bake times and custards, phyllo dough and caramel. There was only whisk this, and roll that, and stir now, and fry later. Her mind was so full of ingredients and numbers and orders coming down the line, there was no room for anything else.

"Hey, Mac," the head chef called out, hours later, when the restaurant was blissfully empty and the only thing left to do was clean. He was the only person aside from her father who used that nickname, and she found she sort of liked it. "Go home."

McKenzie froze, elbow-deep in suds, and looked over her shoulder. The head chef was a big man and Italian of all things, working in a French restaurant. There was an aura of grandness around him that everyone in the kitchen felt, as though he took up extra space no matter where he stood. Right now, he met her gaze with stark approval, the hint of a grin across his lips. Her heart did a flip inside her chest. "I just have a few more dishes to clean and then I'll head out."

He closed the distance between them and turned the water off. "The line chefs are going to finish up. Head chefs, even acting head chefs, don't have to do their own dishes. And you did good today. You earned a break. So go home, celebrate, get some sleep, and come back ready. You've got a big day tomorrow."

McKenzie was afraid to breathe. *Tomorrow? Does that mean— Is he implying— Did I get the job?* She opened her mouth, unable to stop the question from stirring at the back of her throat.

He nudged his head toward the door with a wink, and cut her off before she could ask. "Home, Mac. You're not getting anything else out of me tonight."

She felt her chest deflate.

He turned away with a laugh.

McKenzie tried to fight the buzz rising beneath her skin as she rinsed her hands off and toweled them dry, but it was no use.

I got the job.

I'm going to be head pastry chef, at twenty-five.

I did it.

I actually did it!

She grabbed her purse from the lockers in the hall and eagerly reached for her cell phone. There were only two people in the world she wanted to talk to right now.

@TheGourmetGoddess: I got the job! I think I actually got the job! And I'm using exclamation points! Jo, you should be proud...and here's a smiley face for Addy :) Yes!

McKenzie tried to press *send*, but an alert popped up. *Please turn off airplane mode to access the messaging app. Click settings for more information.* She blinked and shook her head. *Wow, that Fed really did throw me off my game. I've been in airplane mode all freaking day.*

McKenzie opened her settings and shifted her cellular data back on. The phone in her hand started vibrating immediately.

Missed call from an unknown number.

Missed call from Jo.

Missed call from Jo.

Missed call from an unknown number.

Missed call from Mom.

Missed call from Jo.

You have seventeen new messages.

"Jesus," McKenzie muttered under her breath and shook her head, too tired to deal with it right now. She closed the alerts and returned to the chat with her friends, but paused as a series of new messages flooded the screen.

@TheBakingBandit: McKenzie, call me!

@TheBakingBandit: Are you okay? Did you get this?

@TheBakingBandit: I sent someone to help you! Please call me as soon as you see this.

@TheBakingBandit: Addy is okay, I swear. And I'll explain everything. Just call me.

@TheBakingBandit: Leo's plane landed in New York. He should be to you soon. He's my friend and I trust him. Don't be scared.

@TheBakingBandit: Okay, little miss punctual. WHERE ARE YOU?

@TheBakingBandit: Leo hasn't called. You haven't called. I'm seriously getting worried here. CALL ME!

@TheBakingBandit: CAAAALLLLL MEEEEEEEEE

@TheBakingBandit: Nate just spoke to Leo. He said you're okay. Thank god someone in New York knows how to return a freaking phone call!

@TheBakingBandit: Sorry...

@TheBakingBandit: Clearly, I have no ground to stand on here. But please, call me. Even if you're mad or pissed or whatever. Give me a chance to explain.

@TheBakingBandit: McKenzie...?

What the hell? McKenzie shrugged off her chef's coat, hung it in her locker, and lifted her purse over her shoulder. As she made her way toward the back door of the restaurant, she dialed Jo's number.

"McKenzie!"

"Are you trying to take my ear off?"

"Sorry! Sorry. I'm just excited to hear from you."

"Yeah, I know." She snorted. "The slew of missed texts and calls sort of indicated that you wanted to talk. What's up?"

"Where's Leo? Didn't he explain?"

McKenzie wrinkled her brow as she pushed the door open and stepped onto the dark street, taking a deep breath of New York City air to clear her mind. It wasn't exactly fresh, or particularly clean, but it did the trick. "Who?"

"Leo!" Jo's enthusiasm was on another level. Every word came out a shout. "Oh! Wait! He probably introduced himself as Agent Alvarez to you."

"The Fed?" McKenzie froze. With the hustle and bustle of dinner service, she'd completely forgotten he existed…and was probably still inside waiting for her. *Oh, well. Serves him right.* "You sent him?"

"Yes! Leo's the best. Did he tell you he was on his way to Hawaii? And then Nate called, and poof! Just like that, he's on his way to New York to do us a favor and keep an eye on you. I mean, who does that? He's the nicest guy in the world."

McKenzie frowned. "Hawaii?"

"I know! I mean, I love you, and I don't even know if I would've done that."

McKenzie leaned against the side of the building for support, cold stone rough against her back as her mind whirled. *He was on his way to Hawaii? And he came here instead? For me?* McKenzie blinked as the world blurred in and out of focus, thinking back to their meeting earlier that day. She'd had a one-track mind—pastries, and getting to work, and preparing for her presentation. There'd been no room for anything he'd said, but now her thoughts were wide open. What was it he'd told her?

"That was a joke, by the way," Jo continued to prattle on, filling the silence. "I would've come after you if I could've, but this plea deal with the Feds means I need approval to travel, and well, Addy was sort of kidnapped so she's the priority right now, and—"

"Wait," McKenzie cut in. "You're really a hacker?"

"Reformed."

"And an art thief?"

"Again, reformed."

"And now you're working for the Feds?"

"Uh-huh."

"And the Russian mafia is after you?"

"Well, not me so much as my partner, Thad, but didn't Leo go over this with you? He must've. He—"

"Addy was really kidnapped? Oh my God, is she okay? Agent Alvarez, he said—he told me—but I didn't believe him. I mean, we spoke this morning. We were joking around. You were both fine. You were talking about code browns for Pete's sake. I thought he was misinformed. I thought—"

"It's okay," Jo cut in, trying to soothe. "I would've thought the same thing. Addy is with my partner, Thad. She's been with him since last night, and that whole code-brown conversation this morning was him sending me a secret message through her. *Code brown* is one of our code words—I know, I know. We came up with it when we were twelve, that's my only excuse. Anyway, I spoke to her and she's fine. And now I want to make sure you are too. I know this is a lot to take in, and—"

"A lot to take in?" McKenzie barked, surprised with the bite in her voice. Her heart pounded inside her chest. Her pulse raced. She was losing control—and she never, ever did that. "What the hell is going on? I mean, who the hell are you, Jo?"

"I deserve that." For the first time since McKenzie had known her, Jo's voice was hollow, void of its natural verve. "But I swear, I'm still Jo, the same Jo I've always been. Inventor of the coopie. Aspiring home baker. Your best friend who loves you, and nothing will ever change that, even if you don't want to be my friend after this. The person I am with you and Addy is the real me, the realest version there is, and all this other stuff is just a hurdle I'm trying my best to move past. Please, believe me."

The heartfelt words helped ease McKenzie's panic. She'd always felt the same way. To the outside world, she was the daughter of a criminal, the girl who fell from grace, the ice queen, the poor little rich girl, the Upper East Side bitch. Addy and Jo had always seen through that. With the two of them, she was just McKenzie, just herself—a take-no-prisoners pastry chef. They were her escape. They'd always had her back, no questions asked. Didn't she owe them both the same loyalty, at least until she had all the facts?

Okay, so the circumstances were a *little* more extreme in this case, but what other choice did she have? If what Jo said was true, and the mob was involved, she needed all the help she could get.

McKenzie took a deep breath and counted to ten, finding her calm. "I don't really understand what's going on, Jo, but for right now, I have no choice but to trust you. Agent Alvarez said something about the mafia to me earlier, but I didn't believe him. Are dangerous men really after me?"

"They might be."

McKenzie sucked in a sharp breath.

"Listen," Jo hastily added, sympathy drowning out every other emotion in her voice. "I know this must be terrifying to you, but I promise, it will be okay. Addy is with my partner, Thad, and I trust him to keep her safe. The Russians are following them, so I highly doubt they'll have any reason to approach you. Leo is in New York out of extreme caution and as a favor to me. In a few days, all of this will be over and you won't have anything to worry about anymore. Okay?"

"Okay." McKenzie nodded. Her pulse was already calming. *Focus on the task ahead. Make a plan. You're better with a plan.* "What do I need to do?"

"Go find Leo," Jo said slowly, enunciating each word clearly to break through any lingering panic. "Nate—my new boyfriend, the Fed, you remember him, right? Anyway, he's paying for a hotel room for you. Leo will take you there. It's secure, and no one will be able to find you. Just lie low for the rest of the night, and I'll call you first thing tomorrow to explain everything. Okay?"

"Okay."

She could do this.

Find Agent Alvarez. Follow him to a hotel. Try to get a good night's sleep. And talk to Jo in the morning for a new set of instructions. A simple, easy plan.

She could do this.

"I'm sorry, McKenzie," Jo whispered, a slight tremble in her voice. "I really am. I never meant to involve you or Addy in any of this."

McKenzie squeezed her eyes shut, not quite ready to forgive, not quite sure if this was still her Jo or a complete stranger. But she wasn't ready to throw the towel in on their friendship just yet, not when a true friend was so rare. So all she said was, "I know."

"I'll call you tomorrow. Go find Leo."

"Okay, will do. Bye."

"Bye."

McKenzie dropped her head against the wall at her back and kept her eyes closed for a second. This was crazy. This was insane. It couldn't be happening—but it was. She'd learned long ago that the only thing to do when the world flipped upside down was hunker down and ride out the storm. Denial was for the weak, and she'd already traveled down that road today. It was time to face her problems head-on. The first step was to swallow her pride, find the Fed, and let him do what he'd come to this city to do—save her life.

At least, that was the plan.

But even the best-laid ones tended to go awry.

Tires screeched on asphalt. McKenzie tore open her eyes as a black van hopped the curb and two thick men with guns jumped out. Her instincts kicked in. She pushed off the wall and ran, pumping her arms and her feet, putting those morning jogs to good use. But they were too fast. Or she was too slow. A tree trunk of an arm snaked around her waist and pulled her back into an iron chest, stealing the breath from her lungs. Duct tape covered her lips, muffling her scream. A bag dropped over her head. Twine scratched her skin as it was wrapped around her wrists, clenching them painfully tight behind her back. She struggled, but in thirty seconds it was over. Hands grabbed her biceps and her calves and tossed her into the van. She rolled once, twice, before slamming into something hard.

With two thunks, the doors closed.

The van lurched into motion.

And she was gone.

- 7 -

Leo

Leo turned the bend just in time to see a blonde head disappear into the shadowy depths of an unmarked van. As the doors slammed shut, he reached for his gun and charged.

"Stop right there! This is the police!"

The van took off like a rocket blasting into orbit. Leo emptied his clip, aiming for the tires, keeping the bullets low. They pinged uselessly off the road as the van barreled down the street, but he couldn't risk aiming any higher. If he hit the engine, the car might explode. If he hit the siding, the bullet might pierce the metal and hit McKenzie. He stuffed the gun back into its holster and took off at an all-out sprint. The one good thing about midtown New York was that it made for a bitch of a getaway. The light ahead was red, and the streets were too busy to blow through it. The van slowed…and the head of a semiautomatic rifle poked through the open window.

Leo dove to the side.

Bullets hissed in the air all around him.

He rolled, ignoring the pain as his backpack dug into his skin, and didn't stop until he found cover in an alcove near the side entrance to the building. Dust stung his eyes as bullets ricocheted off stone. Leo pulled another clip from his bag, reached carefully around the corner, and returned fire. He kept the barrel low, aiming to frighten more than anything else.

The bullets stopped.

Tires squealed.

Leo jumped to his feet and ran. The light ahead was green. The van raced through the intersection, going from zero to sixty in a matter of seconds. There was no way he'd keep up on foot, so he grabbed the first thing he could, which was, in typical New York fashion, a taxi. The cab was stopped at the light. Leo yanked open the door and flashed his badge at the driver.

"I need you to follow that van right now."

The man looked over his shoulder, eyes going wide. "I can't, man. I'm in the right lane. I can't make a left turn."

Just his luck—Leo found the only rule-following cab driver in New York City. "Do it. Now!"

He slammed into the seat as the driver pressed the gas and peeled into the middle of the empty intersection. Horns blared. A pedestrian screamed bloody murder.

"Which van?"

"The black one, straight ahead. Don't let it out of your sight. I don't care if you have to run a light. You won't get in trouble. It's a matter of life and death. Do you have a phone?"

The cabbie dug into his pocket and slid the phone through the plastic divider. Leo dialed Nate's number. His partner picked up on the third ring.

"McKenzie's been taken," Leo said, not giving Nate a moment to answer. "A black van with at least three occupants pulled up to the back door of the restaurant as she was leaving. I was waiting by the front door and didn't realize she'd left until a waitress told me. By the time I got around the corner, it was too late. They duct-taped her lips, put a bag over her head, and threw her into the back of the car."

"Do you have eyes on?" Nate asked, slipping into business mode immediately.

"I'm following behind in a taxi. They opened fire—"

"Opened fire?" the cabbie repeated from the front seat.

Leo ignored the outburst. "—so I had to get off the street. License plate is Alpha-Tango-Yankee-One-Nine-Eight-Charlie. I can't tell the make or model."

"I think it's a Nissan," the cabbie added.

"The cab driver thinks it's a Nissan."

"Any idea on destination?"

"We're traveling west on…"

"Fifty-Third Street," the cabbie chimed in again.

"Thanks," Leo muttered. "West on Fifty-Third Street. I see Times Square ahead. My guess is we're heading over the river—probably the George Washington Bridge, though they could be headed upstate via the West Side Highway. They have New York plates."

"Okay, Leo, stay on the line. I'll get the tech team to start tracking your phone, and I'll keep mine on speaker. If you get more information, just say so. I need to step into the other room for a minute to grab the landline so I can call this in, and then I'll be back. Don't lose sight of the target, okay?"

"I won't, Parker. I promise you, I won't."

He heard a click on the other side of the line, then some static shuffling. He dropped the phone into his pocket as the light ahead turned red. The van slowed.

"Don't get too close," he told the cabbie. They screeched to an immediate halt, and Leo's forehead slammed into the plastic divider. "Shit, man. I meant slow down, not stop."

He rubbed what he knew would be a bruise come morning and stared through the windshield. If he got too close, they might shoot. If he got out of the car, they might shoot. If he didn't do either of those things, they might get away. The cab was too obvious. As soon as they reached the highway, the yellow paint would be a beacon to the Russians. It would be impossible to tail them discreetly. He had to find new transport. He had to—

The light turned green and the van took off again.

The cabbie chased after them.

As they flew through the intersection, Leo found the answer he'd been searching for.

"Stop!"

The cab slowed.

"No, I mean stop this time!"

The brakes screeched. Leo held his forearm up to protect his head as he careened forward again. *I really should use a seat belt in situations like this.* He tossed the door open and jumped out.

"Hey, my phone!" the cabbie yelled.

"I'll get it back to you," Leo shouted over his shoulder. There was no time to explain. He had to get back to that intersection before the traffic started moving again. He took off at a sprint as the light changed, flashing a yellow glow over the asphalt. He stepped onto the crosswalk and grabbed the handlebars of the motorcycle as it turned green.

"What the hell, asshole?" the man yelled. "Let go,"

He was dressed in a charcoal suit, and a gleaming Rolex decorated his left wrist. Two recently shined leather shoes rested on the foot pegs. If Leo had to guess, he'd say the guy was a Wall Street banker headed back to his fancy uptown apartment, someone who was used to getting his way.

"I need your bike," he said, lifting his badge with one hand and holding on with the other.

"Fuck off, man. Do you know what this is?"

Leo did, in fact, know what it was. A Ducati 1299 Superleggera, one of the fastest street-legal motorcycles on the market, worth a whopping eighty-nine-thousand dollars—and he'd been itching to ride one.

"Do you know what this is?" He moved the badge closer to the guy's face.

The man sneered.

Horns blared as traffic built from the holdup. Down the street, Leo knew the black van holding McKenzie raced farther and farther away. If he didn't act now, he might lose her. So he did the one thing he knew, as an officer of the law, he probably shouldn't do, but the one thing he deep down found extremely satisfying—he grabbed the guy by the collar, tossed him from the seat, and hopped onto the bike.

"I'm going to sue!"

Leo rolled his eyes and hit the gas.

Damn, this thing is fast.

He sped around the corner and back onto the street where he'd last seen the van. It was nowhere in sight.

Fuck. Fuck. Fuck.

He revved the engine, blazed through the next light, and weaved through the traffic. Up ahead, he caught sight of a black van at the other end of the street turning the corner. He pursued, cutting through the gridlock in the intersection. He turned, realizing they'd reached the West Side Highway, and took off. Leo didn't slow the motorcycle down until the van was comfortably in sight. Then he hung back, careful not to get so close they might notice they had a tail. He followed as they took the exit for the on-ramp to the George Washington Bridge, and reached for the phone in his pocket.

"Parker, we're taking the bridge."

There was no response.

Leo spared a moment to glance around, searching the dark sky for floodlights and scouring his rearview mirrors for any red or blue flashes. "Do you have backup coming? Choppers? Police vehicles? A blockade? Anything?"

Silence was his only answer.

"Parker, are you there?" Leo shouted into the receiver, worried the combination of the wind on the bridge and the speed of his bike were drowning out his words. "Do you copy?"

Nothing.

What the—?

Leo pulled the phone away from his ear and stared at it. The screen was black. He rubbed his finger over the glass, but the darkness remained. He pressed the *on* button. The screen flashed with a low-battery symbol and turned back off.

Dammit!

He had no idea how long ago the call had dropped, how long ago he'd lost contact with his partner, and the bureau, and the only chance of backup he had.

Leo stuffed the phone back into his pocket and gripped the handlebars tighter. A white flash caught his peripheral vision and he glanced back. An NYPD chopper cruised along the edge of the river, beaming a spotlight over the cars on the West Side Highway. Leo turned forward again. The van was almost at the end of the bridge, and Leo was three-quarters of the way across it. The chopper would never find them before they crossed over state lines and into New Jersey, which was probably what the Russians were counting on—switch jurisdictions as much as possible to royally screw the police. Well, there was one agent they hadn't lost yet, and he planned to keep it that way.

Leo followed them down the highway for another fifteen minutes, off an exit, and over a few side streets. He stayed back, always keeping at least a car or two between them, until the van slipped into a warehouse at the end of a block. Leo turned down a side street and cut his engine, using a building as cover. Poking his head around the corner, he waited for their next play. This area was too public, too crowded. It was the sort of place where a pedestrian might hear if McKenzie screamed. Leo suspected they were exchanging vehicles, but there was no way to be sure.

Ten minutes later the black van pulled back onto the street.

Leo hastily rolled the bike behind a parked car and crouched low so he wouldn't be seen from the main road. The van sped past, not slowing down as it zipped by.

His heart thundered.

What if they weren't changing vehicles?

What if it was a ploy?

What if they were waiting me out? Making sure they weren't being followed?

What if McKenzie is in that car right now, praying I'll find her?

What if I just sealed her fate?

His fingers fidgeted, dancing through air as his energy spiked, pulsing through his system with a rush of adrenaline. They itched to wrap around the handlebars and fly into the night. They itched to chase. But his gut was steady, solid, and it told him to wait.

Five excruciating minutes passed.

Leo walked back to the corner, keeping an eye on the warehouse down the street. Another minute ticked by before the nose of a new van poked onto the street, slate gray this time. There was a name painted across the side door. Leo couldn't make it out, but he suspected it was the name of a phony business, meant to ease the minds of laymen who might see the van parked outside their house. He went back to his hiding spot behind the car.

The gray van rolled by, each foot slower than the last. The driver was clearly taking his time to study the streets around him. Leo let go of the breath he'd been holding as relief coursed through his system.

I was right.

I haven't lost her.

I was right.

The only reason they'd be moving so slow was to make sure they weren't being followed, and the only reason they'd be worried about that was if they had precious cargo. Leo ignored the scratch of asphalt against his cheek and kept low to the ground, gluing his gaze to the van as it made its way slowly down the street, almost daring any onlookers to come out of hiding. He wasn't an idiot. Right now, he was outnumbered, outgunned, and lacking the element of surprise. He needed to wait for the opportune moment to strike, and this clearly wasn't it. Actually, he had no idea when that time would come. He didn't have backup. He was facing the most well-armed criminal enterprise active in the United States today. And he had no way to contact his team. Leo was breaking just about every inch of protocol the bureau had hammered into his brain. But there was another code of honor that was drilled even deeper into his core, sewn into the very fiber of his being—leave no man or woman behind. If he abandoned McKenzie now, no one would ever find her again. There wasn't a doubt in his mind that he was her only hope, and he'd promised his friend and himself that he'd protect her no matter the cost.

He planned to keep that promise.

The gray van slipped around the corner. Leo climbed back on the motorcycle and eased it into motion, keeping his lights off and the purr of the engine as quiet as possible. He would wait and watch and follow for however long it took for that perfect window of opportunity to arise.

- 8 -

McKenzie

McKenzie stumbled as her kidnappers pushed her forward. She couldn't see anything with the bag still over her head, but at least now she was on solid ground. They'd helped her out of the van a few moments ago and were now leading her to an unknown destination. Muffled voices caught her ear, too low to decipher. She tried to slowdown to listen, but a palm pressed into her back urging her on. After a few more steps, fingers gripped her tied wrists, jerking her to a halt. They ripped the bag from her head and shoved her through a door. McKenzie tripped over her feet and fell. With her hands still bound, she rolled twice before coming to a stop. She blinked a few times, trying to regain her composure.

Stay focused.

Stay sharp.

She steadied her breathing. If she fell into hysterics, she'd never get out of this. Her only chance was to keep a level head, take in every detail, and wait for her moment. One would come eventually—she had no choice but to believe it would. The key was in making sure she'd be ready to capitalize on it.

McKenzie darted her gaze around the room, cataloging every detail. It was small, no more than eight by eight, maybe a closet of some sort. Two men with guns stood blocking the door—she assumed they were the same ones who'd prodded her in here like a cow into a pen. Though she was tough, she also knew her limits. They were armed and each had a hundred pounds on her. There was no chance she'd be able to break her way through. Pushing the idea from her mind, she studied the space around her, searching for anything to work with. The room was awash in gray. The floor was cool beneath her and smooth from a coat of shiny epoxy. The cinderblock walls were impenetrable. There were no vents and only a single light switch, controlling the bare bulb dangling from the ceiling overhead. A small mattress sat against the wall with one pillow and a set of white sheets.

How long do they expect me to be in here? Her stomach sank, but then she paused and swallowed. *I guess it's better than the alternative.*

Shaking the thought from her mind before fear could stifle her focus, McKenzie turned her attention back to the door. The guards spoke quietly with each other, tossing intermittent glances in her direction. An uncomfortable tingle crept down her spine, but she ignored it and looked past them, to the room barely visible through the gap between their bodies. The first thing she saw was a red convertible with a tan hood and gleaming silver wheels. It definitely looked expensive. Behind it, there was a silver sports car, also pristine and seemingly pricey.

Am I in a garage?

She didn't have a good enough view to see anything else—no tools, no doors, no one besides her guards. Yet she had the sense she was somewhere private, not industrial. The walk from the van hadn't been very far. They'd been outside for a few brief seconds, long enough for McKenzie to hear the wind through the trees, before coming inside. Chances were she was in the basement of someone's home. If she could just get out of this closet, a door outside might not be too far away.

That was a big *if.*

"Water?" one guard gruffly asked, voice deep, with an accent she couldn't place.

McKenzie flicked her gaze to meet his and nodded. She wasn't thirsty—her stomach was tied in too many knots to drink—but she'd do anything to keep the door open a little while longer.

One of the men walked to the side and disappeared from view. The other stepped forward, reaching for her face. McKenzie flinched back. He didn't pause. He grabbed her chin roughly, with no care, and tore the duct tape from her lips. She couldn't help the cry that slipped up her throat. Her skin stung, on fire. The man's hard eyes didn't soften in the slightest. He spun her around, sliced through the ropes binding her wrists, and pushed her toward the bed. Fear cut like an open wound across her chest. McKenzie curled her hands into fists, ready to fight with everything she had, but when she turned around, he wasn't paying her any mind. The guard leaned against the doorway with his arms folded across his chest, watching something out of sight. He blocked maybe half of the opening, which meant the other half was free.

There was no way she'd escape, she knew that much, but maybe escape wasn't the point—not yet. She needed to see what lay beyond her small cell. How many armed men waited out of sight? Was there a door outside anywhere within reach? Could she locate a weapon of some kind? Information was the only tool she had to work with.

So, she ran.

McKenzie lunged through the opening headfirst, taking in everything she could. An arm grabbed her around the waist, catching her midair. Two seconds flat and she was thrown back into the tiny room. She rolled across the floor, closing her eyes before the endless gray washed away the image in her mind.

There were two more cars parked in the other room, and in front of each were massive garage doors. The wall to the left was covered in gadgets of all kinds, household items like brooms and rakes. There'd been a door on the far side, probably leading into the house, and a man stood within its frame. He had coifed white hair and tanned, wrinkled skin. He'd been wearing a collared, button-down shirt, white with blue pinstripes. The moment she lunged through the door, he glanced up, and through his thin-wire-framed glasses she'd met his dark brown eyes, so deep they seemed black from that distance. The contact had been brief but charged, and she'd never forget the expression on his face before she'd been catapulted back into her prison—alarm.

He was panicked.

But why?

Heavy footsteps thudded. McKenzie pushed against the floor and rose to a seated position, glancing over her shoulder as the guard who'd disappeared tossed a plastic water bottle into the room. It crunched as it landed and rolled across the floor, then stopped at her feet. The door slammed shut with a resounding *bang*, leaving McKenzie locked up and alone.

She snatched the water from the ground, took a long sip, and then got down to business. If she was going to get out of here, she'd need some sort of weapon. McKenzie went to the bed first, but it was just a mattress—no frame, no wood, no anything. She glanced up and studied the ceiling, then the walls, then the floor, but the only gap was the sliver of space beneath the door, which didn't have a handle from her side. She pressed her ear to the opening, but the voices speaking on the other side came through as nothing but muffled groans. Even with her cheekbone pressed painfully against the floor, she couldn't see through the crack. All she saw were two spots of shadow that she suspected were the feet of one of the guards.

She rolled over, lay flat, and stared up blankly.

What am I going to do?

What am I going to do?

There were no weapons. There was no way out. There were armed men on the other side of the door, and she had no idea where the hell she was. If what Agent Alvarez had told her was true, she wasn't dealing with fools. The men on the other side of that door were part of the Russian mafia and probably had more experience with making people disappear than she could even imagine.

Oh God.

Oh God.

Panic bubbled beneath her skin. McKenzie was good at keeping her cool. She knew how to compartmentalize, how to focus on what was important and leave the rest for later. But her distractions had run out.

Despite being called an ice queen, she was only human, and she was scared out of her mind.

"Oh God," she moaned softly and rolled onto her side, entire body trembling from the bone-deep chill spreading down her limbs, not from the cold floor, but from desolation. McKenzie hugged her knees into her chest and rocked softly.

Think of something else. Think of anything else.

McKenzie closed her eyes, drawing on the first thing that came to mind—a recipe for palmiers, little cookies made of puff pastry. They were one of her favorites, and they were an absolute bitch to make from scratch, the perfect distraction. Now she just needed something to do with her hands… She forced her eyes open and eyed the mattress one more time.

Sheets. I'll make some sort of a weapon with those.

I've got to.

McKenzie grabbed the top sheet, trying not to think about the last time it'd been washed, and clenched the edge between her teeth. Then she pulled, ripping a strip free. Mindlessly tying knots to keep her fingers busy, McKenzie went over the recipe in her mind. A palmier lived and died by its puff pastry, and the key to that was patience—something she was currently desperate for. The baker needed to make the dough, then flatten the butter, then fold the two together, then refrigerate, then fold, then refrigerate, over and over and over. She imagined she were in a kitchen, not a cage, with a rolling pin, not ripped sheets. She pictured the angles of the folds, the temperatures, the ingredients, the timing, until in her mind's eye, she was pulling a tray of golden heart-shaped goodies from the oven. McKenzie could almost taste the flaky yet smooth cookie, could almost hear the crunch as she bit down, could almost feel the sweet crumbles dissolve on her tongue.

Going through the steps soothed her racing heart. The familiar routine calmed her, until her head cleared enough to see reason. She stared at the makeshift rope in her hands. It looked more like something Rapunzel would've used to repel from her tower than a weapon McKenzie could use to choke someone, but it was better than nothing.

Maybe I can turn it into a lasso or tie their hands or— McKenzie sighed and rolled her eyes. Who was she kidding? She wasn't freaking Wonder Woman. She was just a girl who was in way over her head. *I should've listened to Agent Alvarez when I had the chance. I should've believed him. Why didn't I believe him?*

Because she hated the police and she loved her job, and in the moment, it had been naively easy to let old prejudices blind her. The prospect of becoming the youngest head pastry chef in New York had gone to her head, ambition too heady a drug to ignore. After all, her job was her life. She didn't have any friends aside from

Jo and Addy. She didn't have lovers. Her family life consisted of fifteen-minute phone calls with her father and the occasional trip to Greenwich to visit her mom. The kitchen was her all—the one thing that had always been there for her. Kidnapped, alone, and uncertain if she'd survive the night, McKenzie had a realization—if she could go back, she'd give up head pastry chef in an instant to be safe. She would've followed Agent Alvarez to that hotel room as soon as he'd offered. She would've listened. Jobs came and went. She only had one life.

What if I've been wasting it?

McKenzie had no idea how long she sat on the cold floor, holding her makeshift weapon and contemplating the what-ifs, but the heavy thud of a body slamming into the door yanked her awake in an instant. She flinched and jumped to her feet, muscles aching in protest at the sudden shift. Something banged against the metal door again. A pained groan sifted through the crack, finding its way to her ears. Then a grunt, a wheeze, and a strangled sort of cry.

It was silent for a moment.

McKenzie blinked, wondering if she'd imagined it as the second stretched into two. She took a tentative step forward, lured by morbid curiosity, and held the rope taut between her hands, not exactly sure what she would do with it.

The door flung open.

McKenzie leapt back in surprise, catching the scream in her throat before it had the chance to burst out. She stared into those deep hazel eyes brimming over with concern, unable to believe they were real. Agent Alvarez's gaze dropped to the knotted sheets clenched between her fists. The ghost of a smile passed over his lips, there and gone in a flash, as he looked up.

"Let's go."

He didn't have to tell her twice. Not this time.

McKenzie dropped the rope and took the hand he'd offered, gripping his warm, firm skin like a lifeline. The touch of another human being had never brought her so much comfort. He was real. He was tangible. He was going to save her.

They stepped over the body lying across the door together. McKenzie didn't know if the guard was dead or knocked out. She didn't ask. She kept her gaze glued to Agent Alvarez, studying the curve of the biceps visible beneath the edge of his black T-shirt, the V his shoulder blades made beneath the dark fabric, the sinewy muscles along his forearm, flexed from the pressure of his strong grip. His steps were confident. Authority and experience oozed from his powerful frame. It had been a very long time since McKenzie had felt able to trust another person, but right there in that garage, with his hand guiding hers, she let go of her fear of allowing another person close enough to hurt her.

For the first time in a long time, she knew she couldn't do it on her own.

The door behind them swung open.

A voice called out.

"Get down!" Agent Alvarez shouted, and tugged on her arm.

McKenzie listened.

They dove behind a car, then landed in a tangled heap. He pulled her into his chest and rolled them over so he was on top as bullets sailed overhead. The shots thunked as they hit metal, burying into the side of the car, and glass shattered.

"Not the Aston Martin," the Fed whispered with a wince.

Is he seriously worried about the car right now?

Before she could say anything, he reached behind his back and retrieved his own gun, then returned fire. Shouts filtered through the open door. Boots stomped like thunder.

"We have to go," he muttered.

"No shit." She couldn't help herself.

He glanced down, offering her a wry smile as though he didn't have a care in the world and they weren't being shot at right now. "Think you can keep up?"

Maybe the point was to distract her via frustration— it was working. She forced the words through her teeth, more confident than she felt. "Try me."

He leaned up, using the car as cover, and fired a slew of shots in the direction of those pounding feet. Silence stretched. She wasn't sure she wanted to know what it meant. He crouched back down, pulled another set of bullets from his pocket, then met her gaze. Their faces were so close their noses almost touched.

"On my signal, I need you to run through that open door over there as fast as you can and hang a sharp left. I have a motorcycle hidden in the trees on the side of the house. You won't be able to see it, so just go into the woods and I'll find you, okay?"

"You aren't coming?" The panic in her voice made her wince. It was unnatural to her ears.

"I'll be right behind you," he said, words crisp and clear and infused with unspoken promise. He deepened his gaze, moving a little closer as he reached out and gripped her forearm. Gold flecks glimmered in the depths of his eyes. "Trust me."

McKenzie nodded.

Agent Alvarez spun, peeking over the top of the car.

A door crashed open.

"Now, McKenzie," he shouted as he pulled the trigger. Her fingers trembled. Her heart thundered. "Now!"

She ran.

Her vision tunneled until all she saw was the open door and darkness beyond. There were no guns. No bullets zipping through the air. No shouting voices. There was only freedom. She sprinted, determined that this time she'd be fast enough.

She was.

McKenzie sped through the door and across pavement, until she heard sticks crunch beneath her feet. She darted between trees, not stopping, not slowing, diving farther and farther into the shadows beyond the lights of the house.

"Over here!"

Agent Alvarez's voice was a beacon to her ears, and she turned. He stood behind a large tree, firing his gun toward the house. A motorcycle rested against his hip. As soon as he saw her, he lifted his leg over the seat, then revved the engine.

"Hop on."

It was a death trap, but she didn't care. McKenzie threw herself onto the bike and wrapped her arms around his waist, trying to find solace in how solid and sturdy and invincible he felt. She closed her eyes, buried her face against his back, and focused on the heartbeat thrumming beneath his warm skin as they raced into the night.

- 9 -

Leo

Holy shit! I can't believe I pulled that off, Leo thought as they sped through the forest. Okay, they weren't out of the woods yet—literally or figuratively. But the hard part was over.

He'd hid in the trees surrounding the property for nearly four hours before making his move, taking in every detail. There'd been two guards inside the garage at all times and a third that emerged from the house every half hour or so to circle the perimeter. The trees were dense enough to provide cover and the garage was well lit, making it easy to see through the windows. He'd knelt in the shadows as long as he could, until the barest hint of sunrise lightened the sky, slowly shrinking his hiding place. When the second interior guard marched upstairs, Leo took the opening.

One-on-one he knew he could win, and he did.

He got her out.

Now the only thing left was the getaway.

Leo pushed down on the gas, trying to keep an eye out for tree roots as dawn continued to brighten the sky. McKenzie pressed solidly against his back. Her arms were wrapped in a death grip around his waist—but hey, at least she was finally listening to him. The inability to breathe was negligible compared to the relief bursting like a firework inside his chest.

A break in the trees caught his eye.

"Hold on!" Leo shouted over his shoulder as he swerved around two more tree trunks and then burst through the clearing. He swung the handlebars to the side then slammed the brakes, reaching his right foot out and pressing it against the asphalt to pivot. They cut sharply onto the road, leaving black burn marks in their wake. The tires protested the rough handling.

I know, he wanted to soothe, as though the motorcycle were a child instead of an inanimate object. The way he was treating this ninety-thousand-dollar bike was criminal, and in any other scenario, he'd stop. Right now, there was no time. *I'm sorry.*

He shifted gears and they jetted forward again.

Banging and screeching noises followed behind. He glanced into his side mirror, spotting the same gray van from before hurtling out of the driveway followed by the red Aston Martin peppered with bullet holes. No gunshots rang in the air, which meant one thing—they wanted McKenzie alive. Leo stored that snippet of information in the back of his mind for another time, along with all the other aspects of the night that made no sense at all—the expensive house, the address that had never come up once in the two years he and Nate had been tracking the Russian mob, the fact that they'd even gone after McKenzie in the first place. It was too much to get into now—he had to stay focused. There'd be time to mull over the facts later.

At least, he hoped there would be.

That Aston Martin was creeping a little too close for comfort.

On this old country road, the only place to go was forward. Leo leaned on the gas and pushed the bike harder, muscles contracting to keep the powerful machine in line. Behind him, a bigger engine purred. They raced—fifty miles an hour, sixty, then eighty, up to a hundred. The trees were a blur. Without goggles, the wind brought tears to his eyes. Leo blinked them away, keeping his grip on the handlebars. The van quickly dropped back, unable to keep up, but the sports car pressed on. Every time he glanced at the side mirrors, those bullet-shaped headlights grew bigger and bigger.

The road swerved.

They started to climb.

The convertible changed lanes, ignoring the threat of oncoming traffic as it crept up. Leo darted his gaze from the mirrors to the street, helpless to do anything as the car pulled alongside them. He glanced over, meeting the driver's eyes. They promised death. The man reached underneath his jacket and retrieved a pistol. He fired a warning shot that disappeared into the trees. McKenzie's arms tightened.

Is he bluffing?

Does it matter?

Leo ran through every scenario in a split second. If the man shot McKenzie, she was dead. If he shot Leo, they were likely both dead. A crash at this speed would be fatal. If he was bluffing, well…how long would that last before he got pissed and forgot the game he was supposed to be playing? There were no good options— not when staring down the barrel of a gun. The man straightened his arm, extending the gun closer. Leo glanced forward, calculated the odds, and decided the risk was worth it. He'd never been one to play it safe anyway.

The road turned.

The motorcycle didn't.

"Hold on!"

He jerked on the front of the bike, lifting the nose as they ran off the side of the road and went airborne. There was no guardrail, so he took a gamble that though the drop looked steep, it'd be manageable. They landed hard. McKenzie screamed. Leo kept hold of the handlebars, using every ounce of strength he possessed to keep the front tire straight as they careened downhill, slipping over dirt and leaves and sticks. They were almost near the bottom. The trees thickened. He pressed the brakes as hard as possible to slow their rapid descent. Something popped inside the bike. Leo looked down for a split second, trying to locate the damage. The front tire hit a rock and they went flying.

Leo lifted his arms to cover his face, years of training having drilled into him the importance of protecting his head. He rolled roughly over the forest floor until his thighs hit a trunk and his body spun out, coming to a hard stop. He didn't take a second to breathe. Ignoring the pain, Leo jumped to his feet.

"McKenzie!"

He ran forward and dropped to his knees beside her body, which was as still as—

No, don't even think it.

He forced the memories from his mind and cupped her face, careful not to move her spine as he gently rubbed his thumb across her cheek. It was warm. "McKenzie, wake up."

She didn't stir.

"McKenzie," he whispered, unable to deny the strained, pleading edge to his voice. Leo pressed his fingers to her wrist. The pulse beneath her skin was strong. He leapt over her chest and knelt on the other side of her body. From that angle, he saw the blood dripping from a cut in her forehead. *Dammit, she hit her head.* Leo reached out and lightly pressed his fingers to the already swelling area around the wound.

"Ow," McKenzie groaned and stirred.

"You're all right." A heavy breath pushed the words out in a rush.

"Depends on the definition."

He arched a brow, feeding off her combative tone. "You're alive."

"Barely."

"You're safe."

"Safely in the middle of nowhere."

"You're in one piece."

"Despite your best efforts," she drawled again.

Leo sat back, unable to keep an indignant huff from slipping through his lips as he rolled to his feet. He couldn't win with her—why even bother? Yet just as he was about to turn around and march back to the bike currently in shambles on the forest floor, her voice stopped him.

"Agent Alvarez?" These words were softer than the wind, barely there and raw with a sort of vulnerability he hadn't heard from her yet. Leo hesitantly glanced down, meeting her bright eyes, which were wide and beaming with gratitude. "Thank you for saving my life. I don't—I don't know what I would've done without you."

All the fight left him. Leo reached out his hand. "You can call me Leo."

"Leo," she repeated slowly, as though testing how it sounded on her tongue. McKenzie reached up and grabbed the fingers he'd offered. He pulled her easily to her feet, forgetting how tall she was until she stood nose to nose with him. Her body weighed practically nothing at all she was so slender. Their eyes met across the small distance. Even with that ugly bruise on her forehead, growing more and more purple by the second, she was breathtaking. It took Leo a moment to remember he still held her hand. As soon as he did, he dropped it and turned back to the bike.

"I'm not setting foot—or, well, ass—upon that thing again," she called to his back.

Leo rolled his eyes. "It's not the bike's fault we crashed."

"No. It's yours."

Well, I walked right into that one. He sighed, trying to ignore the amused smile tugging at the corners of his lips. "It's your lucky day, Miss Harper."

"McKenzie."

He ignored the comment—it just felt wrong to chastise someone by using their first name. "This poor, innocent, beautiful bike is well and truly wrecked."

"Good riddance."

"Shh," he admonished. "She might hear you."

McKenzie rolled her eyes. "So that's your thing? Motor vehicles?"

The judgment was thick. He was almost surprised she didn't end the sentence with, *How cliché*. Leo knelt and put his hand against the soft leather seat in silent apology. *She doesn't understand.* Then he looked over his shoulder at McKenzie, unable to halt the grin widening his lips. "A guy who's into cars is no more or less surprising than a woman who's into baking."

Her jaw dropped. Her eyes narrowed. "I'm not *into* baking. I'm a French-trained pastry chef with a bachelor's degree from the Culinary Institute of America."

Leo shrugged and turned his gaze back to the bike. "Then it sounds like you're a woman who's *really* into baking."

"I'm the youngest head pastry chef in New York City, thank you very much."

"Impressive," he answered with honest admiration. McKenzie released an audible breath, like a deflating balloon. Leo tugged his backpack out from the storage box under the seat and pounced on the opening. "Let me see your eyes."

She flinched back. "What?"

Clearly, she had some issues about personal space.

Leo lifted his hands, palms out. "I just want to shine a flashlight in them to make sure your pupils aren't dilated. You probably have a concussion, and I want to make sure it's not anything worse."

Her brows twitched together and she tugged her lower lip into her mouth, but she nodded. This time, when Leo stepped closer, she let him. He cupped her chin with his fingers, then tilted her head up and held it steady. With his other hand, he clicked the flashlight attached to his key ring on. Her pupils immediately contracted. They were maybe a bit dilated, but not by much, and more importantly, they were the same size. He turned the flashlight off but didn't let go. "Do you feel light headed or dizzy?"

McKenzie shrugged. "No, not really."

"Do you have a headache?"

Her right eyebrow arched high, dripping with attitude.

Right, right, the bleeding head wound. "Sorry, stupid question. Are your ears ringing?"

"No."

"Do you feel nauseous? Like you have to vomit?"

"No."

"Can you say 'Peter Piper picked a peck of pickled peppers' five times fast?"

She frowned. "Can anyone?"

Smart-ass. "Just do it."

McKenzie sighed and rolled her eyes dramatically. Pushing her buttons was growing on him. "Peter Piper picked a peck of pickled peppers. Peter Piper picked a peck of pickled peppers. Peter Piper pecked a pike of peppered pick— Argh!"

He pressed his lips together and coughed. "I think you're okay." Leo dropped his hand and stepped back, but McKenzie's probing stare held him captive. He didn't look away. "What?"

"It's just—" She broke off with a shake of her head and dropped her gaze to the floor. Leo didn't move. She lifted it back up a moment later. His heart pinched at the shrewd consideration in those eyes, as though she could see right through him. "How do you know all of this?"

The bureau. He wanted the easy answer to roll right off his tongue, but it lodged in his throat, stuck. Maybe if she knew a little more about him, she'd be able to drop her walls. They were in this together now, for better or worse, and it would be so much easier if she could just learn to trust him. Besides, he'd dug into her past and asked about her father, crossing a line he hadn't known was there. It was only fair she learned a little bit about his past too.

"I was a marine," he said. McKenzie tilted her head to the side with what seemed like genuine interest. "While I was overseas, one of my brothers was— We were— He—"

"It's okay," McKenzie stepped in. "You don't have to tell me."

Speaking about those memories was difficult, near impossible, but the more he did, the less power they had over him. Leo kept on, even as his voice caught and the words stumbled. "A bomb went off and he was thrown back in the blast. He hit his head pretty hard, but when I got to him, he said he was fine. He said the helmet caught the worst of it. I believed him, told him to see a medic when we got back to base camp, and then I forgot about it. That night, he fell asleep and didn't wake up. Internal bleeding, the doctors said. His head injury was a lot worse than any of us realized. After that, I studied what to check for in case it ever happened again. And when I got back home, I took a course in emergency medicine so the next time I was in that sort of situation, I'd at least have a better idea of what to do."

McKenzie watched him. Her expression froze for a moment, and then every inch of it softened. "I'm sorry, Leo."

"Wasn't your fault." He turned away and hefted his backpack from the ground. For some reason, he'd never been able to stand the sight of sympathy.

"Still, I—" She stopped herself, maybe sensing his disdain, and instead said, "That really fucking sucks."

"Yeah," he replied, breathing out a dark laugh. "It really fucking does."

"So." She paused and took a deep breath. "What do we do now?"

"Well…" Leo glanced up the hill toward the road they'd just catapulted off, a little surprised the Aston Martin hadn't already made it back and started shooting. Then he turned his face to the opposite side, staring into dense trees beyond. "The guys who were following us will probably be back any minute, and we want to be as far away as possible before that happens. I say we take our chances with the woods and get some distance between us and them."

McKenzie looked up toward the road, shuddered, then turned back to him. "Sounds like a plan to me."

Leo shrugged his bag over his shoulder and started walking. McKenzie kept pace at his side. He chanced one more glance back to make sure they weren't being followed, unable to quite shake the eerie tickle scratching down his spine.

"I'll call for help as soon as I can," he said—for her benefit or to reassure himself, he wasn't sure. "We have to find another road or a house eventually, right? I mean, we're only an hour or two outside of New York City— how big can this forest be?"

- 10 -

McKenzie

Let's take a stroll through the forest, he said.

It can't be that big, he said.

We'll find help soon, he said.

Well, these damn woods could kiss her ass. They'd been walking for hours, and nothing. Not the hum of a car. Not the smell of a diner. Not the sight of another human being. Nothing. And McKenzie was exhausted.

She considered herself decently healthy, aside from all the taste-testing of her desserts. She ate well. She exercised daily. She slept eight hours every single night. But nothing had prepared her for the exhaustion of mortal terror paired with sleep deprivation, followed by a near-death joyride and an endless hike in whatever godforsaken forest they'd ended up in. She was a city girl through and through. Give her a latte. Give her a taxi.

Give her horns and car exhaust and crowds any day over this. Central Park was about as outdoorsy as she could handle. *To think, people actually pay to go on vacations to do this stuff.*

McKenzie shuddered. The only small favor was that she was miraculously well dressed for the occasion. Who knew that being a chef was such good preparation for a life on the run? The boat shoes she'd picked out for maximum comfort in the kitchen were holding up surprisingly well in the middle of the woods. The long pants she wore to keep her legs safe from boiling splatter now kept her calves safe from scratches and bites. Her white undershirt was a little see-through with sweat and her arms were already a little pink with sunburn, but on the whole she couldn't complain—wardrobe-wise, at least.

Everything else was fair game.

"I'm dying."

Leo didn't pause his stride. He glanced briefly over his shoulder, arched a brow, and turned back around. "You look mighty lively for a corpse."

"Obviously, you've never seen *The Walking Dead*."

The comment earned her a snort.

McKenzie's lips twitched with a smile before she pressed on. "Can't we take a break? Aren't you tired?"

He shrugged and kept marching. "I've been through worse."

McKenzie opened her mouth with a retort, but forced it closed before the biting response could pop out. *He was a marine, you idiot. Of course he's been through worse. He's been through more than you can imagine.*

With a sigh, McKenzie fought through the ache and carried on. Sarcasm was her natural fallback when she was uncomfortable or frustrated or defensive, but she owed him better. He was doing all of this to help her, to save her. The least she could do was quietly try to keep up. Her silence, though, seemed to bug him more.

Leo glanced briefly over his shoulder. McKenzie kept her eyes focused on the forest floor, thick with sticks and leaves and roots, but she felt his gaze without looking. The touch of his eyes was as palpable as a caress, moving around her face, her frame, bringing a heat to her skin. He sighed and stopped walking.

"Let's rest."

"No, it's okay," McKenzie said, and kept going. "You're right. It's not so bad and we should probably take advantage of the daylight while it lasts."

"We're lost with limited provisions," he countered, not loud, but his deep voice still penetrated. "We don't want to push ourselves to the brink of injury."

"How limited are we talking?" McKenzie asked, successfully keeping most of the bite from her tone. She'd thought about asking for water or a snack a dozen times, but managed to refrain.

She assumed if it was available, he'd offer.

Leo nudged his head to the side, pointing out a fallen log a few feet away. They both walked over and sat down. As McKenzie's sore muscles cheered with sweet relief, Leo shrugged his backpack off and plopped it between them.

"We've got..." He reached in, then rummaged around. "Twizzlers." After tugging out a red packet, he handed it to McKenzie. "Chocolate-covered almonds." He took out another bag, blue this time, and gave it to her. "A pack of gum. And, oh, half a bottle of blue Gatorade."

She blinked a few times, staring at him. "Did you steal this backpack from a twelve-year-old on his way to the movies?"

"No. I was—" He stopped abruptly and frowned, returning his attention to his backpack.

"You were what?" she asked, partly curious, partly just wanting to pry.

He shook his head. "Nothing."

"What?"

"No, really. It's nothing."

The wistful edge to his tone made her remember her conversation with Jo moments before she'd been grabbed outside the restaurant. "Plane snacks." She sighed. His gaze jumped up, finding hers, surprised. "You really were on your way to Hawaii?"

"How'd you—"

"Jo."

"It doesn't matter."

Leo glanced away and retrieved the Gatorade from the bag, then lifted it to his lips. He tipped his head back, drawing her eyes to his Adam's apple as he took a long sip. His bronze skin glistened in the sun, covered with a fine layer of sweat. She dipped her gaze lower, noticing the way his black T-shirt stuck to his chest and molded to the contours of his muscles, bringing definition to what must have been very cut six-pack abs. She looked away as her throat, and maybe another part of her, tightened.

"Have some."

He offered her the bottle. McKenzie took it and stared.

How much of this is backwash and how much is actual Gatorade? She wasn't a germaphobe necessarily. Good hygiene just made sense. But her throat felt raw it was so dry, her lips were one step away from cracking, and in the heat, she was already feeling a little light headed. Now wasn't the time for her neuroses to come out of hiding. She took a tentative sip. As the liquid rushed down her throat, all her tension eased away and her shoulders dropped. She tilted her head back for more.

"Not too much," he told her gently. "I'm not sure how long we'll need that to last."

She hastily ended her sip and shoved the bottle back in his direction. Leo offered her the opened bag of chocolate almonds, and she took a handful. Holding her palm before her face, McKenzie arranged the pieces by size, smallest to largest, then popped the tiniest in her mouth first.

"Do you always do that?" he asked, gesturing toward her hand as he reached into the bag, grabbed a few almonds, and threw them all into his mouth at once.

The very sight made her shoulders writhe. "Um. I guess."

"Why?"

McKenzie stared at her palm, wondering who between the two of them was the odd one. She'd been by herself for so long, with no one else to compare her quirks to, that she honestly didn't know. The longer she considered the answer, the more her skin began to crawl. So she took the heat off herself, and shot back, "Why aren't you in Hawaii?"

He held his hands up like a peace offering. "It was just a question."

"So was mine."

He stared at her. She stared right back.

Leo cocked a brow and lifted the edge of his lip in challenge, as though silently whispering, *I'm game if you are.* "I'm not in Hawaii because while I was at the airport, I got a call from my partner, Nate, who also happens to be Jo's new boyfriend. He said one of her friends was in mortal danger and he didn't trust anyone else to keep her safe. So I came, simple as that."

"For a lot of people, that situation wouldn't be so simple."

He shrugged, looking away. "I guess I'm not most people."

No, she thought, studying his profile. His dark hair spilled over his forehead. The barest dusting of scruff coated his cheeks. His jaw muscles ticked as he clenched them, uncomfortable with something about this question, though she couldn't for the life of her guess what. *I guess you're not.* "Why didn't you want to tell me? That doesn't seem like an answer you should have any reason to feel ashamed of."

His head whipped up. "I'm not ashamed. I just…" Leo paused as his brows twitched. "I don't like being praised for things that I think should be deemed common sense."

Are you even real? McKenzie silently asked, studying the golden centers of his eyes as he held her gaze. He was too good, too kind, as though some magic spell had brought a GI Joe to life just in time to come save her. If the situation had been reversed, if she'd been the one to ditch a vacation to come save his life, McKenzie would've thrown it in his face so fast. It was the perfect guilt trip.

That's because New York turned me into an asshole, she thought wryly. *Or maybe I've always been this way.*

McKenzie sighed—she didn't want to focus on herself. Instead, she brought them back to neutral territory, and quipped, "It's a good thing I wouldn't have praised you then."

He snorted, all signs of discomfort wiped from his face. "Oh, really?"

"I've been to Hawaii," she drawled. "The black sand beaches. The turquoise water. The cocktails. Only an idiot would give all that up for me."

He stared at her in amused disbelief.

McKenzie let her knee fall to the side so it nudged his gently, then retreated into her own personal space. "Thank you, Leo, for being that one-in-a-million idiot."

"My pleasure."

He took a Twizzler out of the packet and tore off the end with his teeth. McKenzie looked back down at her almonds. *I need to stop watching him eat.*

"So..." Leo trailed off, leaving the air thick with innuendo.

"So, what?"

"So, what's with your eating habits? I thought we had a deal."

"You know what they say when you assume?" McKenzie dropped another almond into her mouth, relishing the creamy sweetness as it dissolved on her tongue. No matter how many creative desserts she made or tasted, there was nothing quite like the simple pleasure of chocolate. She sucked the coating off before finally biting down on the almond hidden inside. "You make an ass out of you and me."

"Pretty sure we were both assholes already."

A laugh slipped through her lips before she could stop it. "Touché."

"So, are you going to tell me? Or are you going to suck all of the chocolate off yet another almond and pretend you don't know what I'm talking about?"

Something in his tone made McKenzie glance over. The heat in his eyes made her freeze, a deer caught in the headlights one second before impact. An unfamiliar burn spiked down her back as his gaze dropped to her lips, then rose back up, silently questioning what else she could do with her tongue.

McKenzie started choking on her almond.

Karma, you vindictive bitch.

"Whoa!" Leo jumped over and slammed his hand into her back until the piece dislodged enough for her to swallow.

"Thanks," she muttered and drew in a long breath.

"Saving your life is becoming a nasty habit I can't shake."

She glared at him. Leo just widened his grin.

McKenzie relented.

I guess I owe him this much.

"The food thing is… I don't know what it is. When I'm eating a meal, I like to keep all the foods separate so the flavors don't contaminate each other. Then I eat one pile at a time. When I'm eating snacks, I usually find some way to organize them. If it's Skittles or M&Ms or something with color, I divide it by that and eat one group at a time. If it's something more like mixed nuts, I'll divide by type before I dive in. With the almonds, size was the first thing that came to mind."

"Smallest to largest," he commented.

She half-heartedly shrugged. "I like to save the best for last."

"And bigger is…better?"

McKenzie stared at him pointedly, but there was earnest curiosity in his gaze. She couldn't help it. She winked. "Isn't it always?"

His brows drew together with incomprehension. A moment later, the lightbulb went off. He rolled his eyes so hard she thought they might fall out, but there was honest humor sparkling in his eyes. "Can you tell me why?"

"Do I really have to explain it to you?"

"Not that," he interjected, shaking his head as her lips wobbled. "Why with the food? Have you always eaten like that?"

"Sure. I guess."

She looked away instinctually as the lie rolled off her lips. McKenzie knew exactly when the habit started, but she wasn't ready to get into the truth right now. How could she explain that her need for control popped up sometime between when her father was arrested and when she got to school one day to be greeted by the words *Daddy's little see-you-next-Tuesday*—only, the NC-17 version—keyed into her locker? Were there enough words to describe going from a normal teenager one day to a pariah the next? Would she explain that it started small—cutting her sandwich for lunch into cubes, then her grapes into halves, then separating her vegetables by color, then giving up salads because the mixing of all that food made her uncomfortable? Or would she say how she quit playing soccer because the girls iced her out, and suddenly, the rigid rules of ballet, the isolation and precision, became her norm without a team sport to balance it out? Or maybe her baking was the best descriptor, how she'd graduated from messy brownies in the oven to only wanting to work on the most complex French pastries, because the measurements and the temperatures and the times were all that made sense? It boiled down to a sad truth—one that was so common it was trite. As her world unraveled, McKenzie had latched on to the few things within her power to control, and even now, years later, her grip hadn't let up. She didn't need a shrink to tell her that.

"The world can be an unfair place," she finally murmured into the silence, not sure how long Leo was prepared to wait for an answer she wasn't quite ready to give. "I guess I like to hold on to a little bit of order when I can."

McKenzie hesitantly met his gaze. Leo's sharp eyes probed, digging beneath her words, reminding her that his job was to pick apart people's lies. "I'm sorry I asked my partner about your father. I should've come directly to you."

Wiping her hands together, she brushed off any crumbs as she stood. "It's okay. I didn't give you much of an opening to even try."

"I'm sorry about that too," he said.

She felt his gaze on her back but she didn't turn around. Instead, she reached her arms over her head and stretched, lengthening her aching spine and returning some life to her tired muscles. They'd been sitting and talking for too long. If they didn't start walking, she might do something she'd regret, something foolish like let him behind her defenses.

"I should've had a little more patience outside of your apartment," Leo continued, ignoring her attempts to shut the conversation down. "I had no idea the memories my presence might dredge up, but that's no excuse. My training taught me better, taught me to be calm. Instead, I let my exhaustion and frustration get the best of me."

"I'm sure I didn't help."

"No, you didn't," he admitted. She could hear the smile in his voice, a little whisper of joy. It was the only reason she turned around. "But neither did I. And look where it got us."

"Lost with limited provisions?"

"I was going to say abso-fucking-lutely nowhere, but that works too."

She returned his grin. "Should we start over?"

He extended a hand. She slipped her fingers into his, ignoring the way her heart flipped in her chest as he tightened his hold. They shook in the middle of the woods as the sun beat down and smiled at each other like a pair of idiots.

"Leo."

"McKenzie."

They bobbed their clasped palms up and down for far longer than was necessary. She arched a brow. He arched one right back. She pressed her lips together to keep them from widening farther. He didn't bother, and instead beamed across the small distance between them. The warm summer air grew hotter.

"You going to let go?" he asked.

"Are you?"

"I asked you first."

"I—"

Before she could finish the retort, he tugged on her hand and twisted her around so her back pressed against his chest. Their whole bodies touched from head to toe as his strong arm wrapped around her stomach, holding her in place. The air fled her lungs in a whoosh.

"Be careful what you wish for," he whispered into her ear, lips a hairsbreadth away as his breath teased with a ghostly caress. McKenzie jolted away in the exact same moment that he let go. "You know, I was going to offer a piggyback ride since you were so tired, but now I'm not so sure."

McKenzie spun, feeling flames blaze to life in her eyes. "Over my dead body."

"Technically, under it." He winked.

She flushed, which just made her angrier…and him more annoyingly amused.

"Don't be crass," she jibed haughtily, even though she'd been the one making dirty jokes a few minutes before.

Leo shrugged. "Don't give me the opening."

That truce lasted about, oh, ten seconds. McKenzie didn't care if she was going in the right direction, she just started marching, a fire lighting under her feet as his laughter echoed through the empty forest around them.

- 11 -

Leo

It took all his self-control not to shout after her as she stomped deeper into the woods, *I hate to watch you go, but I love to watch you leave.* Cheesy, obviously, but he knew it would get under her skin, which, for some reason, had become his new favorite form of entertainment. Leo suspected the feeling was mutual.

But in honor of their newly established and clearly fragile peace, he put the food into his backpack and ran a few paces to catch up.

McKenzie didn't glance in his direction as they marched through the forest, but Leo found his gaze constantly slipping toward her. Sticks scratched at her arms, bringing red lines to her fair skin. Mud stained her shoes. A thin layer of dirt covered her entire body. The cut on her forehead had started to scab, framed by a nasty bruise. Yet McKenzie hardly seemed to notice. She didn't complain. She didn't cry. She didn't succumb to hysterics. Concentration lit her blue eyes, and Leo couldn't help but admire her tenacity.

He'd been a street kid, then a marine, then a federal agent. He'd seen people get shot, and he'd done the shooting. He'd had much better times, and much, much worse. Situations like this had lost their ability to faze him, but to McKenzie this was all new. In the past twelve hours, she'd been kidnapped, held hostage, shot at, run off the road, and now lost in the middle of nowhere, yet she persevered. The sight of her being so strong made his helplessness an even more bitter pill to swallow.

His brother used to say he had a hero complex—a joke laced with both appreciation and concern. Leo didn't think it was that, but he never told Manny otherwise. He took the hit with a smile on his face and a laugh on his lips, the same way as always. Because in order to explain the truth, he had to go back to a time his little brother probably didn't remember, one Leo loathed to revisit.

The apartment they'd grown up in had been small, with a kitchenette that was little more than a closet off the living room, a bedroom for his parents, and one for him. The hiding places were few and far between. Under the bed was Leo's favorite—the curtain his sheets and comforters made was almost enough to make him feel protected. But there was no spot so safe he didn't hear the smack every time his father's fist landed true, the cries that spilled from his mother's lips, the crash of their already meager possessions shattering upon impact. After Manny had been born, it became easier in some ways, because Leo could focus on his brother instead of the horrible things happening on the other side of their bedroom door. He'd keep his palms flat over Manny's ears and hold him close. He'd wipe the tears from his brother's cheeks and kiss him good night when it was mercifully over.

Helping Manny became Leo's lifeline—which was probably why he snapped the first time that fist turned in his brother's direction. It had been Christmas Day. Leo stood by the door waiting for Manny with his new baseball bat and glove, dying to get outside. His mother sat at the dining table preparing *tamales*. The pork had been slow-cooking all morning, and the entire apartment smelled of chili and cumin. His father was on the couch, watching basketball with a beer in his hand.

Come on! Leo shouted toward their room.

Manny jumped through the door and juggled his new set of toy cars in his hands as he ran down the hall. He was still so young and gangly, all flailing limbs and enthusiasm without a lick of control. Leo remembered it as though it happened in slow motion, even though he knew it wasn't possible, but it seemed that way. Manny tripped on one of the baseballs Leo had left on the floor. His small body flew. Leo remembered thinking, *No, no, no*, as his brother crashed into the TV. The screen wobbled, teetering on the old wooden stand, before toppling to the floor.

No one moved. The silence deafened.

Then his father roared.

Their mother jumped to her feet, trying to reach Manny, but she was too far away. That fist stretched back. Even though he was small, a boy with hardly any muscles at all, Leo reacted. He raised the bat and swung as hard as he could, slamming it into his father's arm. Bone crunched as his father wailed, spinning on his eldest son. Leo saw red. Every ounce of fear and frustration fled the cage he'd crammed them into. He was a child possessed and his father was a half-drunk old man. There was no contest. He swung the bat again and hit his father in the side. Then again, and the man crashed to the floor. He yelled at him to get out. He screamed at him to leave. *I'll kill you if you ever come back. I'll kill you!*

Their father fled.

Leo never saw him again.

Manny had been too young to remember, but Leo would never forget. He'd never spoken about it with his mother. The closest they'd come was later that evening, after she'd put Manny to bed. She walked into the living room, sat next to him on the couch, and took his hand, squeezing it so hard she cut off circulation. The silence spoke louder than words ever could, and they sat there together for hours. Neither of them slept. They just watched as the sky outside shifted from dusk to dark to dawn. It was the first time he could remember looking into his mother's eyes and finding no trace of fear within them. It was the first time he realized how life-changing one action by one person had the power to be. It was the first time he understood how moving it was to see gratitude in another person's gaze.

Leo became a man that day. But no matter how old he grew, he never forgot the boy hiding deep inside—the one hiding under the bed, helpless, alone, and terrified out of his mind. The one with nowhere to go, no way to help, and nothing to do but sit there and listen.

He'd vowed to never be that person again.

"McKenzie?" he called ahead, breaking the quiet that had settled between them.

There were facts he couldn't change. They were in the woods. They were tired. They were lost. They had no idea where they were going. Food was low. Water was nonexistent. The sun was going down. And members of the Russian mob were probably still after them.

But there was one problem he could still do something about.

"Do you mind if I ask you a few questions?" he said, stepping a little faster as she slowed to let him catch up.

"What about?" Her tone was cautious.

"What you saw in that garage."

Relief flooded her face as she turned to look at him. The meaning was clear—business, she could do. Personal, at the moment, was off limits. Leo was just fine with that as he shoved those dark memories back down and settled into a more comfortable role—federal agent.

"Did those men say anything to you?"

She shook her head and shrugged. "Not really. One asked if I wanted water, but that was it."

"Was there anything distinct about his voice?"

"It was deep, a bit gravelly. But no."

"Did he have an accent?"

"Not one I could place."

"Did they speak any other languages?"

"I think so, but I'm not sure what it was. It could've been Russian, but I don't know enough to be positive."

"What did they look like? Would you recognize them in a lineup?"

"Um, I wish I could say yes, but honestly, I'm not sure. It all happened so fast. I didn't see anything when they grabbed me, and there was a bag over my head most of the time. In the garage, one of them was wearing sunglasses, but he had short black hair, light skin, the beginnings of a beard."

"That's good."

"No, it's not." McKenzie snorted. "Don't agent-speak me, Leo."

"Sorry." He met her gaze apologetically. "Force of habit."

She opened her mouth as though to retort, but then stilled. Her brows twitched and her eyes glazed over, just for a second, but he recognized the signs.

"What?"

She turned her face forward, staring at the trees. "It's probably nothing."

"I'll determine that. Tell me, what?"

"It's just— There was one man…" She paused, licking her lips. "I wanted to see more of the room, so I ran through the door and lunged." The edge of his lip quirked into a smile at her foolish bravery. "Before they shoved me back inside, I made eye contact with this man. He had white hair, and leathery skin, like he spent too much time in the sun. He wore a button-down shirt, and he had these really dark brown eyes. Something about him seemed, well, familiar."

That caught Leo's attention. "Familiar how?"

"I'm not sure, like I'd seen him before, in a movie or something. Maybe in the news? There's been so much about the mob on TV these past two weeks. It must've been that."

It was possible.

Leo didn't remember that house or a man of that description being on the bureau's radar, but that didn't necessarily mean they weren't. He was only one agent—he couldn't possibly know everything the FBI was investigating, or hell, even everything his own department was currently investigating. Still though, he couldn't shake the feeling that something was off about this entire situation. It didn't fit the MO. The Russians didn't kidnap civilians, not unless they had to. Ryder had just been spotted in South Carolina, hundreds of miles away. And the mob had nothing to gain from kidnapping McKenzie. So why now? Why her?

"Do you remember anything else?"

"Just the look in his eyes." She reached her hand out and placed it on his forearm, stopping them both. Leo met her gaze, reading the confusion and the questions swirling within her eyes. "He was afraid. I know he was, but I don't know why. And don't give me some smart-ass excuse like it's because he knew you were coming."

"I don't know," Leo teased, trying to lighten her mood. McKenzie had been through enough. She didn't need more weight on her shoulders. "I can be pretty intimidating when I want to be."

"Guess I'm immune." Her tone was flat and sharp enough to cut through all his crap.

So much for that. Leo sighed. "Have you ever heard of Nikolai Sokolov?"

"He's the boss, right?"

He was impressed. "Yeah, and—"

"Was that him?" Her eyes bulged.

"No." She deflated. Leo dipped his head, catching her gaze before it fell. "You should be happy it wasn't him. He's a cold-blooded bastard. We put him in jail two weeks ago, and I have it on good authority that his bail is about to be denied. With him away, there's no clear leadership. The pieces haven't started falling yet, but it's only a matter of time before the tower crumbles from within. Without Sokolov to enforce loyalty, someone will turn, then another, until it's chaos. For them, at least. I prefer to think of it as justice."

"And that's why this guy is scared?"

"Probably."

McKenzie picked up on the hesitation in his tone. "But you think it could be something else?"

Yes?

No?

He settled on, "I'm not sure. But it's not something you should concern yourself with."

"Why the hell not?"

"Because you've been through enough," he told her, making his voice firm. For her own safety, she needed to understand what he was saying. "When we get out of these woods, I'm going to call my team, and the Feds will handle it from there. You'll go back to your apartment, back to your life, and you won't think about it anymore. Don't go digging for answers you shouldn't find, especially where the mob is concerned. It's a good way to get yourself killed."

She gritted her teeth as her nostrils flared. Then she paused and took a deep breath before opening her mouth. "Fine."

"Fine."

"But—"

"No buts." *I saw that coming a mile away.*

She pursed her lips in frustration. "Why—"

"None of that either."

"How—"

"No," he said, unable to quite stifle the laughter in his tone as he reached out and placed a finger over her lips. They were soft and plush and undeniably alluring, even when twisted in a frown—or perhaps especially so. Leo dropped his hand. "Let's change the subject. Tell me about those doughnut-hole things you made—what were they called? Profiteroles?"

She stared at him for a prolonged second, and then rolled her eyes and started walking. "Don't call them doughnut holes. It's a crime against baking. Profiteroles or cream puffs, but for the love of God, not doughnut holes."

His mouth quirked as she visibly shivered. "What was that tower you were making? What was it for?"

"It's called a croquembouche," she corrected, not in a snide way, more of an informative one. The passion in her voice was undeniable, which was exactly what he'd been banking on. The easiest way to shift a conversation was to turn it to something the other person couldn't help but talk about. He used the technique in interviews all the time, to force a victim out of their shock, or to get a tight-lipped informant to open up. "I was making it as a job application of sorts. The head pastry chef of my restaurant quit, and the head chef and owner are interviewing new candidates. That's why I was in such a rush to get out of my apartment when you showed up. I didn't want to be late for my presentation."

"Wait, wait, wait," he goaded. "I thought you were already, and I quote, *the youngest head pastry chef in New York City, thank you very much.*"

She tossed a glare in his direction. "Well, I'm about to be."

"I like a woman with confidence." He elbowed her gently, and the ghost of a smile passed over her lips. She hastily stifled it. "So how do you make them?"

"Well..." McKenzie launched into a recipe. Leo listened, asking questions to keep her talking, genuinely interested.

Yet in the back of his mind, he pictured the man she'd described—white hair, leathery skin, and wealthy enough to own an Aston Martin—running through the headshots and profiles he'd practically memorized he'd been looking at them for so long. Two years spending every waking minute hunting the Russian mob, and Leo came up with nothing.

So what was he missing?

And what did it mean for McKenzie?

- 12 -

McKenzie

"—so I dropped out of Cornell after a semester and told my mom I was going to culinary school instead."

"You dropped out?" Leo asked, mouth agape. "Of an Ivy League education?"

McKenzie snorted. "You sound like my mother."

"I'm sure that went over well."

"You have no idea." She sighed, thinking back to that conversation. McKenzie had been home for two weeks over Christmas break before she decided to break it to her mother that she wasn't going back.

Oh, yes, you are, her mother had shouted.

No, I'm not. McKenzie's voice was stone—she could be pretty stubborn when she wanted to be. Clearly.

You are a Harper! Harpers are not college dropouts, McKenzie Kathleen! I will not accept it.

Yeah, well, I thought we weren't criminals either, but Dad already saw to that.

She'd regretted the words the second they'd passed through her lips—even now, the memory made her wince. But they'd done the trick. Her mother had stormed off, leaving McKenzie alone at the dining table. The slam of that door still brought a scratch down her spine.

"I had a trust fund," McKenzie pressed on, trying to keep her tone as nonchalant as possible. "So there wasn't really anything my mom could do. I don't think she's ever forgiven me for deciding to become a pastry chef instead of a doctor or a lawyer, something that might restore the family name."

Leo frowned at that. "But you're kicking ass, and you clearly love it. Isn't that more important?"

"You'd think," she commented, unable to quite keep the bite from her voice. "But chefs are the *help*. Nothing's going to change that, at least in my mother's eyes."

"Wow." The word slipped out, dripping with disdain.

"Yeah, wow." Sometimes, she hated rich people.

Okay, I'm rich people. Clearly, we're not all bad. Pretentious people—that's who I hate. Pretentious, up-their-own-asses, pandering-to-society, always-worried-what-people-might-think douchebags.

"Anyway, what about you? You must've gone to college to become a Fed. Where?"

"University of Houston, in their honors program. I wanted to stay close to home."

"You're from Texas?" The question blurted out.

Leo arched a brow.

"Not that there's anything wrong with that," she hastily added. "I just— I'm surprised. You don't have an accent."

"The bureau trained it out of me." He shrugged, then grinned. "Agents can't go around saying *y'all* in the middle of an interrogation."

"Are you being serious?"

"No."

She frowned at him.

"Okay, okay." He laughed it off. "Yes, the bureau tries to train people out of their accents, because the best thing an agent can do is always try to blend in, no matter the surroundings. But I grew up in a pretty Hispanic neighborhood, so southern accents weren't our thing."

"Well, you've got the rest of the southern-boy thing down."

"What does that mean?"

McKenzie stared at him. *Really?* Could he possibly not see how annoyingly perfect he was? "You know—the chivalry stuff. Saving the damsel in distress, defending the innocent."

He stopped and put a hand to his chest. "Was that—
I mean, could that possibly have been a compliment?
Coming from you?"

"Of course not," she mocked. "I'm a New Yorker.
We think chivalry is dead. Life is every man or woman
for themselves." *But damn if I couldn't be convinced
otherwise...*

"I'm touched, really."

"So..." She dragged the word out, turning the
conversation back around. "You went to college, then
joined the marines, and now you're a federal agent. Your
mom must be proud."

All that mirth on his face fell right to the floor with
a splat. Okay, the actual *splat* was from his backpack,
which slid from his shoulder and dropped heavily to the
ground. But the effect was the same.

"She is," he answered in a measured tone. "Now."

That little slip of a word instantly sparked her
curiosity. "But she wasn't before?"

"It's nothing."

"Come on—I told you all about my mommy issues."

Leo glanced up at the sky, drawing her eyes to the
same spot. They'd paused in a little bit of a clearing, and
without a thick layer of tree branches overhead, it was
evident that the blue sky was quickly giving way to
sunset. Orange-and-red beams reached out like fingers
dragging ice into fire.

"It's getting dark," he said. "We should probably make camp for the night, and this is as good a place as any."

"Nice try." McKenzie tossed him a pointed look. They were similar in a lot of ways—getting him to reveal personal information was like pulling teeth. Guarded hearts couldn't hide from one another. She knew all the tricks. "Spill."

He took a sweater out of his bag and laid it over the dirt in the small clearing they'd wandered into. Then he sat and patted the spot by his side. McKenzie sank down just as he fell back, crossing his hands behind his head. She grabbed the Twizzlers from his bag and slid one out of the package, then took a bite while she waited for him to fill the silence.

"I didn't...grow up the way you did. I'll put it that way."

McKenzie snorted. "Lucky you."

"I'm not sure I'd say that," Leo murmured softly. A sad laugh spilled from his lips, landing like a drop of water in a still lake, causing ripples.

McKenzie shut her mouth as the wakes washed over her. He was right. And she was being a brat. All things considered, her life hadn't been that bad—and there were plenty of people who had it much worse. Her father was still alive, and she could visit him as often as she liked. Her mother was, well, her mother. She had a great job, good friends, a beautiful apartment, and enough money in the bank to never be concerned. A few tough years as a teen did not a sob story make.

"Sorry," she whispered, glancing over her shoulder. His eyes were glued to the sky. "I'm prying. You don't need to tell me."

"My mom raised my brother and me on her own," he said, as though he hadn't heard her. There was something wistful to the tone. "She was an immigrant and she didn't speak very much English, but she never let that hold her back. She cleaned houses. She worked for a department store for a while. She babysat around the neighborhood. Her favorite job was as a barista at the coffee shop in this botanical garden, because she loved looking out at the flowers all day. She worked two jobs most of the time and kept a tight lid on the finances, trying to save as much as she could so my brother and I could live out the American dream."

"She sounds like an amazing woman."

"She is," he agreed, flicking his gaze toward her. His eyes sparkled in the fiery light of the setting sun. "But she's also a proud woman, and I think that's why she got so mad when I threw everything she gave me away."

He paused. McKenzie extended her hand, offering him an almond, which he took and chewed for a few seconds, lost in thought. The muscles in his jaw clenched, but she waited. It would do nothing to push.

"You see, my brother was—well, still is—a genius. I always knew it. He understood computers before they were even a thing. While I was learning how to do email, he was going into the back end of the software and making adjustments to make it run more smoothly. I knew he was going places, and I didn't want anything to hold him back. So when I got to college, I signed up for the naval ROTC and gave all the money my mom had saved up back to her, so my brother could have it instead. Oh man, was she pissed." He sucked a long breath through his lips, sounding like a boy again, and then tossed a wicked grin in her direction. "She didn't speak to me for months. You've never seen angry until you've seen Latina-mom angry."

"I'll take your word for it."

He laughed—not at her words, but at whatever memory played on behind his eyes. "She said so many curse words in Spanish to me that day. I mean, there were some I'd never even heard before. Half were things I think she made up. But mostly, I think she was scared. She left her family behind, her life, her culture, everything she'd ever known, to come to a strange country so her kids would be safe, and then I turned around and did the one thing that pretty much guaranteed I wouldn't be. I liked being a marine. I liked the brotherhood and I liked believing in something bigger than myself, but I hated the fear I saw in my mother's eyes every time I said goodbye, the worry in her voice every time we spoke over the phone. When my four years were up, I spoke to some of the officers at Quantico about my options. The marine base also houses the FBI Academy, and they recommended me to the bureau. The job still has its dangers, clearly, but I'm not in a war zone. My mom's always been proud of me, at least I think, but now she can be proud without being so afraid, which is a compromise I was more than happy to make. And I like the work I'm doing—it's rewarding, it's challenging, it's always changing and it's important. I get to put evil men in jail for a living."

He shrugged casually.

Is that what the guys who put my father away thought they were doing? Just taking another evil person off the street? Just locking up another monster?

Something in her face must have betrayed her thoughts, because he turned sharply toward her. "I'm sorry. I didn't mean—"

"It's okay," she cut him off. She didn't want to talk about her father, what he may or may not have done. Not now. One messed-up parental confession was enough for the evening. "So what ended up happening with your brother? Did his genius pay off?"

Humor filled Leo's face, making her muscles loosen. "The little bastard went to MIT, wrote an app while he was still an undergrad, and sold it a few months after graduation. He used the money to build a start-up that was later bought by a major corporation, and now he lives out in California. He's worth millions."

In any other situation, she would've spit out her drink. As it was, she glued her lips shut and choked on her Gatorade for a few seconds, until she had it under control enough to swallow. Every ounce of liquid was precious.

"Are you serious?"

He held his hands up. "No joke."

"I hope he didn't forget where he came from."

"Nah, he'd never. He bought me my first Harley-Davidson. She was beautiful. Red paint, silver rims. The engine purred like a cat in heat. I'll never forget the first time I rode her—right back to the dealership. Then I gave him a noogie and told him not to waste his money on me again."

She wasn't surprised. He was exactly the same as the mother he'd described—proud. Too proud to accept a gift like that from his little brother. Too proud to accept her gratitude. If everything he'd told her was true, and she was beginning to believe it was, he possessed that rare sort of kindness that truly didn't want or expect anything in return. The act of having done good was enough.

McKenzie looked away, back to the bag for another handful of almonds. She was a little damaged, she knew, but being around someone who seemed so put together, so flawless, so noble, made her feel all the more broken.

"My mom, though, was more than happy to accept his gift," Leo continued with a delighted sigh. "He bought her a small house near him, so she'd be somewhere safe, with a backyard, so she could grow all the flowers that remind her of home. She won't let him pay anyone to clean it or cook for her or anything like that, but she says she earned that house after putting up with the two of us for so long."

"I'm sure she did."

McKenzie brushed her palms together, trying to wipe off the dirt and crumbs. Her only solace was that it was so dark she couldn't see the grime she was sure was caked all over her body. Leo put the little bit of food they had left into his backpack, then put it under his head like a lumpy pillow. The air was cooler without the sun, and it brought a shiver to her skin.

He mistook it for fear. "We're pretty safe out here, all things considered. I wouldn't worry."

"I wasn't."

Until you said something…

McKenzie shifted her gaze to the trees, which were little more than silver and shadow, streams of moonlight cased in folds of darkness. The leaves rustled. Sticks snapped. The wind whistled, an eerie sort of cry. She turned back toward Leo.

"I'm fairly confident that as soon as you fall asleep, every animal within a one-mile radius will run away in fear."

"Ha. Ha."

She shrugged. "I'm just saying."

A breeze swept through the clearing, bringing goose bumps to her skin. McKenzie rubbed them away.

"Come here."

She glanced down to where Leo was stretched across the ground. Starlight brushed his skin, outlining the contours of his biceps, highlighting his cheekbones and his jaw, a face that could've been cut from stone. He held an arm to the side, an open invitation.

"I don't bite."

"That's a shame." She fought a wince. *Now is not the time for inappropriate sexual humor. Stupid defense mechanisms!*

He arched a brow, as though to say, *Really?* "Body heat. It's survival 101."

She sighed.

He was right and she was being an idiot. They were still lost in the middle of the woods. Getting hypothermia out of sheer stubbornness would get her nowhere.

McKenzie lay down cautiously, putting her head against his arm. His muscles stiffened at her touch. She swallowed, suddenly finding her chest was tight.

He didn't give her time to protest.

Leo rolled over, closing the distance between them, sealing her back to his stomach in an airtight embrace. His other arm slid around her hip, cradling her close, encasing her in a cocoon of warmth. Her heart thundered in her chest, but she was bone tired and exhausted. Before any of her instincts had time to kick in, McKenzie fell sleep, at peace against all odds with her current situation.

- 13 -

Leo

Leo couldn't remember the last time he'd spent the night with a woman. Sex was one thing. It was fulfilling a need. It was meet someone at a bar, go to her place, and leave a few hours later. It didn't need to be personal. But spending a whole night curled in a woman's embrace, holding her close—that was something else entirely.

He was terrified.

Night was the only time when he felt truly vulnerable. During the day, he could pretend all he wanted. He could feign confidence. He could laugh things off with a smile. He could fool everyone. In sleep, his defenses were down, and that was when the demons crept out of hiding.

He'd suffered from nightmares for as long as he could remember. As a boy, he imagined monsters. As a teen, he envisioned his father coming back to seek revenge. They were just dreams, easy to shake off as soon as he woke up and remembered where he was. The war changed everything. Whenever he closed his eyes, he was back there in the desert, back with the gore and the screams. They weren't made-up fantasies. They were memories that took hold of his mind and didn't let go, claws that dug so deep he couldn't shake them off. The terror was real because his body remembered it, his mind clung to it, a self-inflicted punishment for all the bodies he'd left behind.

Leo had never been to a doctor—he knew plenty of guys who had it worse—and when he'd applied for a job at the bureau, he kept the information to himself. The last thing he needed was to fail the psych evaluation. Hiding it wasn't all that hard. He never screamed that he knew of. He never cried out or made noise. He thrashed occasionally. Sometimes he'd wake up on the floor or with his sheets in a tangle or with bruises he couldn't place. It got better over time. He read up on therapies and learned different techniques to help control it. None of his roommates at the FBI Academy ever commented. Nate was the only person who Leo suspected of knowing the truth, but his partner didn't ask questions. And his job made it easy to avoid relationships—to make sure no one got close enough to see the cracks in his shell, to get cut by them.

Tonight with McKenzie, though, there was nowhere to run. She needed his body heat, they needed to stay together, and if he was being honest, he enjoyed the feel of having another person so close. Isolation was safe, but was also lonely. As soon as he closed his eyes, he'd be laid bare. There was no way to know what might happen. Would he hurt her? Would she see the hurt he tried to hide?

Those questions haunted him as he fought to remain awake long after McKenzie's body went slack within his arms. Her breathing was smooth and even, a soothing rhythm. Her heartbeat echoed in his chest, thumping against his skin until his own slowed to match. She was tall and made of lean muscle, yet somehow, still soft in that way a woman's body was made to be. Her waist seemed crafted to hold his arm.

Their bodies molded together, each curve so perfectly aligned there was no space in between. They were both dirty and sweaty, but as he settled his head behind hers, a floral scent still clung to her hair, fresh and vibrant. Those blonde locks were molten silver in the moonlight, her pale skin a creamy white, both bright against the dark forest beyond.

Leo wasn't sure when he eventually succumbed to sleep, but he woke at the sharp pain of an elbow jabbing into his ribs.

"Leo, shut up," McKenzie grumbled, hardly awake.

"What?" He came alive in an instant, eyes flying open as he breathed deep, pulling air into empty lungs. He'd been right on the edge, right on the precipice of something. It was as if she'd caught him right before he'd gone tumbling over a cliff. "What?"

"Shut up."

"I didn't say anything."

"I can't sl—" The words faded as a long yawn took her voice captive. "—with all that racket."

He blinked, bringing the world back into focus. The sky was still dark and speckled with stars. The woods were quiet. He'd rolled over onto his back, but McKenzie was still in the exact same position on her side. He released a long breath and smiled. *Snoring. I must've been snoring.* "I'm not entirely sure how your inability to sleep is my problem."

She groaned in protest. "Just...shut..."

She was out before she finished the sentence. Leo rolled his eyes. *We're in the middle of the woods sleeping on hard dirt, and I'm the thing keeping her awake?* But it was just snoring—not talking or screaming or shouting. Just a little snore or two—practically nothing. He calmed his thrashing heart and rolled over onto his side, bringing his arm around her waist again. She shivered and wriggled closer, burrowing against his chest. He surrendered to her warmth and her curves, slipping back to the sleep before he had a hope to fight it.

He came alive again at the sound of McKenzie's scream.

Leo was on his feet immediately. His mind was still on a battlefield. Bullets popped in his ears. Men shouted. Agonized cries filled the air. A mix of sand and dust and ash dried his throat. Leo's hand went for the gun at his waist, fingers clicking the safety off on instinct. In a blink, he'd dropped to the ground and pulled McKenzie behind him, then lifted his weapon in the air.

He blinked.

Once.

Twice.

But there were trees. It was light out. It was quiet, nothing but rustling leaves and chirping birds. The world was calm, serene even. Because he was in the woods with McKenzie on American soil, and no one else was around. With a sigh, Leo dropped the weapon and squeezed his eyes shut, trying to shake the potent memories from his head as the real world came back into focus.

"I'm sorry, Leo," a pained voice whispered behind him. "I didn't mean—"

"No, it's fine."

"I overreacted. It's just— I woke up and that fucking thing was sitting on my head!"

He turned around and looked down, watching McKenzie run her fingers through her hair and shake her head back and forth with a wrinkled look of disgust on her face. *She's not paying attention to me. She has absolutely no idea that I'm the one who overreacted.* The realization calmed him enough to let a smile quirk the edges of his lips. "What fucking thing?"

"That—" She snapped her head up, eyes slightly wild as they scanned the leaves. "Where'd it go?"

"I'd be more helpful if I knew what you were looking for."

"A squirrel." She said it as though the animal were the devil incarnate. "A fucking squirrel."

"You're freaking out about a squirrel?" he asked, unable to keep the hilarity from his tone. She'd kept her cool during a kidnapping, a gunfight, and a high-speed chase, but a squirrel was her undoing? He couldn't believe it. "The ones with the cute bushy tails?"

"Don't be fooled by a bit of fluff," she muttered, holding her hands before her as though one might come flying through the leaves at any moment. What was she going to do—judo chop it to the ground? "I *hate* squirrels. They're the assholes of the animal kingdom. One step above rats, one step below pigeons. I had a dog growing up, a golden retriever named Beau. He was the best. Anyway, there was a tree outside my bedroom window, and this fat, instigating mofo of a squirrel would just sit there every day and stare into my room, taunting Beau. Every fucking day. And Beau would lose it, barking and going wild, and that *thing* wouldn't move.

It'd slowly chomp on a nut, as though Beau was the entertainment and it had all the time in the world. I swear, the fucking thing smirked."

"I don't think they can do that."

"Well, that one did. And the one I woke up to was the same way, sitting on my head, lounging—hell, plotting. I'm telling you, it was up to no good."

He crossed his arms and lifted his brows in disbelief as she walked around him in a circle, a hunter on the prowl.

"You laugh now," she accused. "But just wait."

"I didn't say a word."

She grunted.

A ruffling sound sliced through the quiet, like papers being shuffled.

McKenzie whipped her head around, finding Leo's eyes. "What was that?"

"Probably a squirrel…in a tree…because we're in a forest."

"No, it sounded like plast— Aha!"

She pointed triumphantly toward the ground. Leo slowly dropped his gaze to follow, seeing nothing more than his flattened sweater and his backpack.

"There's noth— Whoa!" He jolted back as his backpack moved. "It's in my bag?"

"It's in your bag."

They locked eyes and both shouted, "The food!"

"Shoot it!" McKenzie demanded.

He stared at her. "I'm not going to shoot it."

"Okay, then what's your grand idea?"

"I'll just— I'll—"

McKenzie put her hands on her hips. The backpack continued to move around. Leo scowled and stepped forward. He grabbed the bottom of the backpack, flipped it upside down, and shook it. The squirrel tumbled out— along with everything else in his possession—and landed on its feet with a Twizzler between its teeth. They stared at it. It stared at them. Leo took a step closer. The squirrel hastily stuffed four chocolate-covered almonds into its cheeks, until they were so full they might pop, and took off into the trees.

"Ballsy little bastard," he grumbled.

"I told you, they're assholes." McKenzie sighed and knelt next to Leo, surveying the damage. "Did it get all of our food?"

"Just about." Leo held up the empty pouch of Twizzlers, then jiggled the almonds. "There's a few of these left."

"Dump 'em."

He shrugged. "They're probably—"

"Leo, I'm dirty. I'm tired. I could use an IV drip of coffee, and I'm starting to get hangry. If I could, I would grab that bag out of your hands, stuff every one of those almonds in my mouth, and eat them in front of you. I wouldn't even share. But that thing could've had rabies. It could be diseased. We don't know. Without a hospital nearby, we can't risk it."

Damn, she does hate squirrels. "Okay."

He turned the bag over and a handful of almonds dropped out.

Whelp, there goes our food.

He stuffed the empty plastic into his backpack and grabbed the Gatorade. There were maybe one or two sips left. He downed half and handed it to McKenzie, who finished the rest. Then he picked his stuff up off the ground—one broken phone, one wallet, one set of noise-canceling headphones, his last two magazines of ammunition. McKenzie helped, handing him the paperback that had fallen out—a Tom Clancy novel—and his gum—cinnamon, because he didn't mind a little heat. He stuffed the charging cord for his broken phone back in, then froze when he heard McKenzie snicker.

"What?" He didn't bother to look up.

"Nothing, it's just a, well, an interesting juxtaposition."

Leo turned. McKenzie wore a shit-eating grin and held her hands out. A condom rested on one palm and a set of rosary beads on the other.

"I didn't know that was in there."

"Which one?" Amusement was thick as honey in her tone, sickly sweet.

"The condom." He glowered as she grinned, and snatched it from her palm. "The rosary I take everywhere."

"Really?" Surprise colored her voice. "I didn't peg you as religious."

"I'm not." He shrugged and took the rosary from her palm, a little more gently this time. He tucked the string of beads into a zippered pocket and carefully sealed it tight. "But my mom is. This was hers. It was a confirmation gift from her mother. My grandpa carved the crucifix from a tree in their backyard. She gave it to me before I left for the Middle East on my first tour. For good luck, she said. I've carried it with me everywhere I go ever since."

He kept his gaze on the ground, feeling the weight of McKenzie's stare. There was no reason to tell her, no reason she had to know. He wasn't really sure why the explanation popped out. The more time he spent around her, the more natural it felt to open up, as though maybe deep down he'd yearned for companionship, even as he'd pushed people away. But there was no pushing her away—they were stuck with each other, whether they wanted to be or not.

"I didn't mean to make fun," she murmured, voice soft, vulnerable. He glanced over, eyes drawn to the spot where her lower lip was pulled nervously between her teeth. A sudden urge to kiss it loose punched through him, striking like a blow and knocking the air from his lungs. He tore his eyes away. "That's really beautiful. And hey, maybe it's working. I mean, divine intervention is as good a reason as any for how the hell we ended up here."

As soon as she finished speaking, thunder crackled, booming and breaking and tearing like something trying to rip through the heavens. They both snapped their heads up, noticing for the first time the thick clouds blanketing the sky.

"Divine intervention, huh?" he teased.

McKenzie found his gaze. Her bright eyes sparkled. "It's just a working theory."

He shook his head and threw his bag over his shoulders. "Come on. We want to be somewhere safe by the time the storm hits."

McKenzie held his gaze and pushed her brows together. "How far do you think we are from civilization?"

Leo had no idea.

A few miles, maybe—if they walked in a straight line. In the woods, it was hard to tell. They could've been moving in circles all day yesterday without realizing. The landscape blended together. Without a compass or a trail at their disposal, east became west, north became south. He'd tried to follow the arc of the sun the day before, but now with the cloud coverage, it'd be more difficult. Of course, he didn't tell McKenzie any of that. The look in her eyes whispered faith—she believed he'd get them out of this mess. He didn't want to give her reason to doubt him.

"Tell me about this Beau character," he said as he turned and took a confident step forward. Leo had no idea where they were going, but he'd get there with conviction. The trick to good bullshit was dressing it up with bravado.

"Oh, Beau." McKenzie sighed. The soles of her shoes scuffed on dirt as she hastily followed behind. The sound was music to his ears because it meant she trusted him. "He's the only man who's ever had my heart."

Leo snorted.

"Don't tell me you're a cat person," she retorted. "I bet you are, aren't you?"

He was a marine. It was almost sacrilegious to not love dogs—he'd seen canine units in action firsthand. He had friends who owed their lives to dogs. But he wouldn't knock cats either. To each his own, though he'd never tell McKenzie that. It was too much fun to ruffle her feathers. "Who doesn't love a good pus—"

A fist whammed into his biceps, shutting him up. The edge of his lip quirked as he rubbed the spot. The woman packed a mean right hook. "Ow."

"I won't have you defiling the memory of my beloved dog."

She scowled at him, which, of course, made his smile widen.

"So I take it Beau was a good boy?"

"Yes. He was a very good boy."

As her eyes glazed over with a memory he wasn't privy to, her expression transformed. He'd never seen McKenzie so overtaken with love. Everything about her softened. An inner glow brightened her skin. A silly smile pinched her cheeks. Her eyes twinkled like brilliant sapphires. For a moment, he wondered what it might be like to be the subject of that affection, rather than a secondhand witness. Would he melt under the heat? Would he mind?

Another bout of thunder rattled the sky.

Leo glanced up as an ominous feeling scratched down his spine, but he forced his mind to clear. There was nowhere to go but ahead, so he put one foot in front of the other and kept his gaze level, silently praying they'd find shelter in time.

- 14 -

McKenzie

Over the next few hours, the forest transformed. The cloud coverage thickened, shifting to a sinister gray that cast the woods in shadow. Without the sun filtering through the leaves, the forest lost its color. The trees were a muddy brown, no longer glittering with honey highlights. The dirt, sticks, and leaves littering the floor blended to form a deep umber. The lively green canopy overhead shifted to dark evergreen. That had been dour enough… Then the rain came. It was slow at first, a few drops here and there, enough to annoy but not to bother. Fog crept through the trees, eerie and haunting, growing denser with each passing minute. The calm broke instantaneously. A bright stroke of lightning sliced through the sky, thunder tore the world in two, and the floodgates opened. Just like that, it was a downpour.

McKenzie kept one hand on Leo's back as a guide and used the other as a visor to shield her eyes. Every time she blinked one raindrop away, ten more came, turning her into a human waterfall. She couldn't see. Her limbs were going numb from the wet and the cold. Trembles racked through her. The ground turned slippery and each step became ten times more difficult. Their progress slowed.

Divine intervention, my ass. We are never getting out of this alive.

"Keep an eye out for anything we can use as shelter!" Leo shouted above the din of the storm.

She could hardly see a foot in front of her nose. It was as though the clouds had decided to fall right along with the rain. Even the trees were nothing more than dark shadow.

"Okay!" she yelled back anyway.

"We need to find a place to wait this out. It's getting bad!"

"Ok—"

McKenzie broke off with a scream as a fiery bolt of lightning sizzled through the fog, exploding like a bomb against a tree. A *crack* split the air as a branch crashed to the ground. The trunk splintered and flames erupted from the center. She stumbled back in fear. Her foot tangled in something, and she went down with a cry as pain flared in her ankle.

"McKenzie!"

Ow. Ow. Ow!

She reached down, trying to free her foot from the object she'd stumbled into.

A slick, wet tube wriggled against her fingers, and a hissing sound filled the air.

"Oh my God, it's a snake!"

He dropped to the ground anyway.

"Leo, be careful, it's a snake!"

"No," he muttered, glancing up with a joyous glint in his eyes that she couldn't for the life of her understand. "It's a hose."

"Like, a garden hose?" McKenzie frowned. The hissing noise had disappeared—she realized it must've been the sizzle of rain dampening the fire. The implication of his words hit full force. "A hose! We must be near a house. There's got to be a house close by!"

"Exactly." He grinned as he unwound the tube from her leg. "Can you stand?"

Leo offered his hand and McKenzie grabbed it. As soon as she put weight on her foot, she cringed, biting her lip to keep from making a sound. He must've noticed. Before she had time to say a word, Leo's arm wrapped around her legs and he swooped her into his arms.

"You don't—"

"Just be quiet and hold on."

"You know," she couldn't help but quip, spirits lifted at the mere prospect of shelter, "the last time you told me to *hold on*, we went catapulting off the road and over what seemed like the side of a cliff. So…"

"Hold tighter this time."

She snorted, but wrapped her arms around his shoulders, nestling her head into the nook below his neck, relishing the warmth emanating from his skin as she shivered. His body was firm but comfortable. Beneath her arms, his muscles writhed, taut and unyielding. He made her feel light as air as he marched determinedly forward, eyes focused and acute.

"Do you see anything?"

The wind howled and the trees groaned in protest. McKenzie shook her head against his chest. "No, I—"

They both froze at the same time as a set of steps appeared through the haze, leading nowhere, like the very edge of a stairway to heaven. Leo ran. After two steps, the squish of mud was replaced with the slap of boots on asphalt. A driveway—they'd reached a driveway. With each step closer, the house gained more and more detail—a wide uncovered porch and great sweeping windows, brown shingles and a sharply angled roof, but mostly, a bright red front door. Leo tried the knob, but it was locked. He rang the doorbell, once, twice. There was no response. He pounded his fist into the wooden surface.

"Hello! Is anyone home? This is a federal agent! We need help!" He waited a minute, then two, but the house seemed empty.

"Can't we just break in?" McKenzie asked.

Leo tossed her a look.

"Trust me, burglary isn't my first choice either, but we have to get out of this storm. They might have food. We can use their phone. If an alarm goes off, then half our work is already done—the police will be on their way to come save us."

He sighed, face twisting, then relented. "We need a wire or something."

"Done. Put me down."

Leo eyed her warily, but slowly set her back down on her feet, keeping one of his hands on her waist to help steady her. McKenzie reached back and slipped her fingers beneath her shirt to unlatch her bra. She tugged the straps over her shoulders and down her arms, then slipped the whole thing out and handed it to Leo triumphantly. He eyed the nude lace resting in his palm for a moment and swallowed slowly.

"The underwire," she explained.

"Right!" His body twitched. "Right. Just let me…"

He lifted the cup to his lip and bit down on the edge, then tugged the material in two. The muscles in her stomach tightened. Suddenly, being cold wasn't so much of a problem anymore.

"Okay," he murmured as he pulled the wire free and knelt in front of the door. He twisted his wrist back and forth, jiggling the wire in the lock and trying the knob, until—

It swung open.

Leo stood and reached one arm around her waist, then pulled her toward him. Lifting her off the ground, he stepped into the house and kicked the door shut behind them. The world went from wild chaos to taut silence in an instant. McKenzie's now-freed breasts pressed against his hard chest, nothing but two slips of wet fabric between them. She looked up. He glanced down. The heat in his eyes was a furnace, warming her to her core. The arm wrapped behind her back loosened, and she slid slowly down his frame. They held their stare the entire time, even as the toes of her unhurt foot landed softly against the floor. Leo didn't let go.

A drop of water slid off his nose and splashed hers.

The spell broke.

He stepped back and looked away, gaze jumping in every direction except for hers.

"No alarm." His deep voice cut through the quiet. Leo reached his arm toward the wall and flipped a switch she hadn't noticed. "No lights. Electricity must be out. We should try the phones."

His voice fell to a whisper as he turned around to face her. McKenzie stood in place, not entirely sure what to do. His gaze dropped to her toes, then traveled slowly back up, taking its time. Midway up her chest, it stopped. He spun on his heels. McKenzie glanced down, immediately understanding the sudden shift. White shirt, no bra, plus torrential rain, meant unintentional peep show.

Well, that's...fabulous.

She crossed her arms over her chest, shivering again.

"There've got to be towels around here somewhere," he grumbled, searching the closet near the door. "Aha!"

He shoved one in her general direction, careful to keep his eyes focused on the opposite wall.

"Thanks," she muttered, taking it and turning around.

McKenzie wasn't normally a modest person, but as she peeled her wet shirt off and slid her pants over her hips, her pulse raced. Her nerves were on overdrive. The wet slap of cotton hitting stone made her entire body jolt. *Was that his shirt, his pants, or...something else?* McKenzie bent forward and shook her head back and forth as she rubbed the towel against her scalp, drying her wet hair. *Doesn't matter.*

She scrubbed at her arms and her legs, drying every inch of her cold skin. Finally, when there was nothing more to do, she wrapped the towel around her torso, cinching it with a knot, and turned around.

"What now..." Her voice vanished into nothing.

Leo faced away from her, shirtless, head hidden beneath a towel as he scrubbed the water from his hair. Those broad shoulders were on prime display, muscles flexing and coiling as he moved his arms back and forth. Her gaze traveled down the deep cut of his spine, following the trail all the way to the edge of his boxer-briefs, and back up. She'd been told she had iron in her blood, but now, McKenzie wondered if there was maybe too much as a magnetic pull lured her hand closer. She couldn't resist. Taking a step forward, she pressed her fingers against his bronze skin, marveling at the rich hue. Leo stilled, but McKenzie didn't. She traced the deep black swirls of ink that had caught her attention, watching as the image writhed beneath her touch.

"You have a tattoo."

It was a set of wings that stretched from one side of his back to the other, feathers curling around his shoulders and covering the top half of his biceps. She'd never noticed it beneath the edge of his T-shirt, but now she couldn't look away. With his arms still stretched above his head, the wings were spread wide, as though he were flying.

Leo didn't respond.

McKenzie slowly drew her hand back, worried maybe she'd crossed a line she hadn't realized he'd drawn. "I have one too."

"*You?*" The surprise in his tone was obvious.

McKenzie grinned.

Leo turned, still holding the towel in his hand, and watched her with interest.

"It's not that big, so you probably didn't notice it before."

She tried not to let her eyes linger too long on the cut edges of his abs as she stepped closer, pushed her bracelets farther up her arm, and held out her wrist. Leo reached forward and lightly traced the black loops before looking up to search her eyes for the meaning he didn't understand. McKenzie swallowed, finding her voice.

"It's, um, two M's intertwined to look like a Celtic knot. My dad's full name is Charles MacDonald Harper the Fourth, and he picked out the name McKenzie Kathleen to sort of match. I think he always knew one child was all he'd ever get out of my mom. Anyway, we used to joke and say he was the Big Mac and I was the Little Mac. It was this whole thing. Sometimes when he didn't have too much work, he'd surprise me at school and take me to McDonald's for lunch as like a daddy-daughter date. Or, well, he did, before everything…"

Leo held her gaze, not letting go as something almost sad passed over his face. "You really love him, huh?"

"Of course, he's my dad," she answered automatically, pulling away a little and glancing to the floor, the urge to retreat overwhelming. Then, for some reason, words tumbled from her mouth before she had the right mind to stop them, spilling out in a rush, as though desperate for life. "He—he's not like the press and the news and the media made him out to be, during the trial and the case and everything after. He's not a criminal, at least, not to me. You see, my mom never wanted kids. I think she did it more out of obligation than anything else, because it was expected. She was never warm or motherly the way you'd expect, which is okay. Women, especially moms, don't have to all be the same. And I'm a lot like her, actually, *ice queen* and all."

She released an airy laugh, rolling her eyes at his former description. But it was apt, in a lot of ways. It was one of the reasons she and her mom had such a difficult time getting along—they were too similar, too used to freezing people out and keeping things in, too guarded.

Leo took a breath as though to interject, maybe to apologize, but she stopped him.

"My dad's the affectionate one, and I love that about him. When I was little, he was the one to give me a hug and a kiss when I cried. He was the one who'd toss me in the air and play with me outside and ask me about my day. He came to all my soccer games, hooting and hollering from the sidelines. Sometimes, he did the same thing at my ballet recitals too, much to my mortification. But it always made me laugh. My mom too. I've never seen her laugh the way he used to make her laugh. Her whole face would change, and soften, and light up, like she was an entirely different person. When he went away, we both lost that feeling, and we sort of fell apart. I love her, I always will, but the two of us don't work so well without him around. He was the life of our family, the rope that tied us all together and made us whole. So, I got the tattoo because it made me feel better to think he wasn't so far away. I mean, I know he's not dead or anything. I talk to him all the time, but it's different, you know, to not have him close by? I have this dream that when he gets out, everything in my life will go back to normal, even though I know that's not possible. But there are some things, maybe, that will…"

She thought back to the last time she and her mother had gone to see him. Her father greeted them with a big hug, as though they were out celebrating, not in a visitation room under the watchful eye of a prison guard. The sight of his smile brought one to their lips, and just like that, all the tension slipped away. They spoke about everything, about nothing, just trying to make each second count. Then it was over, far too quick. When they left, her mother tried to hide the way she wiped a tear from her cheek. In the car, they pretended they were fine, even though they both felt broken inside, as though ignoring the pain could somehow make it go away. Her mother retreated into her thoughts and McKenzie slipped into hers. They were next to each other, yet somehow, a million miles apart. But in that short hour when the three of them had been together, she'd caught a glimpse of what could be when her father was free. Her family would heal, because he'd find a way to fix them.

McKenzie rubbed her thumb over the tattoo, an old habit, and finally looked back up, meeting Leo's eyes. They were brooding, hooded by the black hair spilling over his forehead. She couldn't read the emotions swirling like molten amber within them.

"I got my tattoo when I got back from the war," he told her, gaze still dark as midnight. "The wings, they have a lot of different meanings. They were designed to look equal parts eagle and angel. The eagle is for the United States, obviously, but also for Mexico, where my roots are, and for the marines, where I figured out who I was. The angel wings are for friends I've lost along the way, who I like to think are looking out for me. And for my mom, for my brother. She used to call me *angelito mío* when I was a kid, her little angel."

He broke off.

McKenzie couldn't fight the sense that he'd stopped himself, that he'd pulled back, too afraid to reveal the next confession that might've slipped out. Leo looked up, blinking the demons away. His eyes returned to their bright hazel, laced with honey.

"Come on," he murmured as he gestured toward the rest of the house. "Let's go find some warm clothes and a bite to eat. If we're going to break in, we might as well do a thorough job of it."

McKenzie watched him walk away, unable to stop from wondering what words he'd left unsaid. What could possibly be buried so deep he hesitated to tell her? She studied his tattoo again, the unfurling feathers about to take flight.

Guardian angel, she thought, following as he disappeared around a bend, deeper into the shadows of the house. *You should add that one to your list.*

- 15 -

Leo

He'd almost told her about his father, about why his mom thought of him as her angel, her saving grace. *Angelito mío.* Leo shook his head and marched down the dark hallway. *What was I thinking?*

There was only one explanation. The dehydration was getting to him. That, plus the lack of food, the sight of her wet clothes clinging to her skin, the feel of her fingers gliding across his back, the soft vulnerability in her voice as she'd finally let him in. Leo was dizzy, and confused, and most definitely not thinking straight.

Clothes. We need clothes first. Everything else can wait until later.

That towel barely covered McKenzie. Her shoulders were bare, her thighs were too, and every time she took a step, the fabric pulled a little farther apart. In fact, the whole effect just served as a reminder of all the things she wasn't wearing—a bra for one, pants for another. He didn't want to know if she'd kept her underwear on.

Dear God, I hope she kept her panties on.

Why did I think about that?

Why did I even let that thought enter my mind?

He shoved open the door at the end of the hallway and stepped into what he'd guessed would be the master bedroom. Judging by the vaulted ceiling, second fireplace, and floor-to-ceiling windows, he'd guessed right. Leo stepped inside, unable to keep his attention from slipping to the massive king bed to the side of the door. He promptly stalked deeper into the room.

"I'll find us some clothes," he muttered.

"Okay." Her voice was annoyingly unaffected.

Leo didn't turn around. He tried the first door he saw—bathroom—and then went for the second—a walk-in closet. The hangers were mostly empty, and so were the drawers, save for a few somewhat haggard-looking options.

"So, do you want plaid, plaid, or more plaid?" he called out.

McKenzie popped her head into the closet. "Ooh, is it flannel? I love a good flannel."

"I can't tell if you're being sarcastic or not."

"What?" She raised a brow. "You only like your women in silk negligees?"

Why did you have to put that image into my head? He snorted to keep from having to actually formulate a response.

McKenzie pushed her way into the confined quarters, nudging him with her hip. Leo pressed as far back into the wall as he could, but it wasn't enough to avoid the graze of her elbow as she reached forward to inspect the clothes. The spot burned. He took a deep breath, trying to quell his reaction, but the heady scent of her hair made the space seem smaller. Leo looked up toward the dark ceiling, pulling his focus away from the graceful curve of her neck.

If only Nate could see me now…

His partner would've never let him hear the end of this—reduced to middle school urges with absolutely zero self-control.

Pull yourself together. This is a rescue mission, not a vacation, as you well know.

"I'll grab these," McKenzie said, pulling a few things off the shelves.

Leo nodded.

She glanced over her shoulder, eying him strangely for a moment, but didn't say anything as she walked back into the bedroom. Leo turned around, trying not to think about the fact that she was changing right behind him, and took his own set of plaid pajamas. The pants slid on fine. The shirt was another thing entirely. He couldn't get the damn thing to button—the sleeves barely fit up his arms. Leo folded it and put it back on the shelf before opening a few more drawers. He finally found a T-shirt. It was a little snug, but it was plain and it was clean. By the time he stepped out of the closet, McKenzie was fully clothed and standing by the windows, silhouetted by the light of the storm.

"I can't believe how bad it is," she said, looking outside. Raindrops landed on the roof and hit the siding in a dull hum, a peaceful sort of melody now that they were safely inside. She pressed her finger to the window and traced one of the rivulets of water cascading down the glass. "I mean, we got really lucky."

"Or unlucky," he countered, unable to stop himself. "Depending on how you look at it."

McKenzie turned around with a roll of her eyes, giving Leo a look at her outfit for the first time. Her flannel pajamas were mostly hidden beneath a plush oversized robe she'd cinched at her waist. Her feet had been swallowed up by socks that gave fuzzy a new definition. Her hair fell in loose wet waves around her shoulders. Though she was all covered up, he didn't think she'd ever looked more attractive. There was something sexy in seeing her so undone, so carefree and at ease, no longer the closed-off woman he'd met in that stuffy New York hallway. The view through the window was chaotic and untamed, but there was something wild inside too—the look in her eyes, the invisible current simmering in the air between them.

"How's your ankle?"

McKenzie shrugged. "Just twisted. It'll be better by morning."

"Come on."

Leo walked over and presented her with his back—a safer option that being face-to-face. With a laugh, she hopped on, wrapping her arms around his shoulders as Leo hooked his elbows beneath her knees.

"Are you my chauffeur now too?"

"Apparently." He glanced toward her, catching her eye in his peripheral vision.

"In that case, to the kitchen!"

He took off running, unable to fight his grin as she yelped and held on tighter. By the time they zipped around the corner and entered the open living area, she was laughing.

He deposited her on the island. "Stay there. Let me check the phones and see what supplies I can gather up."

Leo walked back into the living area and grabbed the phone on the end table. There was no dial tone. He tried the other set on the opposite side of the room, but that was dead too.

Okay, power is definitely out. We need light.

He checked all the drawers and shelves first, but couldn't find a flashlight. Fighting his better judgment,

Leo gathered all the candles and placed them around the living area, lighting them one by one with the box of matches he'd seen near the fireplace. It was too romantic, but there was no way around it. He'd just have to keep his head on straight and power through. Tomorrow, they'd be able to call for help. Just one more night with McKenzie and then everything would go back to normal.

You've got this.

Leo found a pantry filled with nonperishables and grabbed a bag of chips and an unopened can of salsa.

"Hey, can you tell if the stove is gas?" he called out.

"Um…" McKenzie answered, clicking her tongue. "Yeah, I think so."

"Excellent," he muttered to himself as he went back into the pantry for more. A few minutes later, he returned to the kitchen with his arms overflowing.

McKenzie practically tore the chips from his hands. She ripped the bag open and stuffed one into her mouth. Midchew, she nudged her chin in his direction and asked, "What's all of that?"

"Black beans," he said with a grin, placing the cans onto the granite countertop. "Kidney beans. Diced Tomatoes. Tomato sauce."

"Yum?"

"Just wait," he countered, quickly crossing the room toward the freezer. The power was out, so he felt less bad about pillaging their resources since it would all go bad anyway. He found ground beef—*major score!*—and some frozen corn, and tossed them both onto the counter.

McKenzie pulled her brows together, scrutinizing the supplies. Her eyes widened, and she looked up at him. "Chili?"

"Damn straight."

She snorted. "You *are* from Texas."

"Well, *real* Texas chili doesn't have beans, but beggars can't be choosers, right?"

He kept scrummaging, this time through the spice rack on the counter, and grabbed some chili powder, cumin, red pepper flakes, salt, and cayenne. Then he pulled a pot out from one of the drawers. Using a match, he lit the stove. When he started cooking, McKenzie fell back against the counter, crossing her ankles as she continued to munch on chips. He handed her a glass of water, which she finished in about three sips. He refilled it and kept watch on the thawing ground beef.

"I could get used to this letting-the-man-do-all-the-work thing," she mused.

"Seems like you already have."

"Hey, I'm injured here." She crunched on another chip. "My stomach is growling like crazy. How long until it's ready?"

A laugh slipped through his lips. "I haven't even started yet. I'm just browning the meat."

"Did you add some spices though?"

"Some cumin, some cayenne, and a little chili powder."

"Smells good." She inhaled deeply and a soft smile widened her lips, making him wonder at the memory playing behind her eyes. "Did your mom teach you how to cook?"

"She tried," he murmured with a shake of his head. "Don't let this fool you. I definitely wasn't the best student."

That secretive grin still played on her lips. McKenzie closed her eyes. "What sort of things did she make?"

"The usual—*enchiladas, tamales, empanadas, mole, croquetas*. My favorite, though, was her pork tacos. Oh man, she'd put the meat in the slow cooker in the morning and let it simmer all day. The apartment smelled unreal when I got home from school. Somehow she'd know, every freaking time, if I tried a little before she got back from work. *Aye, Emilio, no!* It was like she had eyes everywhere."

"Emilio?" McKenzie asked tentatively. The sound brought a shiver to his skin.

Leo glanced to the side, somehow already aware her eyes would be open and watching him. "It's my name. Emilio Tomas Alvarez, but I've gone by Leo for as long as I can remember. It's a little easier for the, uh, non-Hispanic people to pronounce."

The edge of her lip pulled a little higher. "You mean the white people?"

"Hey." He held his hand up, spatula and all. "You said it, not me."

"And what's your mother's name?"

"Josefina, but sometimes her employers would make her go by Josephine."

"And your brother?"

"Manuel, but everyone calls him Manny."

"And your—"

He dropped a can and it banged loudly against the floor, cutting her off. Leo hastily retrieved it, but he caught her eye on the way up. Whether he wanted it to or not, his gaze gave away everything his lips couldn't. McKenzie sealed her lips and swallowed, shifting her attention back to the ceiling. His father was off limits.

"And you didn't mind going by another name?"

"My mom did, sometimes, back when she was still working, because the Americanized name was sort of forced on her. I think it made her feel farther away from home and a little unwelcome when she was outside of our local community. But me? I don't know. I've been Leo for so long, it's just who I am. A nickname, nothing else."

"Would you rather I call you Emilio?"

No.

No, I wouldn't.

Because every time she said it, a strange rush coursed through him and his heart skipped a beat. Not so much at the word, because her pronunciation was terrible, but at the tender, careful, almost covetous way it rolled through her lips.

"It's no big deal."

"Emilio," she murmured again, shooting another wave of liquid gold down his veins. He turned in time to see her frown. "It doesn't sound as good when I say it."

It sounds better.

He turned back to the stove and stirred the food. They were from different worlds entirely, socially, culturally, monetarily, and it was time he remembered that. "That's because you, McKenzie Kathleen Harper, are about as Anglo-Saxon as they come."

She crossed her arms, still lounging across the island counter. "I'm Scottish, thank you very much."

"For the purpose of this discussion, it's the same thing."

She scoffed, offended. "It is *not*."

"Say, I don't know, *churro*."

"Churro."

"I rest my case."

She sat up, puckering her lips in an attempt to get her R to roll off the tongue a little easier. "Churro."

"*Churrrrrrrro*," he countered with a smug smile. "*Churro. Churro. Churrrrro.*"

She narrowed her eyes. "Oh sure, you can say churro, but can you make churros?"

"What?" Leo shook his head, fighting the mental whiplash. He did *not* see that one coming. "That's not the same thing at all."

She shrugged.

"False equivalency."

She crossed her arms and stared. "Well?"

Leo scoffed. "Can you?"

"Just watch me."

- 16 -

McKenzie

She slid off the counter and hopped on one foot across the kitchen toward the pantry, ignoring the snickering following in her wake. She'd show him. Oh, she'd show him.

Why am I so annoyed right now?

McKenzie paused when she pulled open the pantry door, taking a deep breath now that she was out of his line of sight. It definitely wasn't because hearing him speak Spanish with a sexy, sultry accent had gotten her all hot and bothered. And it couldn't have been the sight of him confidently manning the stove, his muscles pulling tight against that too-small T-shirt, reminding her of the many cut contours she'd seen in the flesh not too long ago.

It was the smell of the kitchen.

Okay, yes, that has got to be why my brain is going haywire.

The cumin, the chili powder, the cayenne—they brought her back to a place she didn't often go, to a home that was once warm, and bright, and full of love.

It smells like Yolanda, McKenzie thought as she reached out and took a bag of flour from the pantry shelves. It had been a long time since she'd thought about her former nanny, a woman who oftentimes felt closer to her than her own mother. When McKenzie was sick, Yolanda was the one who brought her soup, put on her favorite movies, and tucked her into bed. When she was bored, Yolanda was the one who brought her into the kitchen to bake cookies or act as sous-chef while dinner was underway. Yolanda had been the one to pick her up from school and bring her to practices. Her car had always smelled of spices, and whenever she cooked, those same smells would fill the Harper house as well.

McKenzie had been a toddler when Yolanda started working for her parents, and *Yolanda* had been too complicated for her developing brain to understand. So she'd called her Yoyo, and the name had stuck, all the way up until her father's arrest when her mother had fired Yolanda without explanation. Looking back, McKenzie knew exactly why. Her nanny had witnessed the family's shame. She'd held McKenzie while she'd cried. She'd seen her father get dragged away by the

Feds. She'd seen her mother lose control and break the entire set of crystal scotch glasses in her father's study. After that, she had to go. Yolanda was a reminder, to McKenzie's mom, of all their faults. McKenzie had screamed at her mother, had cried for Yoyo to come back, but it was done. The next week, another woman came, mostly to help drive McKenzie around to school and to her practices, but it wasn't the same. That poor woman was the first person she'd iced out, taking after her mom, too blinded by bitter anger to see clearly.

I wonder if she liked it when I called her Yoyo instead of Yolanda... McKenzie shook her head, clearing her mind. *Churros. Think about churros. How the hell do you make churros?*

It had been over a decade since the last time she'd tried, but the memory was still sharp. Yoyo used to put a chair next to the stovetop so McKenzie could watch when she cooked. Even now she could hear the sizzle of boiling oil, could smell the cinnamon-sugar in the air, could taste the crunchy fried dough. They'd been her favorite, back in the day, before the precision of French pastry took over.

Churros were simple, delicious, and messy in the best way possible—something McKenzie hadn't been in a long time. She remembered how to make them. No matter how much time may have passed, that recipe was in her blood.

She grabbed a bag of sugar and a tub of vegetable oil that'd been half-used, balanced them with the flour already in her arms, and hobbled back into the kitchen. Leo had already pulled a deep-frying pan from the shelves and put it on top of a flaming burner. Salt and cinnamon sat inconspicuously on the counter next to the stove, along with a mixing bowl. McKenzie lined everything across the counter, arranging the ingredients from largest to smallest, then spun in search of measuring cups. After three drawers, she found a set and went back to her spot. All her ingredients had been rearranged into total chaos.

McKenzie tossed a silent glare in Leo's direction. He didn't say a word, but the grin on his lips spoke volumes.

Taking a deep breath, she rearranged the items back into height order, then hopped over to the sink to fill her glass of water. By the time she returned, the items had been moved again, but this time into a pyramid. Leo's face was the picture of calculated nonchalance. She jerked her elbow into his ribs with a bit of force. He doubled over, half laughing, half groaning.

"Oh, sorry, I didn't see you there," she quipped. "My mistake."

"You're used to a bigger kitchen." He forced the words out as he stood up straight. Using his palms for leverage, he leapt onto the counter. "My chili is simmering, so I'll give the master room to work."

She wasn't used to having an audience when she cooked. The kitchen at the restaurant was too busy for any of the other chefs to pay her any mind. Now, Leo's gaze was glued to her, a searing touch hotter than the flames currently simmering beneath the pan. McKenzie squeezed her eyes shut and took a breath, pushing the awareness of him away.

Churros. Think about churros.

The memory of Leo carrying her through the rain like some sort of Greek god fluttered to the forefront of her thoughts.

Churros.

She shook her head and reached for the water, trying to dispel the image of him rolling on top of her protectively as bullets flew overhead, trying to forget how good the weight of his body felt against hers.

Churros.

McKenzie poured a cup of water into the hot pan, but as the liquid splashed against the steel, all she saw were water droplets dripping down those bared six-pack abs. The term *washboard* had never been more accurate.

Churros, goddammit! Churros!

She downed the rest of the water she hadn't needed for the recipe and slammed the empty drinking glass back onto the counter, flinching with the force.

"Everything okay?" Leo chimed with a smirk.

"Great," she muttered.

"Because it's okay if you don't know how to make them. You can admit you were wrong, and we can both move on from this."

"I wasn't wrong."

"Or you could tell me I was right."

"Not likely."

"Or—"

"Leo, could you just be quiet so I can concentrate?"

He chuckled softly and crossed his arms, putting his head against a cabinet as he settled in to keep right on watching. McKenzie frowned and returned to her ingredients, picking up the measuring spoons.

Okay, two and a half tablespoons of sugar. Now, a teaspoon of salt and two tablespoons of vegetable oil.

They went into the pan, one after another, with careful exactness. The numbers calmed her. They gave her something else to focus on. McKenzie grabbed a whisk and stirred the mixture until little bubbles appeared on the surface and all the granules dissolved. Then she took it off the heat and added a cup of flour. The world faded away as she sank into the recipe, straining her arm muscles as she churned the ingredients until a ball formed. McKenzie was in the zone—that special place where passion and focus pushed reality away. Time slowed, or maybe it raced. Nothing existed outside of her fingers and the food they brought to life. Not Leo. Not mobsters. Not her past. Not her future.

The only thing that mattered was this recipe, right now, and the endless search for perfection.

She brought a new batch of oil to boil and filled a Ziploc bag with the dough, then cut the end off to make it work like a pastry bag. Piping the churros one by one, she let the thin strips drop into the oil. They sizzled with the heat as the exterior color changed from beige to a crisp golden brown. McKenzie pulled them out, dipped them in a cinnamon-sugar mixture, and carefully arranged them into a pyramid on the plate. She flicked a little extra sugar on top for good measure.

Not bad for the situation. Could've used a little chocolate sauce for dipping, but I have to work with what I've got. While she admired her handiwork, a hand swooped in and yanked the top churro from the pile.

"Hot, hot, hot!" Leo juggled the pastry in his palms.

"They *just* came out of the fryer."

"I know, but they look so good." He broke off to take a massive bit, voice shifting into a pleasured groan instead. "Oh my God."

"You're supposed to let them cool," she chided.

Leo shook his head, stuffing the rest of the churro into his mouth, barely able to talk with his mouth so full. "No, you're not. Try one."

She hesitated.

"I'm serious," Leo said while he took another. "These are better than the ones we used to get at the fair."

"I would hope so."

He continued as though he hadn't heard the snide remark. "I need to make you hate-bake more often."

At that, McKenzie rolled her eyes and grabbed a churro. She blew on the end to cool it. When Leo's gaze dropped to her puckered lips, she hastily stuffed the fried dough into her mouth in what she hoped was the least attractive manner possible. His mouth pulled into a wide smile.

"Good?"

McKenzie shrugged, trying to play it cool even as her stomach audibly growled. *Good? These are fucking amazing. I* am *a gourmet goddess,* she thought, remembering the screenname she'd picked out ages ago. *Maybe I should hate-bake for him more often. And maybe we can hate…other things as well.*

"Where'd you learn to make these? I can't imagine it was on the menu at your fancy French school."

"My, uh…" McKenzie trailed off, covering her pause by taking another bite. Leo and his damn federal-agent senses weren't fooled.

"What?"

"No, it's nothing." She glanced at the floor. Why was this making her uncomfortable to say? *My nanny.* Easy, simple. *My nanny taught me.* Would he understand? Or would he roll his eyes at how stereotypical her wealthy upbringing had been? Because that would hurt, to think she was just another spoiled girl with a nanny who had pretended to love her when really all she'd wanted was to be home with her own kids. McKenzie liked to think it had been more than that with Yolanda, even if the opposite was so often true. Instead, she asked, "What does *mija* mean?"

Leo's brows twitched in for a second. His ever-perceptive gaze sharpened. "It's a shortened form of *mi hija*, 'my daughter.' It's a term of endearment, one an older person might use for a girl he or she cared deeply about."

The discomfort within her eased, loosening enough for the rest of the words to come. "My nanny taught me how to make churros, before she was fired. Her name was Yolanda, but I called her Yoyo because when I was little, I couldn't figure out how to say her name right. And she called me *mija*."

The hope in her voice was embarrassing. McKenzie didn't even know what it meant. Did she want Leo to tell her Yolanda didn't mind the nickname? That she loved her? That she missed her sometimes too? He wouldn't know any of that. He'd probably heard this story a thousand times before, with a thousand different actors playing the same roles.

"God, what I must sound like to you. Poor little rich girl with a money-embezzling father, a mom who didn't care, and a nanny she used to fill the void." McKenzie turned away before he could answer. Leo had been through real trauma. He had real problems. Her life was probably a joke to him. "I check all the boxes, don't I?"

"That's not what I think." He reached out and grabbed her hand. McKenzie shook him off, hating how her fingers trembled, how her voice shook. She wasn't this girl, this weak, falling-apart, lost girl. Not anymore. His palm enveloped hers again, this time for good. "McKenzie, that's not what I think."

He tugged, spinning her around. McKenzie met his eyes, golden highlights ablaze within them. "What then? What do you think?"

"That you're lonely," he murmured, dipping his head so she couldn't look away.

Was he right? She'd spent so many years relentlessly focusing on her career, convincing herself nothing else mattered, that all she needed was a kitchen and stocked pantry to be happy. What if it was just an elaborate lie she'd taught herself to believe? A cover for that hollow place deep inside, empty and yearning to be filled?

"That I'd be lonely too," Leo continued, studying her eyes as she blinked rapidly to fight that uniquely human burn, the only kind of fire that brought water to life. "I may not have had much as a kid, but I always had my mom and my brother, no matter what. I know what it's like to try to go it alone, now, as an adult, but I can't imagine growing up without that security, that safe hold to guide me. And where you've ended up in life, successful, confident, beautiful inside and out, it's a testament to your strength."

The tear that had been threatening to spill dried at his words, and an unfamiliar glow settled inside her chest, bright as the sun, sneaking into all those cracks and crevices, filling them with warm light. He rubbed her hand with his thumb in a soothing rhythm, sending warm tingles up her arm and across her chest, making her feel grounded to something, as though he were her anchor to the shore. McKenzie tore her gaze away, not sure what to do or where to look, just that his eyes were too overwhelming. They saw her, saw through her, straight to all the secrets she tried to hide.

"It wasn't all bad," she whispered, trying to downplay the praise he'd given her. Surface compliments were something she could accept with a smile and a snappy comeback, but Leo's words were something else. They sank deep, too deep. "I told you a little about my father, but my mother and I had some good times too. She loved fashion, and she'd take me on these amazing shopping sprees that made me feel like a princess when I was younger. And she was an event planner before she had me, so she always threw me the best birthday parties growing up. Two years ago, when she was on the committee for a holiday charity ball, she hired me to design the centerpiece for the dessert display. I made this amazing gingerbread replica of the New York skyline, and I heard her telling people all night, *my daughter* this and *my daughter* that. It was the first time I ever really thought she was proud of me, you know? And she is, in her own way…" McKenzie paused, not sure where her words were going, if they made her life seem more full or more barren. It wasn't a road she wanted to travel down anytime soon, so she put her blockade back up to keep her mind from wandering any farther. "So, yeah, that's a long and overly detailed explanation of why I know how to make churros."

"Right." He dropped her hand instantly, as though her shift in tone had snapped him out of a trance. "*Amazing* churros."

"Would I make any other kind?" she teased, not quite feeling the lightness her voice implied. Leo seemed to sense it, or maybe he just knew they were stepping on dangerous ground and needed a swift retreat.

"You know what goes great with churros and chili?" he asked, slipping from the counter and landing easily on his feet. He took a step back, putting much-needed space between them.

"What?" she drawled.

"Alcohol."

"For once, I couldn't agree more."

- 17 -

Leo

He needed a drink. Well, no, he needed a cold shower and an escape route, but with the storm still raging outside, a drink would have to do.

What was it about this woman? Her snappy intelligence? Her clear drive and conviction? Her unexpected vulnerability? It was like all three of those things had interlocked to form an unholy trifecta he couldn't resist. Add her stunning beauty plus the fact that she could whip up desserts that made his toes curl at the drop of a hat, and he was a goner. A fucking goner.

Where the hell was that liquor cabinet?

He walked to the living room, leaving McKenzie behind, relieved to have a little bit of breathing room to get his head on straight. Outside, the sky grew darker. Rain poured down the windows like a gushing river. The fog was still an opaque curtain drawn across the forest, blocking it from sight. The thunder was softer, a little more distant, but the storm still raged. Which meant they were stuck here without any way to contact the outside world for the foreseeable future.

Ah, there it is.

Leo opened the glass-paned doors of the cabinet, taking stock. There was vodka, gin, rum, tequila, and— *aha!*—whiskey. Leo glanced at the label. It was a Macallan 12. Whoever owned this house had fabulous taste. He grabbed the bottle and turned, finding McKenzie's gaze across the softly flickering light of a dozen small flames.

Damn candles.

"Whiskey?"

She narrowed her eyes and tilted her head to the side. "What kind?"

"Macallan 12."

"Yeah, I like that one." She nodded. "Bring it on."

And she knows her whiskey... Another one to add to the frigging list.

He grabbed two glasses from the shelves and closed the cabinet before returning to the kitchen. He poured the drinks and handed one to McKenzie, who had retaken her spot on top of the island. Then he promptly jumped onto the opposite countertop to keep a mandatory three feet between them.

"To what?" McKenzie asked as the edge of her lip pulled into a grin and she lifted her glass. "To not dying?"

"To surviving," Leo said instead. *To surviving this. To surviving our pasts. To pushing through and fighting.*

Her face softened with understanding, and then a wicked gleam fired to life deep in her eyes. "To surviving *each other*."

Ain't that the truth. "Cheers."

He dropped his head back and downed the entire pour in one sip, savoring the burn as it charged down his throat, taking the edge off.

"You do know it's meant to be a sipping drink, right?"

Leo eyed her and raised a brow.

"On second thought," she said, as though having a realization. "You might be right."

"Me? Right?"

"Don't let it go to your head."

Before he could respond, McKenzie arched her head back and finished her glass. As the alcohol hit, she squeezed her eyes tight, fighting the fire.

"Ooh," she exhaled heavily, then looked back at Leo. "Fill me up! And grab me some chili too, while you're at it."

"*Please.*"

She rolled her eyes. "Yes. *Please.*"

He shook his head as he filled her glass and handed her a bowl of food, then retook his place on the opposite counter.

"This is really good."

He flicked his gaze toward her, watching as she pulled her feet up on the counter and crossed her legs, body disappearing beneath the oversized robe draped over her frame. McKenzie lowered her face to the bowl and breathed deep, drawing in the spicy scent of the chili. She took another bite and a subtle smile passed over her lips while she chewed, comfort personified.

He returned his attention to his bowl. "Thanks."

"You know what would make this even better?"

There it is. "What?" He eyed her pointedly. "More cumin?"

"No, no." She shook her head. "Not the food, that's great, just the moment. I want to laugh, Leo. I feel like it's been ages since I had a good laugh. Tell me something funny...*please*. Anything. I don't know, something embarrassing. Something you did as a kid."

"Something embarrassing..." He trailed off, thinking, and leaned back, pressing his shoulders to the cabinets. "I don't know. When I was a kid, I thought Michael Jackson was a god, so one year for Halloween I learned the whole 'Thriller' dance and performed it in random spurts while I was trick-or-treating around the neighborhood. That was pretty embarrassing."

"Oh my God, that's brilliant!" McKenzie leaned in, eyes wide with intrigue. "Can you still do it?"

He shrugged. "I don't know… Maybe?"

"Do it." Her voice edged on possessed.

"Right now? Hell, no."

"Oh, come on!"

"Not a chance."

"Do it."

"I'm going to need a lot more of these"—he held up his whiskey glass—"before I get to that level."

She stared at him for a moment, making Leo question his choice of words as calculations spun deep in her crystal irises. Then she sat back. "Noted. Tell me something else."

"You tell me something," he countered. "Tit for tat."

"Okay…" McKenzie took another sip of whiskey and pursed her lips. "Oh, I've got it. I have webbed toes."

Leo waited a few seconds for her to continue, but she just took another bite of chili. "That's it? That's the whole story?"

"What?" McKenzie shrugged. "They're *really* embarrassing."

"Well, now I have to see them."

"No."

"Come on, take the sock off, Harper."

She grinned when he said her last name and glanced up, meeting his gaze. Then she sighed dramatically and tugged her sock off before holding her foot out. He didn't see anything wrong.

"Wow," Leo deadpanned. "I don't know how you can live with that horror you call a foot."

Her smile shifted to a glare.

"I mean," he continued, "I don't know how you found the strength to leave the house, to show your face in public. What do you do when you go to the beach? People must gawk and—"

"Shut it," she interrupted and stuffed her completely normal toes back into her sock. "I had a complex about wearing flip-flops for years. It's not funny."

"I can see why, with toes like—" He broke off when she lifted her hand and something smacked him clean in the middle of the forehead. "What was that?"

McKenzie coughed under her breath. "What was what?"

"That! What was..." He lifted his fingers to his forehead and pulled them back. A little bit of oily red residue covered his skin. "Was that a black bean? Did you just chuck a black bean at me?"

"'Course not." She took another bite to cover her mischievous smile. "Your turn. Something funny this time."

You're one to talk. He silently huffed, shaking his head. *Webbed feet.* "Okay, I've got one I think you'll like, but it's not about me. It's about Jo."

"Jo?" McKenzie perked.

"Yeah, did she tell you anything about what happened in New York?" She shook her head *no*. "My partner, Nate, and I were in New York, tailing Jo and her partner, Thad, based on intel that they were planning to steal a painting and make an exchange with the mob. Basically, we're following Jo, and she knows it. All week, she's been disabling the bugs we plant in her hotel room, and covering her tracks. So our boss suggests Nate try to get a little closer to her, act a little flirtatious, see what he can drum up. If you know anything about my partner, you should know he's a great guy who happens to have a major stick up his ass. Total square. A stickler for the rules—or he was, until Jo. And she knew it too. So one day, while we're tailing her, she goes into this shop, and it's obvious from the window it's a lingerie shop. We're in the car, waiting. We have her cell phone feed coming through on a tablet, and we see that she turns her cell phone on and opens her messaging app. She types something. She sends something. We don't know what yet because it takes a while to load, but Nate recognizes the number. It's his personal cell phone."

"Oh no," McKenzie murmured.

"Oh, yes," Leo chimed. "Little Jo Hacker managed to somehow steal Nate's private cell number and use it to send him a photo from the dressing room of her in red lace lingerie."

"No!"

"Yes! And that's not even the best part. Nate goes about ten shades of red, and then the photo transfers through the tech team, so everyone in our unit sees, which makes him go more berserk. By the time we got back to the New York office later that night, someone had gone out and bought a red bra and hooked it to Nate's chair. His face! Oh, man, it was so good."

McKenzie shook her head. "That sounds like Jo. She doesn't do anything halfway—it's full enthusiasm, attacking with the force of a tiger, or nothing."

"Well, she went full lioness on my partner, and now they're head over heels for each other, so I guess it worked out."

"Did it?"

Leo stared at her, trying to read the unspoken message in those words. "How do you mean?"

McKenzie paused, glancing down to her chili then stirring it twice without taking a bite. Finally, after a few quiet seconds, she looked back up. "Can I ask you something, Leo?"

"Shoot."

"It's just, I don't trust very many people. After everything that happened with my dad, some of the people who I thought were my friends acted in ways that, well, hurt me. After that, I kept people at a distance."

He could imagine.

Middle school was as much of a war zone as Iraq, more so in some ways. At least his battles were physical—it was the mind games that could really do a number on a person's health. Hell, he should know.

"But Jo and Addy," McKenzie continued softly, "I trusted them. Trust. Trusted? I don't know anymore, with everything that's happened. Jo lied to me for years. She put my life in danger. She—" McKenzie paused to take a deep breath. "Do you think she's a good person, Leo? A few days ago, I would've said yes without a doubt in my mind, but now I'm not so sure."

"I think"—he sighed—"it's complicated, like everything in life is. On paper? I don't know. She was a professional hacker. She stole private information. She aided in the theft of countless works of art, which then went on to help fund some really illicit activities. But in her heart? Yeah, I think she's a good person. As soon as she found out the truth of what her father and her partner were involved in, she turned herself in to the FBI to help undo the damage she'd helped create. She's fun and loving and the sort of person whose enthusiasm makes everything around her brighter. She makes my partner happy. There's a light in him that's never been there before, and the sort of weightlessness inner peace brings. I think maybe she was a girl who loved her father, who was raised in a life that a lot of people would never understand, who wanted out but wasn't entirely sure how to make that happen until just recently. We've all been guilty of that, right? Of doing things we know might not be the best for us, because they're easier than facing the truth?"

He knew he had. Isolating himself, putting on a brave face, shoving the bad times to the back of his mind and powering through—it was easier than facing the truth that maybe he was a little bit broken and maybe he didn't quite know how to put the pieces back together on his own.

"Thanks, Leo. That helps… That helps a lot."

He found her gaze again, wondering what she saw in him—an agent like the ones who took her dad, a man who'd saved her life, a jerk who never let her win? If she knew the truth, would she still look at him with adoration in her eyes? Would she like the broken man he was inside, or did she only like the hero he tried so hard to be?

"I think you should know you're a member of that very exclusive club, by the way," McKenzie continued, as though she could see all the doubts whirling through his mind. "After everything we've been through these past few days, I trust you. And I hope after all this is over, we can still be friends."

Friends… Something within him wilted a little at the word, but he shoved the feeling down with all the others. "I'd like that."

"Good," she quipped, tone changing back to playful with a biting edge as she finished her second glass of whiskey with one long sip. "Because if we don't get out of this alive, you're back on my shit list."

"I'll take those odds." He lifted his glass, inclining it toward her as he raised his brows, and then poured it down the hatch. The burn washed all those pesky doubts away.

- 18 -

McKenzie

McKenzie had no idea how much she'd had to drink. She remembered Leo regaling her with the story of his herculean home run in eighth grade to win the final game of the season. Apparently, he spent the entire summer thinking he would become the next Alex Rodriguez, puffing his chest out for all his friends, only to get a total reality check the first time he stepped foot in their high school. So McKenzie told him about her massive lesson in humility during the transition from being the best in her class at culinary school to the lowest rung on the ladder in a New York City restaurant. She'd actually had the gall to correct the head pastry chef on his sugar work, which led to late-night dish duty for about a month straight. Though, she couldn't help but notice a difference in his sugar molding after that.

They spoke about their families a little, which mostly consisted of Leo telling her more about his brother, Manny. Since he'd been a bit of a nerd, Leo, the older jock brother with muscle mass to spare, became his protector, which didn't surprise her in the least. When someone broke Manny's glasses, Leo broke them—he was just careful not to do it on school grounds where he could get in trouble. They were jealous, he said, because everyone in their town knew Manny with his big brain would go places, places they wouldn't dare dream of. And he had. But so had Leo, though he didn't seem to give himself very much credit for the honorable, admirable life he'd carved out for himself. McKenzie tried, but he wouldn't hear it, so they moved on. She begged him to tell her more, because she had no sibling stories to share, and hearing his made her feel better somehow, a little less alone.

They drank.

And they talked.

And they drank some more.

The world moved forward in disjointed spurts. One moment she was telling Leo about her first trip to Europe as a little girl, how she still remembered walking into an authentic French patisserie and marveling at the brilliant colors in the display, the endless rows of pristine desserts, the delectable smells. The next he was telling her about the time he and his family had gone to Disney

World on their first true vacation, driving all the way from Texas in a road trip he would never forget. Then suddenly, they were arguing about their favorite TV shows. McKenzie would defend *Friends* until her dying days, but Leo said the character development of *Breaking Bad* couldn't be beat, especially by a sitcom. The argument shifted to the merits of a classic American hamburger versus fine cuisine, then to which of the *Harry Potter* books was the best (the third one, obviously), and then they were thumb wrestling.

She must've won, because the next thing McKenzie knew, she was sitting cross-legged on the kitchen island with a refilled whiskey in one hand as she pummeled her other fist into her thigh and demandingly chanted, "Thriller! Thriller! Thriller!"

"That wasn't the deal."

"Thriller! Thriller! Thriller!"

"McKenzie."

She didn't care. She'd waited long enough. Ignoring his plea, she sang the opening notes. "Do-do-do-do-do." *Clap!* "Do-do-do-do-do." *Clap!*

"It's not happening."

"Do-do-do-do-do." *Clap!*

"Give it a rest."

"Do-do-do-do-do." *Clap!*

The next thing she knew, right on cue, Leo jumped off the kitchen counter and belted out the opening lyrics.

"It's close to midnight…"

McKenzie gasped and put her hands on her lips to hide her smile. He ruefully shook his head and leaned close in challenge, raising his brows as if to say, *You asked for this*. Still singing, he placed his whiskey on the counter next to her and gripped the stone edge on either side of her thighs, holding her gaze for a moment. Their faces were close enough for the tips of their noses to graze as he wobbled his head back and forth in a ghoulish manner along with the song. Her heart raced. She kept her hands clasped around her mouth, if only to stop her wayward lips from leaning forward and sealing those few barren inches between them. McKenzie couldn't remember the last time her cheeks had hurt from smiling, but right now they ached. She was sure her eyes must've sparkled just as bright as the irises staring back at her.

Suddenly, Leo pushed against the countertop, hitting an unheard beat in the song he clearly knew from heart, and spun on his heels. He snapped his fingers and shifted his feet into a dancing sort of skip as he traversed the length of the kitchen, making it to a wide-open space just in time for the chorus. That was when McKenzie really started laughing. He was Michael Jackson reincarnated, first twitching his head like a zombie, then shaking his hips side to side with his arms out, then adding some dramatic hand movements, then some dips and spins while he shifted his head back and forth as though it were disconnected from the rest of his body. Leo managed to keep a straight face for about the first half of the dance, and then he completely broke down. He fought through the rest of the chorus, but as soon as he hit the classic Michael Jackson tippy-toe pose near the end, he collapsed to the floor and held his forearms over his eyes to block out the sight of her.

"I cannot believe you made me do that."

"I don't know," she teased, struggling to find her voice between the laughter spilling through her lips. "The agent doth protest too much, if you ask me."

"Those were smiles of mortification."

"They looked pretty self-satisfied."

He let his arms drop over his head and turned in her direction as the edge of his lip quirked up. "Okay, maybe it was a *little* fun. I haven't done that in years."

"I'm pretty sure you do it all the time when you're alone in your apartment. You probably have a red leather jacket hidden the back of your closet for just the occasion."

He barked out a laugh. "You caught me. I'm a secret Michael Jackson impersonator."

"It's almost criminal that you're keeping this talent from the rest of the world. You need to take this show on the road. I'm sure your partner—" McKenzie broke off when all the color drained from his face.

Leo groaned and rolled to his feet. "No one from the bureau can ever know about this, McKenzie Kathleen Harper. They'd never let it go. This is a secret you will take to your grave."

"Scout's honor." She held her hand over her heart. *Though I can't promise I'll let you live it down.*

"Clearly, you were never a Boy Scout," he drawled and stepped closer to the kitchen island to peel her hand from its spot against her chest and hold it aloft. He repositioned her fingers gently, until her thumb and pinky were pressed together and her other three fingers were raised—the official salute. He didn't let her hand go as he shifted his gaze to hers, a glance that smoldered. "A promise between friends?"

"A promise," she whispered, voice coming out breathier than she'd intended.

Why did I use that damned word friends *earlier?* She could kick herself. *Friends* was just about the last thing on her mind.

"Okay," Leo said loudly and shook his head, stepping back. He snatched his drink from the other side of the island and jumped up next to McKenzie before gesturing toward the open space in front of them. "Your turn."

"I thought I was on injured reserve?"

"Nuh-uh. Not after you made me do that, you aren't. Do some spins, hop on one foot, anything. I don't care, just entertain me."

McKenzie took another sip, questioning for a moment what it meant that the alcohol had stopped burning on its way down, then slid off the counter. *Spin. Hop on one foot. Spin.* She had it. McKenzie tried to stifle her satisfied grin, but she'd never been very good at hiding her swagger. Turning back to Leo, she shrugged off her robe and tossed it onto his head like a human coat rack. When he pulled the cotton off, a curious grin lit his face. McKenzie sauntered back, testing her bad foot, but it took her weight okay, and she'd hardly need to use it. She assumed fifth position and extended her hands to the side. Transitioning to second then to fourth for some force, she spun, and spun, and spun, extending her leg for extra momentum. Pirouettes had always been her favorite. After seven spins—her personal best was double that—she landed gracefully in an extended fourth position and raised her arms above her head, flicking her wrists with a bit of flair.

Leo gaped.

Then he reeled back as his entire face twisted in a scowl. "That's not even fair."

"I took ballet for nearly a decade," she said with a shrug, suppressing the grin threatening to break forth in order to maintain her aura of nonchalance.

"Well, you could've mentioned that."

"And miss that look on your face?" She lost her battle with her lips. "Not a chance."

"Do something else."

"Something else?"

He took another sip and nodded.

Something else? Oh, I know!

McKenzie reached down and tore her socks off, not entirely sure why every idea she came up with included the removal of another item of clothing. But this was good. She had a feeling Leo would like this one. "Okay, so you know the movie *Titanic*?"

"A classic." There wasn't a hint of sarcasm in his voice.

"Exactly," McKenzie said, equally as serious. Rose and Jack were the stuff of legends, and for once, she was happy not to have to argue with her Fed. *My Fed?* McKenzie shook her head. "Well, I loved that movie as a kid. It was one of the reasons I couldn't wait to learn pointe when I first started ballet."

"Ooh, you can do the thing!" His eyes widened.

McKenzie smiled. "I can do the thing."

She rolled her ankles, loosening the joints, wincing as a pang traveled up one of her calves. It would be fine. She'd only be on pointe for a few seconds.

"I haven't done this in a while," she prefaced, then aligned her feet in first position, with her heels together and her toes facing to the side. She held her hands before her waist, just like in the film, and lifted, first her hands, then her body, higher, higher, higher, pushing from the balls of her feet, to the edge of her toes, and up, until all her weight rested on the very tips of her big toes. When she was still regularly going to ballet, the move didn't hurt, not really. She'd been used to spending hours practicing on pointe every week, but it had been a long time since then. After a few seconds, a sharp pain seared from her twisted ankle. With a yelp, McKenzie fell, balance suddenly gone. Leo was there.

She didn't know how he jumped off the counter so fast, but one second she was falling, and the next he was catching her in his strong arms, just as she'd come to expect he would. The hands that had been above her head fell around his shoulders. McKenzie looked up, Leo glanced down, and just like that, all her willpower faded.

She leaned up and kissed him.

Leo's arms tightened around her and he pulled her closer. McKenzie's fingers dug into his hair. He tasted of sugar and spice and oaky afterburn. She shifted her head slightly to the side to deepen the kiss, needing more. His lips were soft yet demanding. His tongue went on the attack, and McKenzie met him fire for fire.

"We shouldn't—" He broke away with a pant.

She'd rarely agreed with him before, and now didn't seem like a very good time to start. "Why not?"

"Because, because…" He darted his gaze back and forth, looking everywhere except her eyes. "I had a *lot* of reasons."

"You can tell me when you remember."

McKenzie sealed their lips together again. With a groan, Leo gave in. He dipped his hand beneath the edge of her shirt, hot fingers grazing the curve of her hip. She inhaled sharply, but the sound was lost in his lips. Leo sank the rest of the way to the ground, taking McKenzie with him. She landed straddling his lap, which worked just fine for her—she had no problem taking charge. Her fingers found the hem of his shirt and tugged it up.

"This isn't our house," he stammered as she broke apart for the brief second it took to yank the cotton over his head. "That was one of the reasons."

"I'll pay for damages," McKenzie murmured, unable to focus now that his chest was on full display. She'd been fantasizing about it in the back of her mind since the second they stepped through that door, and now those hard edges were all hers for the taking.

"Damages?"

McKenzie was too busy peppering kisses down the side of his neck to answer. Her fingers gained a life of their own as her palms flattened against his stomach and ran over the deep grooves carved into his abs. She loved the way his muscles flexed beneath her touch. Next thing she knew, her shirt was hoisted over her head.

"Jesus," Leo muttered with an almost pained voice.

No bra, McKenzie thought, grinning into his skin as he gripped her hips.

Leo rolled so she was beneath him with her spine flush against the wood floor. Her thighs tightened on instinct, wrapping around his waist. His forearm rested on the floor, taking most of his weight as his other hand traveled up the soft curves of her stomach. McKenzie gripped the backs of his shoulders, imagining how the wings painted into his skin writhed beneath her touch, wild and untamed.

He broke away again, yanking his face up and meeting her gaze through the shadows. "You're in shock."

McKenzie pushed against his chest and rolled them back over so she was on top. "I know exactly what I'm doing."

"You're—"

"Leo," she cut him off, pressing her palms against his pecs to hold him to the floor. She was heaving, half-naked, and highly aroused. She didn't have time for this bull. "Either shut up and kiss me, or shut up and get the hell out. Either way, for once in your life, stop talking."

He stared at her, at war with himself.

McKenzie stared right back.

Leo sat up so they were at eye level and searched for something in her gaze. She wished she knew what—what words she could say, what emotion she could share, what she could do. For once in her life, she wanted to be enough. She wanted someone to stay. Everyone left her.

Everyone abandoned her, discarded her like trash in a bin, as though there were something wrong with her. Not her looks or her body—hell, the flannel pants were thin enough that she knew the truth of that. Something else, something rotten inside, something she didn't know how to fix. For a moment, McKenzie thought he was going to leave.

Then Leo lifted his hand to her cheek and ran the backs of his fingers over her skin in a gentle, coveting touch that made her feel more precious than she had in all her life. He leaned in, pressing his lips to hers, slowly, softly, deliberately, as though he waited for an answer to a question he'd forgotten to ask. She kissed him back, and that was response enough. Leo slipped his arms beneath her thighs and stood, bringing her with him. He turned and placed her gently on the island before stepping into the open place between her thighs. She arched up, refusing to let go of his lips. Leo was unhurried. His time as a marine had taught him too much control. He worked her into a frenzy, those burning hands touching every inch of her exposed skin, until she was so dizzy, her mind so full of stars, McKenzie couldn't tell if her eyes were open or closed. His body was her road map and she slipped her hands lower and lower until finally, he gave in to the madness.

Just like that, he swept her off the table and carried her down the hall. They banged into one wall, then another, breaking apart at a loud crash. Their gazes met through soft candlelight, one word visible in both of their twinkling eyes.

Damages.

Leo shrugged. McKenzie grinned. They collided, meeting in the middle, and stumbled the rest of the way down the hall, smiling and kissing and laughing, until they fell onto the bed, and the world gave way to a different pleasure instead.

- 19 -

Leo

The steady beat of helicopter blades pounded in the distance. Leo looked past the blazing fire and the debris of the building to the black sky above.

"Chopper is almost here," the sergeant said.

Leo shook his head, gaze returning to the open doorway glowing orange with the promise of flames. There were still two bodies unaccounted for inside, and he refused to leave them behind. "I'm going back in."

"You've already been back in four times. The walls are about to collapse."

"I'm going in."

"I'll go too," another man said.

"Me too," one more added.

"Go quick," Sarg said. "The chopper won't wait very long."

It was too big of a target. Leo knew it and so did the two others, but they also knew the bodies of two marines closest to the blast still hadn't been recovered. And their loved ones deserved to have a piece of them brought home.

Leo took the lead, and the other two men followed. They raced back into the flames, guns held aloft, night-vision goggles on. The previously crowded main hall had already been cleared of bodies, living and dead, so they ran quickly through, steadily progressing deeper. There were a few enemy men down, and they stepped over the still forms blanketed across the floor. The heat was overwhelming. The glare from the flames turned their goggles almost white. Leo ripped his off his head, blinking as the scorch hit, but at least he could see. When they got to the blast site, he signaled to the others to go through an open doorway to check for bodies, while he provided cover. They pulled a disfigured, charred form out a few moments later. The silver gleam of dog tags was all Leo needed to see. After they passed hand signals back and forth, one of the men peeled off to carry the body out while Leo and the other soldier proceeded forward. They found the final body around the next corner and each took a shoulder strap by the hand.

A man leapt onto Leo's back.

Sharp metal nicked his throat. Before the knife could slice deep, he shuffled back, slamming the unseen attacker into a wall. The building groaned.

"Leo!"

"Go! Go!" he shouted.

Hands scratched at his skin, but he grabbed the knife, twisted it free, and slammed his elbow back, hitting ribs.

"Leo!"

He rolled, reached for his gun, and spun onto his back. Then he—

"Leo!"

He blinked and suddenly, the real world returned. There were no enemy fighters, no fires, no burning buildings. Just darkness and quiet and two big eyes looming over him.

"Leo," McKenzie said, softer this time.

He didn't move. His mind was still racing out of that building. His skin still itched with the heat of the fire.

"Leo."

The cut on her forehead had started bleeding again, deep maroon in the shadows of the room. Her eyes softened, so sympathetic he had to look away. That was when he realized his fingers dug into her biceps, deep enough to bruise. Leo snapped them off with a sharp inhale. Was her skin darker than before? Had he left marks?

"What'd I do?"

"Nothing, Leo," she cooed, but the words were too soothing to be real. McKenzie kept her palms pressed against his chest, holding him down and watching him.

"Did I hit you?"

"By accident."

But in the back of his mind, all he heard was the slap of his father's fist striking his mother and the piercing pitch of her cry. Only this time, it was his fist and McKenzie's scream striking like an knife to his heart.

Oh God.

Oh God.

Leo rolled out from underneath her and set his feet on the floor, leaning over to cradle his head in his palms. He tried to breathe but his lungs held no air. His chest was empty. His throat burned.

I hit her.

Oh God.

I hit her.

It was his worst fear come to life, his greatest nightmare—only this time it was real.

I'm no better than him.

I— I—

"It was my fault, Leo," McKenzie murmured, pressing a warm hand to his back.

He flinched. "No. It wasn't."

Fue mi culpa, Emilio, he could hear his mother say in the back of his mind. *It was my fault. You know your father.* It had been the same every time. She shouldn't have said this, or done that, or made this, as though the blame could have somehow been on her shoulders. But it was his father's fault, his father's demon, his father's lack of control. And this time, it was Leo's. He never should've fallen asleep. He never should've stayed in the bed. He never should've let any of this happen in the first place.

Leo stood, or at least he tried to, but his legs gave out from underneath him and he ended up sliding to the floor instead. The metal bed frame dug painfully into his back.

"Leo," McKenzie said, her voice firmer this time, but he didn't look. "This isn't some battered-woman thing. It actually was my fault. You were thrashing in the sheets and it woke me up. I thought you were having a seizure or something, so I jumped on your chest and you acted out of instinct. I should've known better—you're a marine, for one, so your body is trained to react. Not to mention that you probably have a hundred pounds on me. I wasn't thinking, and you were asleep. You never could've known."

"Don't make excuses."

"I'm not." Her voice was closer this time. Soft footsteps made their way around the bed, loud in the silence. McKenzie knelt before him, but Leo refused to look up. "Do you really think I, of all people, wouldn't tell you if I thought you were being an asshole? It was an honest mistake, Leo, and I'm fine. And now I know not to touch you if it happens again."

It won't happen again.

He didn't answer. He couldn't. His muscles were clenched so tight his entire body was racked with spasms.

"Leo."

He was too afraid to move, too afraid of what he might do.

"Emilio."

He lifted his face, meeting her eyes. McKenzie gently cupped his cheeks. His jaw was clenched beneath her fingers, and no matter how many times she ran her thumb over his skin, it didn't ease. She knelt before him, refusing to let him glance away. He'd forgotten they were both still naked until he saw the gentle glow of moonlight against her curves. The centers of her eyes were lit with a dusting of bright stars.

"Look at me and hear what I'm saying," she murmured, her voice calm and her words clear. "I'm tougher than I look, Leo. The past few days must've shown you that. It takes a lot to scare me—a hell of a lot more than this. You've saved my life more times than I can count, so my mind is pretty made up on the type of person you are. This hasn't changed that. In fact, it's probably reinforced it. I actually think you're the one who's confused. I'm not a princess in an ivory tower. I'm not a damsel in distress. I'm not made of porcelain, Leo. I'm not so easy to break."

You are, though, so easy to break.

Not your spirit maybe, but other things. He held her stare. Deep in the shadows of her pupils, he saw other scenes play out, ones he was thankful McKenzie would never have to see with her own beautiful eyes. *You have no idea how much damage two human hands can do. But I know. I've lived it.*

McKenzie pushed her brows together as though reading the thoughts in his head, then dropped her hands from his cheeks. She cleared the emotion from her face and cut the sympathy from her voice, trying a different tactic instead. "Come on. You're trembling."

He was numb. He hardly felt her touch as she grabbed his arm with both hands and pulled him to his feet. He followed blindly, unsure where she'd taken him until he heard a shower turn on. The water spat and hissed in the dark.

"The power's still out, but the storm passed," she said, just to fill the silence it seemed. Another moment later, she pushed him forward gently until he felt the hot spray against his skin. "I'll be right back."

She disappeared. Leo didn't notice. He put his hands against the wall, leaning into the tile, and let his head fall forward so the water assaulted the tight knots in his shoulders. He stood like that for he didn't know how long, keeping his eyes closed and his body still, praying the water might wash away the stain. But it was deeper than a simple shower could reach.

"Did your father hit your mother?"

Leo froze.

The words were so soft, so muffled by the shower, they could've been imagined. But they weren't. He knew they weren't.

"You don't need to tell me," McKenzie continued in the same careful tone. "But if you want to talk about it, I'm here. I can be there for you, the way you've been there for me."

He didn't say anything. He just turned his head to the side and opened his eyes. She was silhouetted by a soft yellow glow—candles she must've brought into the bathroom. The curves of her body were blurred by steam. Rivulets of water coursed down the glass divider between them, breaking up her image. As he saw her sitting there, gaze focused on the wall and not on him, lower lip pulled into her mouth, body and soul bared in more ways than one, the shell around his heart cracked. It dropped away. He didn't know why or how or what about her had done the trick, but his mouth opened, and so many of the things he'd kept inside for so long came pouring out.

"My father was abusive," he said, letting the water take the words from his lips. McKenzie didn't answer, but he was sure she heard. "It started before I was born and went on for as long as I can remember. Only ever with my mom, but she never did anything. She just took it. I think maybe she thought it was better it be her than us, not realizing there was a third option—for it to be no one. Then one day, my dad went after Manny. He reared his arm back, and I went crazy. I beat the shit out of him with a baseball bat and kicked him out the house and told him never to come back, and he didn't. But that wasn't the end."

He swallowed, not sure how to continue.

"Your dreams?" McKenzie prompted as though reading his mind.

"Nightmares, more like. I had visions of him coming back for revenge, but they were easy enough to handle, easy enough to control. When I got back from the war, everything changed. I was having a flashback, before, with you. They're—they're so vivid, you can't even believe. It's like I'm back in the Middle East, like I'm—"

He broke off as his throat caught.

"Have you ever seen anyone about it?"

"No."

"Why not?"

"Because—" He paused and shifted his position, dropping his arms to his sides as he lifted his head, letting the water smack him in the face. He rubbed his palms over his cheeks and up into his hair. "Because I didn't think anyone would be able to help."

McKenzie saw through his bullshit. "Why, Leo?"

He turned to stare at her through the water and the glass. Somehow, her blue eyes were crystal clear.

"Because it happened once before, right when I got back from overseas, one of the first times I had these nightmares. I was with a woman and I—I hit her in my sleep, by accident, and by the time I woke up, she was on the floor, curled into a ball, watching me with this look in her eyes, this fear. She was watching me the way my mom used to watch my father, like she didn't know what would come next, like she was braced for impact, too terrified to move, like I was a monster. And I couldn't bear to tell anyone, for fear that they'd tell me the awful truth. That I was just like him."

"You're not." McKenzie jumped off the vanity, fluid in the candlelight.

Leo watched her step closer. His heart pounded, urging him to run, to flee, but his feet were glued to the ground, as though the shower water had turned to chains, holding him hostage. He stared, helpless, as she pulled open the door and stepped inside. The steam wrapped around her body, welcoming her in as his arms hung useless by his sides. McKenzie gripped his jaw. The tips of her fingers dug into the hair at the back of his neck. Catching his eyes, she waited until she knew he was paying attention. It was the tender gleam in those irises that brought him back to life, sending a blast of heat deep into his chest, warming the numbness from the inside out.

"You're not a monster, Leo. You're the furthest thing from a monster I can imagine. In fact, you might just be the kindest, noblest, most amazing man I've ever met."

He dropped his gaze to her lips, wanting to drink the words in, to swallow them, as though somehow that might make them stick.

He did the next best thing.

He kissed her.

McKenzie didn't flinch at his touch or run away in fear. She wrapped her arms around his shoulders and kissed him back, leading where he followed. Leo pulled her beneath the water as his hands roved over her wet skin, closing the distance between them. Unlike last time, this kiss didn't feel like a battle to be won, like a game between opposing sides, each one fighting to come out on top. This time, their kiss felt like two halves of a whole, joining together, not sure how they'd survived so long apart.

- 20 -

McKenzie

When she woke in bed the next morning, McKenzie was alone. A chill spread across her bare shoulders, made colder by the memory of Leo's warm, sturdy arms wrapped around her. She'd had a feeling he would leave after she'd fallen asleep, but the thought made her sad in a way she couldn't explain. He was too good a person to be afraid of himself.

Rubbing the sleep from her eyes, McKenzie rolled over, finding a clock next to the bed. The screen was blank, which meant the power was still out. The storm, though, was long gone. Streams of sunlight coursed through the window, casting the bedroom in a golden glow. The trees outside were bright green and glittering with early morning dew. She had no idea what time it was. Hell, McKenzie hardly knew what day it was. New

York City felt a million miles away, as though she'd spent weeks in these woods with Leo instead of mere days. Without the storm and the dark hiding the rest of the world from view, reality came rushing back. Soon, the power would be on and a rescue team would come with it. Her time with Leo was coming to an end. For all she knew, it might already be over, as though last night were just dream, gone as soon as they both opened their eyes. The very idea made her heart pinch.

With a sigh, she rolled off the mattress, found her discarded flannel pants on the ground, and tugged them up over her hips. Her shirt was still in the kitchen—the memory of Leo yanking it off brought a rueful grin to her lips—but abandoning an unmade bed wasn't in her blood. McKenzie hastily tucked the sheets into place, folded the duvet back over, and arranged the pillows before turning toward the door. Walking around naked in the middle of the night was one thing, but it felt different to be nude in the bright light of day, more intimate somehow. She shielded her chest with her arms and kept her head down as she tiptoed down the hall. Her shirt was on the floor by the kitchen island. McKenzie slipped it over her head like armor, then took a deep breath and spun, ready to face Leo.

She gasped as soon as she turned around. The massive floor-to-ceiling windows on either side of the stone fireplace had been nothing but fog and rain the day before, but now, they displayed a little slice of paradise. Beyond the towering trees, sunlight shimmered across the surface of a still lake. The waters were crystal blue, reflecting the sky. Hardly a cloud was visible. The whole scene was like a postcard, inviting her to dive in.

This must be a vacation home, McKenzie realized, thinking of the empty house, the stocked freezer, and the minimal amount of clothes. *Are we in the Catskills? Maybe? Why would the mob have brought me here?*

The question fled as soon as her gaze landed on the body fast asleep on the couch. Leo was curled on his side, bare chested with his pants slung low around his waist. A pillow was roughly folded between his ear and one arm, while his other arm dangled limp over the side of the cushions. He looked like a boy almost, innocent and scared—completely at odds with the confident, assured man she'd come to know. Part of her wanted to brush his hair from where it had fallen over his face, and remind him with a simple touch that he wasn't alone. Part of her didn't want to wake him. Not out of fear—he could never do anything to make her afraid of him, not after everything they'd been through. A different set of nerves twisted and coiled deep in her stomach. It had been so long since she'd had a morning after, and she'd never had one quite like this. They'd bared their bodies, but more importantly, they'd bared their souls. What could she say after that? *Good morning?*

Instead, McKenzie retreated.

After a few minutes digging around the kitchen, she found a French press in a drawer and a bag of ground coffee in the freezer. While the coffee brewed, she did what she always did when she needed to escape her thoughts but couldn't bake—she cleaned. First the pots and pans from the night before, then the plates and the silverware, then she wiped down the counters, until everything was spotless. She organized the pantry and a few of the cabinets. Finally, when there was nothing left to do, she filled two cups of coffee and faced the inevitable.

Leo's eyes opened as soon as she held the full cup beneath his nose. The shadows gradually disappeared from his irises as he blinked, coming fully awake. He sat up and ran his palm over his face to rub the sleep away.

"Is that coffee?"

"Yup," McKenzie said cheerfully, though her heart fluttered in her chest.

"Are you some kind of sorceress or something?" He smiled and grabbed the cup, then breathed in the smell before taking a slow sip. The tension in his shoulders eased and he leaned into the couch. "Oh, that's good."

"Not a sorceress," McKenzie clarified as she dropped into the open spot by his side, sinking into the plush cushions. "Just generally awesome in every way, I guess."

Leo cut his eyes toward her, raising his brows.

Good, McKenzie thought. *He's still being playful.* "There was a French press in one of the cabinets."

"Ah." He nodded.

"Yeah."

Her mind flashed back to a moment from the night before, with her legs wrapped around his hips, his lips on her skin, the steam of the shower curling between them as the spray of hot water drowned out her sighs.

McKenzie took a sip of coffee.

So did Leo.

The silence extended a bit too long. If they'd been two people who hadn't slept together last night, it would've been normal. Comfortable, even. But it wasn't. And they were. An awkward tingle permeated the narrow slip of space between their bodies.

Is he thinking about the fact that we had sex?

Why I am thinking about the fact that we had sex?

The longer the quiet lasted, the stronger the flashbacks became. The two of them on the bed. The way he'd done that thing with his tongue. The feel of his weight above her.

Speak, McKenzie. Speak!

"Leo, I—"

"McKenzie, I—"

They both stopped at the same time.

"I—"

"I—"

Oh, for goodness' sake. Her nostrils flared and she gripped the cup tighter. *Do I even know what I want to say? I, what? I like you? I didn't mean for last night to happen but I'm happy it did? I'm glad you opened up? I'm not sorry at all?*

McKenzie swallowed all those confessions back down and turned toward Leo, taking the coward's way out. "Leo, go ahead. What were you trying to say?"

"I…" He paused, swallowing a nonexistent sip of coffee as he stared into the brown liquid, searching for the right words.

Beneath her skin, McKenzie's pulse thundered. *Does he regret it? Is he sorry? Oh, please don't apologize, Leo. Please. Please. I wouldn't be able to stand it.* She buried the emotions away, hating how exposed she felt as he finally looked up and met her gaze.

"I feel like I need to state for the record that I did not foresee any of last night happening," he finally admitted, lifting the edge of his lip in a smile. "And that is *not* why I suggested we both get drunk."

She put her palm against her chest and feigned shock, reverting back to jokes because they were oh so easy. "You mean you *didn't* want to have your way with me?"

"McKenzie," he chided. "That's not—"

"Relax," she teased with a wink, keeping their words surface. She didn't want to do deep right now—she didn't know how, not when she was sober and the sun was up and the comfort of darkness was gone. "Maybe *I* wanted to get *you* drunk. Ever think about that?"

He scoffed.

"The Thriller wasn't going to dance itself, you know."

Leo's jaw dropped open. "Did you play me, McKenzie Harper?"

"You were like putty in my hands, Leo Alvarez."

She hid her grin behind her coffee cup and waggled her brows. He rolled his eyes and released a half-hearted puff of air. For a second, she thought maybe he was going to let it go, and maybe they'd move on with the day. Then he put his coffee down and turned toward her, taking her free hand in both of his.

"Leo—"

"Just let me say one thing," he cut her off, keeping his gaze down, studying their intertwined fingers. "Thank you." He looked up, finding her eyes. "What you said last night? It meant—it means—a lot to me. So, thank you."

Her chest tightened, but she kept a carefree smile across her lips, giving nothing away. "You're welcome."

"Okay," he said louder with a heavy exhale. "Time to get you home safe and sound."

Leo pulled his hands away. McKenzie let him go, resisting the urge to tighten her grip and hold on. As he stood and brought some distance between them, she curled her fingers into a fist, hating the way they suddenly felt so empty and cold. Being alone was easier. It was how she'd gotten this far in life, how she'd protected herself for so long. Yet for the first time, watching Leo cross the room to stare out the window, she wondered if it was better. Or if all those people had it right when they said nothing worth having came easy.

"Are you seeing what I'm seeing?"

McKenzie blinked and cleared her mind, glancing toward Leo. He nudged his chin toward the window. "You mean the lake?"

"No," he clarified. "Though it's sort of hard to believe we missed that yesterday. I mean what's happening on the other side of the lake."

"What?"

McKenzie stood and crossed the room to look outside. She took a spot by his side, close enough to see, but not so close she could feel the tempting warmth of his skin. Taking a sip of coffee, she swallowed the lump in her throat. Her eyes widened the moment she saw what he'd seen.

"Is that a wedding?" McKenzie asked, stepping closer to the glass.

Across the lake, a swarm of people ran around like chickens with their heads cut off. Some were clearing branches and leaves from a pristinely cut grass lawn.

Some were setting up rows of white chairs. Some were carefully hanging fresh pink flowers from an arbor. The home behind them was massive—McKenzie wasn't sure how she'd missed it before. Knowing what she knew about the rich, she could easily believe it was a private home. But she suspected it was some sort of club or hotel, which meant...

"They must have a generator!" She snapped her gaze to Leo.

He grinned. "That's exactly what I was thinking."

"Do you think they have a phone?"

Excitement bubbled beneath her skin at the prospect of this nightmare finally being over. Yet at the same time, a tingle slipped down her spine. Every step closer to New York City was one step farther from Leo. She didn't know how she knew. She just did. Everything that had happened between them would remain in these woods, a dream. The process had already begun with their brushed-over conversation, and it would keep going unless one of them dared stop it. McKenzie wasn't ready to make that leap of faith anytime soon. She'd had so few perfect moments in her life, and last night had been one of them. She wanted to keep the memory cased in glass like a snow globe she could look back on and shake anytime she wanted to smile. If they dove any deeper into this thing between them, they'd ruin it.

Wouldn't we?

"There's only one way to find out."

McKenzie turned toward Leo with her brows pinched. She'd forgotten their entire conversation. "Huh?"

"There's only one way to find out if they have a phone we can use," he repeated, eying her as though she had three heads.

"Right, right," McKenzie hastened to say, shaking her head until it was clear. Of course he hadn't read her mind. Of course he wasn't overanalyzing everything that had happened between them. He was a guy. They'd gotten drunk. They'd had sex. End of story and back to the mission. He just wanted to get her home safe so he could return to his normal life. McKenzie lightened her tone. "And what's that?"

"Going over there and asking." He shrugged and turned back toward the window. "This is a lake house, right? There's got to be a kayak or a boat or something."

"I guess…"

"Let's take a look around and see what we find."

Leo strode by her, utterly focused on the job at hand and the new plan circulating inside his head. McKenzie's fingers twitched with the need to reach out and stop him.

Leo, wait. If only she had the strength to open her mouth and speak. He would freeze. He would turn and look at her over his shoulder. She would say all the words bubbling inside. *What you said last night meant a lot to me too. I haven't laughed like that in so long. I can't remember the last time I felt so happy. Thank you for making me feel wanted. Thank you for making me feel seen. It meant more than you could ever know.*

Instead, McKenzie let him pass and lifted her mug to her lips. Taking a long sip, she swallowed all those sentiments back down and buried them deep. In a few hours, everything would be back to normal and she had to be prepared. Leo would drop her off at her apartment, and then he'd say goodbye, turn around, and leave. What else was there for him to do? He lived in DC, she lived in New York. He was a federal agent, she was a pastry chef. He came from a house full of love, she wasn't sure she understood the word. She'd practically thrown herself at him last night, not giving him the chance to say no. Maybe he'd just been acting polite—really, really fucking polite. Maybe this happened with all the women he rescued. Maybe she was nothing special. Maybe they were nothing special. Maybe she'd made it all up in her own damn mind.

Idiot, she thought as she followed him outside in search of a boat.

It had taken Leo a life-or-death situation and days on the run to break down her walls, but it only took a second for McKenzie to build them right back up.

It was better to be the one leaving than the one left behind. She simply wasn't strong enough to have her heart broken again—it had already been split into too many pieces.

- 21 -

Leo

He couldn't help but think McKenzie was quieter than normal as they paddled their way across the lake using an old kayak they'd found tied up behind the house. He'd tried to talk to her about what happened last night. He'd tried to thank her, but she'd shot him down with an easy smile and a breezy *you're welcome*. Part of him had been relieved—the last things he wanted to talk about were his deepest, darkest insecurities and fears. It was easy to return to his usual mode of pretending everything was all right. Yet part of him had been hurt by the brush-off, because he'd meant what he'd said—her words had touched him, deeper than her body ever could've. Yet McKenzie, it seemed, had been unaffected by the whole affair. Now, as they glided toward the wedding on the opposite shore, she was quiet—and he was quietly going crazy. He didn't know what to say. The only topic he wanted to discuss, the only topic on his mind, was off limits.

Was it a trick of the light, or did you mean to look at me as if I were perfect, as if all the scars and damaged bits and rough edges somehow made me better? Was it just the alcohol? The atmosphere? The moment? Or was it something more?

Did you really believe it when you said I'm not a monster? Or were they just words?

Leo tried to focus on the sound of their paddles slicing through the surface of the lake, the trickle of water dropping off the fins as they were lifted into the air, the chirp of the birds hidden among the trees, the gentle rustle of the leaves, but there was an absence he couldn't ignore. The roar of her silence was driving him mad.

"Hello!" Leo shouted as they neared the shore, just to finally speak.

A middle-aged man who'd been clearing a large tree branch paused and stood up. His eyes widened when they landed on Leo and McKenzie in their bright red kayak. Leo could only imagine the sight the two of them made. They'd changed back into their own clothes, which were dirty as hell from the days before—a little bloody and covered in muck. The massive cut and bruise on McKenzie's forehead probably wasn't helping either.

"Hello! You two okay?"

"We're not injured," Leo called back and paddled two more times with a little extra oomph. "But we are looking for some help."

The kayak hit mud and slid, coming to a stop a few feet shy of the dry sand. He jumped out, uncaring as his feet sank in the murky water, then pulled the boat the rest of the way to shore. The man ran over with a curious glint in his eyes and offered McKenzie a hand. She grabbed Leo's backpack from the center of the kayak before accepting the help.

"What can I do?" the man asked as he pulled her to her feet.

"We got stuck outside in the storm yesterday," Leo said and motioned toward their clothes, trying to explain their appearance. The real situation was too much to dive into now. A cover story rolled smoothly through his lips. "The house we rented lost power, so we couldn't get the garage door to open to get back inside, and both of us forgot to bring a key when we went on our hike. We thought you guys might have power? I have my phone, but it got water damaged with all the rain. We want to call our friends so they know we're okay."

"Sure, sure." The man nodded. "I'm John, by the way."

"Leo." They shook hands.

"McKenzie."

"Well, folks, we have power, but phone service is out all around the lake. We're running on our generator—no internet, no cable, no nothing. Trees are down all over the roads. The bride is in a state of panic, as I'm sure you can imagine. But I think the best man, Drew, has cell service—he was calling some of the guests who were supposed to arrive last night and the caterers and the band. Just let me…" He turned and then lifted his hands to his lips, cupping the air around them. "Drew!"

Another guy, probably mid-twenties and closer to McKenzie's age, spun at the sound of his name being called. "Yeah?"

"Get over here!" John screamed, then turned back to them. "Pardon the shouting, but it's effective."

"No problem," Leo said smoothly.

"What's up?" the younger man asked, then turned toward Leo and McKenzie. "I'm Drew, by the way, as you probably guessed."

"Leo."

"McKenzie."

This is beginning to feel like the twilight zone, he thought, stifling a grin. McKenzie wasn't so successful. They made eye contact briefly as a smile widened her lips.

Don't you dare, he silently ordered.

The twinkle in her eye quietly responded, *I wouldn't dream.*

For some reason, it made his chest tight.

"They need to borrow your phone," John said. "They're locked out of their rental house and need to call someone to help."

"Sure thing." Drew lurched into action, pulling his cell from his pocket and rapidly shifting his thumb across the screen. "Let me just… Here you go."

"Thanks."

Leo took the phone and dialed in Nate's number. As the line rang, he couldn't help but notice as McKenzie stepped over to Drew and leaned in close. He didn't like the way his muscles writhed at the sight.

"Did you say the caterers were missing?" she asked softly.

"Yeah," Drew told her in a low voice. A sigh slipped through his lips as he rubbed at the back of his neck with his palm. Then his eyes widened the briefest amount, but Leo knew exactly what it was—it was the look of a man who'd suddenly realized he was talking to a beautiful woman. Drew dropped his arm and straightened his spine. When he opened his mouth to speak, the tone was deeper, more friendly, more inviting. "Did I mention my brother is the groom? He's got a lot on his plate, what with the roads being hell and his bride, Alice, having a meltdown. I'm here all by myself, no date or girlfriend or anything, so I volunteered to run point on fixing this quickly unfolding disaster. But it's not looking good."

"Would it help if I told you I'm a pastry chef?" McKenzie grinned, a wicked little thing that Leo understood immediately—she couldn't wait to get her hands in a kitchen. Dammit if the sight of her so enthused didn't make his pulse race a little faster. Annoyingly, Leo guessed it had the same effect on Drew, whose eyes widened with shocked delight. "And I have nothing better to do right now than come to your rescue?"

Leo fought the sudden urge to gag. Drew, in the meantime, smiled and put his hand on her lower back, guiding her toward the clubhouse. "You might just be the best surprise I've had all day."

Don't fall for that line. Leo snorted, rolling his eyes at the sound of McKenzie's soft laughter. *You've got to be kidding me.*

"Hello?"

The firm sound of his partner's voice pulled Leo back to the phone in his hand. He gripped it tighter and turned around, pushing McKenzie and the doting puppy at her heels from his mind as he let his gaze fall on the lake and focused on the job.

"It's me."

"Leo! Where the hell have you been?"

"It's a long story, Parker."

"Are you with McKenzie? Where are you? What happened?"

I saved her from the Russian mob, we had the most amazing night of my entire life, and then I let her walk away in the arms of another man. That's what the hell happened! Leo wrinkled his nose and took a deep breath through clenched teeth. *The job, the job. Focus on the job.* "Our call dropped somewhere between the Upper West Side and the George Washington Bridge, but I maintained pursuit until the van pulled over into a warehouse somewhere in New Jersey. They switched vehicles, and I continued to tail them to a house somewhere in upstate New York. I'm guessing the Catskills maybe."

"Upstate New York?" Nate broke in. "Why did they bring her there?"

"My question exactly."

Leo nodded as the image of the house filled his mind. The lake, the wedding, and the real world slipped away as he slid back into federal-agent mode. His training took over, forcing his thoughts to compartmentalize, and that pesky bundle of confused emotions was stuffed into a drawer to be opened another time. "The address on the mailbox was 11 Mountainside Drive. It was a big house with expensive cars. They kept McKenzie in what appeared to be an empty closet in the garage that had been cleaned and fitted out with a mattress. It was possibly designed to be used as a cell, possibly not. I couldn't tell. She said she caught a glimpse of the owner—white hair, tan skin, dark brown eyes, glasses, mid-sixties I'm guessing, give or take a few years."

"I'll run the address through the system," Nate commented, as though reading Leo's mind. They had predicting each other's needs down to a science, as the best partners did. "See if I find anyone who matches that description, though no one comes to mind."

"Yeah, I couldn't think of any leads either. The whole thing smells fishy, like there's something we're not seeing. It's slippery. I can't quite get a grasp."

"What happened next?"

"Well, I broke in—"

"Without backup? Leo."

"Don't even start, Parker. It wasn't by the book, but what other choice did I have?"

A defeated sigh came through the line. "Keep going."

"I broke in sometime around dawn and got her out of there, but the guys who initially grabbed her pursued. The only way I could lose them was by taking the motorcycle into the woods. We got lost. A massive storm hit. We found shelter in a house. And just now, we crashed a wedding so I could borrow someone's cell phone to call you."

"Where's the wedding?" Classic Nate—taking everything in unfazed and then straight back to business.

"I'm not sure… Hold on."

Leo turned around, searching for John. Watching McKenzie leave with that guy must've really done a number on him if he'd forgotten to get an address.

"Hey, John!" he shouted. The man in question waved back to signal he'd heard. "Where are we right now? What's this house called?"

"The Balsam Estate," John called. "One Balsam Lake Drive."

"Thanks!" Leo spun to face the water, if only to keep his eyes from searching for McKenzie's telltale form. "We're at the Balsam Estate, One Balsam Lake Drive."

"I'll try to get a team there as fast as I can."

"Take your time," Leo interjected quickly, not sure why his gut reaction was to fight off the rescue. He shook his head. "The roads are shit, or so I've heard. Apparently, the storm brought down a bunch of trees. We're secure here so if it takes a while, we can wait. I mean, don't dawdle, but I just wanted to warn you about the conditions so no one is surprised."

"Maybe the boss will splurge for a chopper."

Leo snorted. "That'll be the day."

"He's been really broken up about your disappearance," Nate continued in a wry voice that made Leo immediately want to roll his eyes. A grin came to his lips instead. "He only called you a *real fucking asshole* about ten times."

"Oh, is that all?"

"The whole New York field office has been scrambling to find you," Nate said, tone returning to its serious nature. His partner never joked for very long, but Leo didn't mind. Sarcasm was his job. "They were nervous. We all were."

That was about as sentimental as the two of them ever got, and Leo could easily read beneath his partner's tone. *I was scared out of my mind that you were dead*, was what Nate was trying to say.

"Unfortunately, it's going to take a lot more than a few mobsters for you to get rid of me, Parker." Or, in agent speak, *I was really fucking scared too.* "Tell Jo that McKenzie is a little banged up and bruised, but she's fine, and I'll have her home soon." Translation, *We barely made it out alive, but we did. And we're both okay.* Leo cleared his throat. That was enough of that. "Any update on Ryder before I go? Or on the third friend, Addison?"

"Negative," Nate growled. "They're still on the loose."

Leo read that snarl loud and clear. "What is it?"

"I'm in Arizona."

"And that stick up your ass is starting to chafe in the dry desert air?" he teased, then something clicked. "Oh! Ryder's mom lives there, right?"

"Right," Nate said. Leo knew his jaw was clenched. He could perfectly envision his partner forcing the words through grinding teeth. "Jo said she had a hunch Ryder was headed here. She wanted to fly all the way across the country, *just in case.*"

"Let me guess," Leo cut in, unable to keep the humor from his tone. "You think little Jo Parker might not be as reformed as she claims?"

"Something like that."

Leo couldn't help it as a laugh escaped up his throat. "You're the one who wanted to date a criminal, Parker. I just came along for the ride."

"She's not— Well, she was— But she—" Nate cut off with a sigh. "Goodbye, Leo."

He shook his head. Jo certainly kept things interesting, for everyone involved. "Call this number when you hear back from the team in New York."

"Will do."

They hung up. Leo dropped his arm and closed his eyes before taking a long, refreshing breath of that crisp forest air. Behind his closed eyelids, two very different scenes played, oscillating back and forth. One of McKenzie below him, ecstasy written across her face as her fingers dug into his shoulder blades. The other of her backside as she walked away.

Leo blinked. *And people say nature is relaxing.* He snorted as a sneer passed over his lips. *I can't wait to get out of these fucking woods.*

As much as he wanted to believe that last thought, he knew the sentiment was hollow—just as hollow as the void gradually expanding across his chest, empty and cold, vacant of all the warmth he'd started to grow used to. His gaze settled on their house across the lake, the windows now dark and swirling with all sorts of hidden desires. Leo pivoted, turning back to the party and the people he'd forgotten were there. He only had eyes for one person, and even though he told himself not to look, he couldn't stop his gaze from scanning the crowd or his heart from sinking when he realized she wasn't there. Worrying about her had become second nature—something he'd need to shake sooner rather than later, so why not start now? She was probably off with that guy Drew, someone whose biggest worry in life was the size of his 401k and how long it would be until his next promotion, someone as uncomplicated as she deserved. McKenzie was beautiful, driven, and at the precipice of achieving all her dreams. Leo was broken inside, unsure if he would ever heal. They'd never work in the real world. If this wedding was a sign of anything, it was of that. So he pushed the discomfort down and forced a smile onto his lips, sliding into the confident mask he was used to.

"Hey, John!" Leo called and marched onto the grass, leaving that house—and everything that had happened last night—three hundred yards behind him. "I've got two hands and nothing to do. Put me to work."

- 22 -

McKenzie

"Oh my God, are you the surprise pastry chef?"

McKenzie looked up in time to see three giggling girls in matching silk robes spill through the side door into the kitchen. *Oh, boy.* "That's me."

"I'm Anna."

"Casey."

"Samantha, but you can call me Sam."

The names were lost to McKenzie almost as soon as they were said aloud. She was too busy trying to remember a recipe for something a little nicer than vanilla cake to focus on three girls she'd never see again.

"I'm McKenzie."

"Oh my gosh." Girl number one stepped forward. "Alice is just so thankful you offered to help. Everything has been a disaster. We told her not to cry, it'll just make her eyes puffy before the wedding, but, well, you spend a year planning the best day of your life, you never expect a storm to sweep through and ruin it."

It was physically painful for McKenzie to refrain from rolling her eyes while keeping a soft smile on her lips. *Isn't it supposed to be about marrying the love of her life? Not a party?* "I'm sure."

"Oh, we're the bridesmaids," one of the other girls said. "Alice sent us down because she needs to decompress. She's having a bit of a bridezilla morning."

"Her mom is trying to calm her down," the third girl jumped in. They all spoke with the same voice, hyper, high pitched, and bubbly in a way McKenzie found incredibly grating on anyone aside from Addy or Jo.

"Anyway, we thought we'd come see if there's anything we can do to help," the first girl said, taking over again.

They stepped farther into the kitchen, then dispersed. One opened the refrigerator, one went through the cabinets, and one started reading the labels of all the ingredients McKenzie had already pulled from the shelves. It was her worst nightmare come to life.

"Please don't touch that." McKenzie stepped over to the stainless-steel island in the center of the room and reorganized the things the girl had moved. Every time she put one bag back in place, something else had been shifted. "Please, I have everything arranged—"

"I found booze!" the girl by the refrigerator cheered.

"I've got glasses!" A cabinet door slammed closed, making McKenzie jolt.

Three drunk bridesmaids are the last things I need right now, she sighed. *All I wanted was a few hours alone in the kitchen, nothing but my thoughts and my food to keep me company. Was that so hard to ask?*

"You want some champagne?" one girl offered.

McKenzie looked at the glass, and then back up. The answer must've been written all over her face. She'd never been very good at hiding her derision.

"Oh, probably not. You're working. More for us!" They clinked their glasses. "So, what can we do?"

"Nothing," McKenzie said through gritted teeth, trying to keep the frustration from leaking into her tone…and failing. She took a deep breath.

"What are you making?"

"Some sort of cake. I'm not entirely sure yet. Maybe some éclairs or macarons too."

"Wow. I made macarons once. They were awesome. All my sorority sisters loved them." *I'm sure they did, and I'm sure you now consider yourself a pastry chef.* "I'm sure I could make them again."

"That's okay—"

"What about cupcakes? Alice loves cupcakes, especially those mini ones from that famous bakery in the city. What's it called?"

"Baked by Melissa," McKenzie supplied. *And they're freaking delicious!*

"Yes! You could make those. You could call them *Baked by McKenzie.*"

Except that would be intellectual property theft. She bit back the retort. Really, she should be used to this by now. That was the thing with jobs people idealized—they always had opinions. Strangers and even friends were constantly telling her what she should cook, what she should call her bakery, what would be the next big thing, as if it were oh so easy. But it wasn't. Her job was hard work. "I'm more of a French-trained chef."

"Ooh, that sounds fancy. Can you make soufflé?"

Not for a hundred people without notice. "I think I'll stick with a cake."

"I can make frosting."

McKenzie slammed the mixing bowl onto the table and they all jumped. "Really, I've got it covered. Thanks for the offer, but I'm sure there's someone else who needs more help than I do."

All three girls shared a look, and her hackles rose. She recognized that look. She'd seen it many times before from the girls who'd once pretended to be her best friends then wrote *slut* across her locker, from the ladies at the country club who'd kicked her mother out of the gardening league. It was a look that whispered, *Outsider. Bitch. You don't belong here with us.*

"Look," McKenzie snapped. *If you want me to be a jerk, I can be.* "I'm not trying to be rude"—*Except, yes. Yes, I am.*—"but I know what I'm doing and I've been doing it for a long time. If you want your friend to have any sort of wedding cake by the time the party starts tonight, I need to get moving, and the three of you will only slow me down. I'm sure there's somewhere else where you can be of better use than in here." *Or, in other words, get the F out.* But her mother had taught her to be more of a lady than that, so she finished it with a simple, yet snide, "Okay?"

The three of them shared that look again.

"Okay."

Their lips wobbled as they quickly snatched their glasses from the counter and took another bottle of champagne. As soon as the door slammed closed behind them, laughter echoed across the sterile hall, obvious and uncontrolled.

"Oh my God."

"Could you believe that—"

The voices died out before McKenzie caught the rest of that statement, but she could imagine. She'd heard it all before. She'd heard worse, but that didn't necessarily mean it had stopped hurting. Curling her fingers into fists, McKenzie took a deep breath and forced the familiar ache back down.

What's the recipe for red velvet cake?

Focus on that. Focus on your food.

How much flour do I need? How much sugar? How much dye?

She ran through the numbers in her head, multiplying them to fit the size of the guest list. The cake would have to be three tiers at least, and no fondant. McKenzie couldn't stand the stuff—it tasted like crap. She'd have to make enough frosting to cover the entire structure. Her piping was passable at best, but it would have to do, and a little sugar work could provide the ooh-and-ahh a wedding cake needed. She'd need to come up with some sort of unique filling so the whole thing didn't become a ball of cream-cheese icing in the mouth.

Oh, how I wish Addy were here with me... McKenzie mused, sighing. *She could pull a romantic, lovey-dovey, flower-draped cake out of her ass, and keep a smile on her face while she did it!*

Even though McKenzie didn't know what her friend looked like, she could picture her so easily. Addy would be in some frilly pink dress, most likely, with one of those '50s-style aprons tied around her waist, something with polka dots. She'd flounce around, stirring and chatting, voice as sweet as the sugar she whipped into a frosting. Jo would be there too, though she'd be isolated to the opposite end of the room where she'd be free to make a complete mess. McKenzie pictured her sitting on the counter with dough and flour splotched all over her clothes, a mad scientist at work. They'd speak in shorthand because they all knew what the others were thinking. They wouldn't have to explain their recipes or what they were doing. They'd just know. She'd offer tips for better technique. Jo would entertain with her crazy antics. Addy would keep the peace. It would be fun.

Fun?

McKenzie paused, blinking the visions away. Nothing had changed in the past few seconds, but the kitchen felt emptier than it had before.

When's the last time I thought of baking as fun? Not a job or a competition or a race to the top, but fun?

She didn't remember. Before culinary school? Back in high school? When her dad was still home? When Yolanda taught her recipes over the stove? Looking around the empty room, McKenzie couldn't help but wonder when her haven had turned into a hideout. The kitchen would always be her safe place—as soon as she stepped inside, everything that was wrong in the world disappeared—but it wasn't warm and inviting anymore, not in the way it once was. There was no joy here, just focus, just perfection and precision. She used to run to the kitchen when things got tough, but now she was the tough thing people ran away from.

Her gaze slid toward the door as though pulled by invisible string. Catty laughter echoed in her ear, a ghostly noise pulled from any number of instances in her past. She looked away, back toward her ingredients and her mixers and her bowls that had no choice but to stay with her.

Would Addy and Jo even like me if they were here? Would they want to be my friend if they knew me in real life? Or would I just push and push and push, the way I always do, until I pushed them right out that door with everyone else?

No, she realized as a smile spread her lips, fully aware of the answer to her question. *Because they'd never let me.*

McKenzie thought back to the conversation that started it all, two long years ago during the premiere season of *The American Baking Championship*. Everyone in the online forum had been raving about one of the contestants for weeks—a grandmother who had always dreamed of becoming a professional baker, but had been unable to chase her dreams due to the societal constraints of motherhood at the time. At least, that was what the woman portrayed, but McKenzie hadn't been buying it. Normally, she was all for a female-empowerment angle, but something about that granny had rubbed her wrong. She never said anything, because, well, she'd been more of a lurker on the page than an active participant. But the more and more the comment thread filled with adoration, the more McKenzie wanted to snap—until finally, she did.

@TheGourmetGoddess: Okay…no one else wants to admit it, but I can't bite my tongue anymore. Who else thinks that old lady would cut a bitch? I don't trust her.

The words had felt so satisfying as she typed them, but as soon as she pressed *send*, her hackles rose. *Shit! I don't want to get into a comment war. Why did I do that? Why? Why?* She hated putting herself out there, even online. Silent observation was much more fun. But then, to her surprise, a reply popped onto the screen.

@TheBakingBandit: Oh, I'm with you! The woman's got evil-genius in her eyes!

@TheBakingBandit: She's a shark in a dainty old lady's body!

@Sprinkle-Ella: She reminds me of my gran…

A grin immediately widened her lips. McKenzie sat up and leaned over her keyboard, pulling her lower lip between her teeth as she eagerly typed.

@TheGourmetGoddess: She's totally going for the nostalgia sympathy angle. Everyone is eating it up!

@Sprinkle-Ella: She is! I totally fell for it in that first episode where she baked that coconut cake! It looked exactly like the one my memaw used to make. (NOT my gran. She's on my dad's side. *shivers*). I got all the warm fuzzies from that…

@TheBakingBandit: It's a great play—she knows what she's doing. Sly old fox!

@TheBakingBandit: Did you see the way she pulled that Le Crueset pan from the bottom oven? She's not as fragile as she looks… I almost respect the hustle, but she's stealing all the attention away from my beloved Joe!

@Sprinkle-Ella: JOE! Cue the sigh… Love him :)

@TheBakingBandit: I was sucked in by that smile and I'm not even sorry!

@TheGourmetGoddess: Smile?! Did you see his petits fours in the second episode? They were perfect. The layers, the edges, the glaze!

@TheBakingBandit: Can I get a hell yeah?!

@Sprinkle-Ella: Heck yeah!

Soon after, the comment thread had been overrun by granny-stans fighting the three of them and commenting about how horrible their accusations were. McKenzie closed the page—online armies were the bullying of the new age, and she didn't have time for it. Right when she'd been about to close her computer, an email popped into her inbox. *Subject: You have been invited to private chatroom by: @TheBakingBandit.*

McKenzie deleted it.

Two minutes later, a second email arrived. *Subject: You have been invited to private chatroom by: @TheBakingBandit.*

McKenzie rolled her eyes and deleted it again, thinking, *Ugh. I just wanted to make a snarky comment. We don't need to braid each other's hair.*

Then a third email came—this time with the subject, *Open me... You know you want to...* The address of the sender was @TheBakingBandit. McKenzie spared a moment to wonder how the hell the girl had found her email address, then clicked.

Dear @TheGourmetGoddess, join us on the dark side. From your new best friends, @TheBakingBandit and @Sprinkle-Ella. PS: I make a mean sugar cookie and it travels well :)

McKenzie thought about deleting it—she'd been late for work and was about to run out the door at the time— but then another invitation to the chat arrived. At first, she'd accepted just to tell them to stop harassing her. But as soon as the chat popped open, she was greeted with...

@Sprinkle-Ella: YAY! You're here :) My real name is Addy, by the way. I'm a wedding cake designer!

@TheBakingBandit: Woot woot! Thought that email might entice you! I'm Jo :) Home baker aspiring to become a pro one day!

Before she knew what she was doing, McKenzie's fingers raced across the keys. She didn't process her response until it popped onto the screen.

@TheGourmetGoddess: Name's McKenzie, French-trained pastry chef in NYC. Now back to the good stuff, what did you think about evil granny's lemon meringue pie?

@TheBakingBandit: Too much meringue!

@Sprinkle-Ella: I prefer more lemon curd, personally.

@TheGourmetGoddess: THANK YOU

The rest had been history. The private chat had been nonstop for the past two years, branching off from the show, shifting to their personal lives and work instead. McKenzie had tried to push Jo and Addy away, but she'd failed. They wouldn't let her put her walls up—they'd bulldozed right through them instead. Now, they were the two best friends she could ever imagine. Even with everything that had happened these past few days, she wouldn't change anything. And she had a feeling that if she ever had the chance to meet them in person, the same thing would happen—they'd weasel their way into her heart. They'd nestle so deep she'd never get rid of them, and she'd never want to. That was true friendship. Not catty whispers or drunken giggles, but something deep. Something real.

A familiar laugh drew her face to the open window, pulling her from her thoughts. Leo stood outside, helping a few guys lift a table. The sight of him drew her back to the night before, to being wrapped in his arms, to his soft eyes and the way they seemed to see through all the defenses, straight into the heart of her. After so many years of solitude, it had felt amazing to finally let someone in, to let him in. Now, he was all the way across the yard, out of reach, right where she'd pushed him.

Leo was joking with another man. He dropped his head back and his shoulders bounced, the picture of ease. One of the guys said something McKenzie couldn't quite make out and Leo brought his palm to his face, covering it as he shook his head.

You'd never know they were strangers, she thought, a little twinge of jealousy curling in her gut. How did he do it? Blend right in? Make it look so easy? He'd been through more horrors than she could imagine, but he still found a way to smile.

Maybe I can too.

What if she didn't push him away? Or her friends? Or the world?

What if she stopped hiding in the kitchen?

What then?

The very thought terrified her, but maybe the fear was a good thing. Maybe it meant she was alive. An idea stirred in the back of her mind—wild and crazy, just the sort of thing Jo would love.

But first, there was something McKenzie had to do, an easy step to proving to herself that she wasn't the bitch the world wanted her to be, to proving to herself that she could change if she tried. She walked out of the kitchen and down the hall, searching empty rooms until she found the three girls in matching silk robes she'd been looking for. They all glanced up with wide eyes when she walked through the door.

"Hey…" McKenzie said as her heart pounded in her chest. *What are their names? What are their names?* For some reason, Huey, Dewey, and Louie were the only things coming to mind. She shook her head. *Improvise.* "…ladies. I'm sorry about before. It's been a long couple of days, and I let the stress get to me. If you're still interested, I'd love some help in the kitchen. I'm sure your friend Alice would love to know that her best friends had a hand in bringing her dream wedding cake to life. I know if I were in her shoes, there's nothing I'd want more."

- 23 -

Leo

The wedding ceremony had come and gone, followed by a heavy-on-the-liquor cocktail hour and a cobbled-together dinner service. Beneath a carpet of starlight, a staticky old stereo system blasted music into the night. No one seemed to care that the floor rental hadn't made it in time. They danced with wild abandon on the grassy lawn, their bared feet growing slick with mud. Despite the storm and the cancelations and the stress, Leo had a feeling that this wedding would be remembered as the best night of the married couple's lives. From what he could tell, there wasn't a frown or a dry eye in the place. After all, it was the people who made the evening, not the things—a fact he couldn't ignore as his heart flipped in his chest upon spotting McKenzie through a break in the crowd.

Up until that moment, he'd been trying to convince himself he hadn't been searching for her every time his gaze scanned the celebration. It was a futile effort. Leo was like an adrift sailor setting sights on land for the first time—the sight of McKenzie filled him up, settled the nerves, and eased the tension. He didn't know how it had happened in such a short amount of time, but seeing her was like seeing home, comforting in a way he didn't know how to explain. He didn't try. He just slipped around the perimeter of the dance floor and snuck up behind her.

Leaning close to her ear, he whispered, "There you are."

McKenzie jumped a little, but the tension vanished almost immediately and she turned to face him with a wide smile on her lips—the smile he'd been yearning all day to see. "Give me a heart attack, why don't you?"

"If I wanted to do that, I would've come over here with the megaphone the best man used to give his speech."

The corners of her lips twitched even as she dryly murmured, "Ha. Ha."

"So where've you been all day?" Leo couldn't stop the words from spilling through his lips. They were supposed to sound nonchalant and slightly teasing, but there was an edge of desperation to his tone. If she heard it, she didn't say.

Instead, McKenzie shrugged. "In the kitchen. The bridesmaids wanted to help with the cake, and I didn't have the heart to say no."

Leo tossed her a pointed look and arched his brows.

"Okay, okay," McKenzie corrected and rolled her eyes. "I told them no at first, but then I changed my mind and let them help. Needless to say, it was a little slow going."

"I'll bet." He snorted. "Why the change of heart?"

"I don't know," she murmured, glancing toward the floor before looking back up and meeting his gaze with a poignant gleam in her eyes. "It seemed like the right thing to do, I guess."

Leo squinted at her, trying to read the emotions behind the words. She was trying to tell him something, in her own guarded way. He knew she was. Before he had a chance to understand, she blinked and looked out at the makeshift dance floor, clearing the expression from her face.

"Anyway," she continued, "after the ceremony, I had to go back to the kitchen to finish up on my own."

"You were at the ceremony? I didn't see you."

And trust me, I was looking.

"You didn't?" McKenzie turned toward him and lifted a single brow. "I saw *you.*"

He frowned at her teasing tone. "What's that supposed to mean?"

"Nothing," McKenzie said, unable to quite hide the humor in her voice. "I just didn't expect a Fed and former marine to turn into a blubbering baby at the first sight of true love."

He nudged her with his elbow. "Hey, that ceremony was beautiful."

"Sure, sure."

"Maybe I have allergies."

"That run on a forty-eight-hour delay? We were in the woods for days."

"Maybe I'm allergic to polyester."

"Well, then"—she paused to fake cough—"I guess it's time you know I'm allergic to bullshit."

Damn, that was a good line. He bit his lips together to keep from laughing, then countered, "I know that's not true."

"Why?" She couldn't help but take the bait.

"Because you would've killed yourself a long time ago."

She pursed her lips to hide a smile.

Ha. I got her.

"Well, I walked right into that one." McKenzie shook her head and sighed, gaze slipping back toward the dance floor.

Leo's followed. The music shifted to something slow. "You want to dance?"

Where the hell did that come from?

McKenzie must've thought the same thing. She snapped her gaze back to his, a slight panic in her eyes. "I thought you only danced to Michael Jackson songs?"

It was a lame attempt to cover up her fear. He wasn't sure why she was afraid, but the very idea of her nerves made his resolve stronger.

"Come on." Leo grabbed her hand and tugged.

"Leo, no." McKenzie dug her heels in. "I—I mean, I look ridiculous in a bloody, dirt-covered T-shirt. There's probably flour in my hair. I don't want to ruin her photos—the photographer is the only person who managed to show up. They don't want us two slobs lurking in the background."

McKenzie was right—she did have flour in her hair, but he found it painfully endearing. Compared to everyone dressed in cocktail attire, the two of them did look like slobs, but she didn't look ridiculous. Even with the bruise on her forehead, the drop of blood on her shirt, and the white powder dusting her cheeks, McKenzie was the most beautiful woman at the party. Hell, she might've been the most beautiful woman he'd ever seen, and the more he got to know her, to see beyond her looks, the lovelier and lovelier she seemed.

Of course, he didn't admit to any of that.

Instead, he lifted her hand around his neck and put his palm against her waist, gently pulling her close. "Okay, then we'll dance right here."

"Leo…" Her tone was chiding, but he ignored it.

He didn't know why she'd decided to freeze him out, but he'd grown too used to the warmth in her eyes to let her turn icy now. And he still hadn't been able to shake that image of her walking away in the arms of another man. The only arms he wanted her wrapped in were his.

"I spoke to my partner again," he said, changing the subject. "They found your friend Addison."

"Really?" McKenzie asked, gripping his fingers tighter. Beneath his palm, her pulse raced in a flurry of excitement. He took a step and she idly followed, holding his gaze. She was too focused on his words to be aware of the dance he was subtly leading her into, which was exactly what he'd been hoping. The stiffness in her body oozed away and she stepped closer, stubbornness subsiding as her curiosity took over. "Is she all right? What happened?"

"She's fine," he quickly cut in. "She's with Jo."

"With Jo?"

"Yup," Leo answered with a grin McKenzie didn't return. "The bureau took Ryder into custody a few hours ago, which is why they haven't come to get us yet. The whole department is focused on bringing him for questioning. Alive, I might add—we need to make sure the Russians don't intercept him mid-transit. I told my team that we'd be secure for a few hours and not to worry too much about us. Nate said Addison is great. A little shaken up, maybe, but alive and well and headed home." Her relief was written across her face, but there was something else too, a slight twinge of envy or maybe gloom. "I thought you'd be happy."

"I am," McKenzie was quick to reply, but that shadow in her eyes didn't retreat. "I am, really—I just, I guess I just always thought that I'd be there when Addy and Jo met, that the three of us would be together." She shrugged, glancing away. "It's stupid. I mean, my friend is safe. Of course I'm happy."

Leo dipped his chin closer, forcing her to focus on him. "It's not stupid."

She rolled her eyes. "Selfish then."

"It's human," he said, squeezing her hand. She was too hard on herself.

"You don't have to make excuses for me, Leo."

He shrugged. "Maybe I want to."

For some reason, those four words were the ones that finally made her smile. The satisfied little grin was gone as quickly as it came. McKenzie looked away as though embarrassed and dropped her head to his chest. Leo wrapped his arms tighter around her waist, holding her close as he continued to sway side to side with the music.

"Maybe this will cheer you up," he murmured into her hair. "My partner said the bureau is sending a chopper for us. I'm not entirely sure if he's pulling my leg or not."

Her muscles tensed and she stumbled on her next step. Leo held her upright as his heart thudded in his chest, waiting for her response, wondering what that little hiccup meant. Was she as reluctant to end their little adventure as he was? Was she dreading their inevitable goodbye? Or was she just afraid of heights?

"As in 'helicopter'?" she finally asked.

"That's what he said," Leo continued carefully, measuring her words and her tone, trying to decipher the meaning behind them. "They should be here soon."

"How soon?" The question came out as hardly more than air.

Leo tried to pull back, to meet her eyes, but McKenzie stubbornly kept her cheek to his chest. Had there been a slight strain to her voice? "Sometime in the next half hour or so."

"Oh."

They danced in silence, nothing but soft music and the laughter of the guests who seemed so far away. The song shifted to something faster and more upbeat, but they maintained their steady rhythm, unhurried and unchanged. Leo and McKenzie were in a different world, in their own pocket at the edge where everyone else ceased to exist. He was unaware of anything beyond the heat of her body pressing into his and the soft kiss of her breath against his neck. She slid her fingers into his hair, curling the strands at the base of his neck, sending a tingle down his spine. He ran his fingers up and down the supple curve of her back. With his cheek resting against the top of her head, the sweet scent of sugar filled his nose. He breathed deep, wanting to remember the smell, the moment, as though will alone could make it go on forever.

"Leo?" she finally whispered.

He pulled back. "What?"

McKenzie adjusted her arms, lifting both around his neck so she could stare into his eyes. Leo's hands fell to her waist and gripped her hip bones as he continued to lead her in slow circles.

"Leo, I—" She paused to lick her lips and swallow. "What happens next?"

He darted his gaze back and forth between her two irises, trying to understand what she was really asking. What happened next with her life? Would she be safe? Would she need to move? Would she recover? Or what happened next with them?

Leo took the safer route. It seemed too much to hope that she meant the latter. "Well, after the Feds pick us up, we'll take you back home. Someone will ask you a lot of questions so we can record a detailed account of what happened. They'll ask me all the same things too. I'll probably keep an agent stationed outside your building overnight, just in case. But with Ryder in custody, I don't see any reason for the Russians to come after you again. You should be able to go back to your normal life, as if the past few days never happened."

"Hmm." She blinked and looked away, into the shadows of the forest to their side.

These one-word answers are killing me.

"Of course," he couldn't stop himself from adding, a hopeful lilt to his voice, "if you're worried, I could give you my number. You can call me if you feel scared or you see something strange."

McKenzie's gaze snapped back to his. The corners of her lips lifted even as she pulled her lower lip between her teeth, biting back the smile. His abs tightened at the sight.

"I'd like that." There was an honesty in her tone he wasn't used to, a vulnerability. She wasn't teasing or playing or pushing. She was accepting him and his offer without a fight.

Leo scrunched his brows together, almost unnerved. A warmth spread across his chest. He tightened his grip on her waist and dropped his gaze to her lips before lifting it back to her eyes. "Consider it done."

"Thank you," she said and glanced away. The fingers against the back of his neck stiffened, digging into his skin. Her chest expanded as she took a deep breath, gearing up for something. His pulse raced. "Leo, there's something I should've told you earlier, before, back at the house. I— I—"

She stopped cold.

No.

Keep going.

Don't stop now.

What? What should you have told me? What do you want to say?

Her body went still, rigid and frozen, and that was when he noticed the dread in her eyes, the acute focus on something over his shoulder. Her skin was pale, drained of color.

McKenzie gasped. "Leo."

Instinctually, he pushed McKenzie behind him as he whipped around, prepared for hitmen or gunfire or a club to the head. His free hand went for the nonexistent gun at his waist—a force of habit. But there was nothing there, no one. They were alone, two dozen or so feet from the closest partygoer. He released a heavy breath.

"Wha…"

Leo trailed off as soon as he saw the orange glow reflecting off the surface of the lake. He slid his gaze across the inky black, drawn by the shimmer, back and back and back to the source. A fire raged on the opposite shore, a burning inferno of hungry flames.

- 24 -

McKenzie

McKenzie swallowed the confession on her lips as she stared into the blaze. An invisible fist gripped her heart and squeezed, bringing a painful pressure to her chest.

"Leo, is that—"

"It can't be."

"It is." There was no way to tell for sure in the dark folds of the night, but McKenzie knew that the burning house across the lake was the one they'd been in only a few hours before. She just knew it. "How'd they find us?"

The panic in her tone was obvious, and she hated how weak it sounded, but there was nothing she could do. She was so good at hiding her emotions, she didn't realize how terrified she still was until she'd seen those flames. One look and she was back in that basement, lying against a cold floor, locked in with no way out.

Those men were still after her. Despite what Leo said, they were here, across the lake, hunting her. They'd never let her get away, not until she was dead.

"Leo—"

"McKenzie." He spoke her name like an order. Two palms encased her cheeks, warm and strong and solid. Leo pulled her gaze from the flames, forcing her to meet his eyes. She lifted her hands to grip his wrists, then held on as though he were her lifeline. Strange how two minutes ago, nothing seemed more difficult than letting him in, but now she didn't want to let go. "Listen to me. No one found us. They couldn't have. There's another explanation for this."

McKenzie shook her head as she swallowed the knot in her throat, unable to speak.

"Breathe," he demanded.

She sucked a shallow breath through her lips as her chest quivered.

"Look at me and breathe."

McKenzie studied his hazel eyes as she took another breath, longer and deeper this time. Those golden flecks in his irises brought her back to earth. Her heartbeat slowed. He rubbed his thumb across her cheek, not letting go but loosening his grip. His features softened.

"It's probably not even the house we stayed in," Leo offered in a soothing voice.

She shook her head, irrationally convinced. "It is."

"We could've left a candle on."

"We didn't," McKenzie countered, unable to stop herself from arguing. She wanted the truth from him—she needed it. "I double-checked—no, triple-checked—every candle before we left. I don't miss details like that, Leo. I carried a cup of water with me and put a little on each wick, just in case."

"That was thorough of you," he murmured wryly.

She glared up at him.

"Okay, okay." His brows scrunched together, bringing a wrinkle to his forehead. "The power's been out all day. A downed line could've easily started a fire."

"Do you really think that's what happened?"

He hesitated.

That brief pause told her everything she needed to know. Before he had a chance to respond, McKenzie jumped back in. "I thought you said it was over."

"It is," he reaffirmed, not an ounce of doubt in his tone.

But McKenzie couldn't help it as her gaze slid sideways. His palms fell to her shoulders as her focus landed on the orange glow turning brighter and brighter with each passing second. Other people at the wedding had noticed too—some pointed, some stared. A shadowed figure ran toward the house, presumably to call for help from somewhere quiet. In the back of her mind, a million questions spun, a vortex spiraling more and more out of control. She had no idea how much terror she'd been suppressing until it was all thrown right back in her face with nowhere to hide. Why did they want her? How had they followed them through the woods? Through the storm? Why a fire? Why now?

"Could they have had a tracker on me or something?" McKenzie turned back to Leo just in time to see the muscles in his jaw clench tight. His gaze wasn't on the burning house—his face was lifted toward the dark sky. "Something that might've fallen off when we ran inside during the storm? Something I left behind by accident?"

"Maybe"—he met her stare with a grin—"if my name were James Bond and we'd stumbled into the middle of a soviet-era spy thriller."

"Leo, I'm serious."

He dipped his chin and squeezed her shoulders, trying to infuse some calm. "So am I. This isn't a movie—a device like that, I mean, it would have to be really advanced technology to go unnoticed by me or by you. I'm talking CIA-level stuff, not something the mob would have access to."

"But it's possible?"

"Anything's possible." He paused to sigh, flicking his gaze up toward the sky for a second before returning it to her. "But is it plausible? The most obvious answer is usually the right one. And what's more likely? That the Russian mafia used some sort of microchip tracker to follow your location, or that a downed high-voltage power line sparked and set something on fire?"

Well, when you put it that way…

"Listen, McKenzie," Leo said, his voice hurried for a reason she didn't quite understand. "You have every reason to be scared, after everything you've been through, but I promise nothing will happen to you. You're safe now. I'll keep you safe."

She couldn't help but get the sense that there was a deeper meaning to his words, something she didn't quite grasp, as though maybe he wasn't just talking about what had happened in these woods, but about more. She'd been alone and terrified for so long, unaware of how much she'd yearned to be saved until he'd come into her life and offered one fleeting glimpse of another life, a happier one, full of laughter and smiles and, dare she think it, love.

Love?

The thought had blossomed as he'd spun her in his arms, and now it stirred again as she stared into his eyes. Before the fire had snatched her attention, she'd been gathering the courage to tell him how she felt. That she'd loved spending time with him. That she'd loved getting to know him. That maybe, just maybe, she'd loved him. But it wasn't possible, was it? To fall in love so fast? To tumble head over heels in one perfect evening?

"Leo," she whispered, trying to find her courage. Inside her chest, her heart pounded like a jackhammer trying to break through her skin. The thudding was so overwhelming she heard it in her ears, a hum that grew louder and louder and louder.

Wait…

She started to lift her gaze, but Leo's fingers dug into her shoulders, drawing her back. "What?" he pleaded. "What?"

"I—"

McKenzie broke off as floodlights stole her sight, painful and blinding. She stepped back and threw her elbow up to shield her eyes as the realization hit. The sound hadn't been her heart. It had been a helicopter. Her rescue team was finally here, one moment too soon—or maybe they'd been right on time. The spotlight was a reality check that slammed into her like a freight train, knocking her from the clouds and sending her back down to earth.

Oh my God, was I really about to tell him I loved him? Mortification struck like an arrow to the heart. *Jesus, McKenzie. Get it together. You were both drunk. You were high on adrenaline. Hell, you had some twisted form of Stockholm syndrome from being trapped inside by the storm. That was not love.*

Leo cursed under his breath and looked up, motioning with his arms. A few seconds later, the brilliant beam slid behind them and shifted over the grass, moving toward the open area on the opposite side of the lawn, away from the party. McKenzie and Leo were cast back into the shadows, but the damage was done.

"What did you want to tell me?" Leo asked, dipping and shifting his head to try to catch her eyes, but McKenzie stubbornly stared at the dirt beneath her feet, feeling a kinship with it she'd never felt before.

"Nothing. Don't worry about it."

He reached for her hand and gently brushed his thumb across the backside of her palm. "Please tell me. It seemed important."

McKenzie looked up and met his pleading eyes, plastering a smile to her lips she didn't feel. "It really wasn't."

John interrupted as he ran over from the dance floor, saving her from having to say anymore. "Is that helicopter for you? I thought you were waiting for some friends to pick you up?"

Leo held her gaze for another moment, a deep knot in the center of his brow. Then he turned, bringing a smile to his lips as he wiped the disappointment from his face. They were both so adept at pretending, McKenzie couldn't help but wonder what, if anything, had been real.

"Those *are* my friends," Leo said, playing into the awe still glued to John's face.

"I need to get me some better friends. Are you guys secret millionaires or something?"

"Nah," Leo answered smoothly. "I just know the right people."

"Alvarez!" a man shouted from across the field. He ran over, decked out in a bulletproof vest with a gun in his hand. John's eyes widened.

Leo spun. "Tommy!"

They shook hands eagerly, and then Tommy turned to her. "You must be McKenzie."

"Apparently, my reputation precedes me," she murmured and shook the hand he'd offered.

"You have no idea," the agent commented, then turned back to Leo. "We thought you guys were dead. You've been dark for three days. What the hell happened?"

"You people have no faith." Leo shook his head, then nudged his chin in the direction of John, who still lingered by their sides. McKenzie was starting to fear his eyes had been permanently frozen in a shocked position. "I'll tell you on the chopper."

Tommy's gaze flicked to John, then back to Leo. He nodded and lifted his fingers to his ear. "The boss wants me to remind you this chopper is costing the department a fortune. Don't dillydally."

Leo snorted. "Tell him I said I missed him too."

The two agents grinned at each other.

McKenzie watched from the sidelines, feeling as though a dam had broken somewhere and life was rushing back so fast she might drown. She'd stopped seeing Leo as a Fed, as one of them. He'd become Emilio, the rugged knight in shining armor, and she'd been the princess in her ivory Upper East Side tower. Now the truth oozed through the cracks he'd created in her shields, sealing them back up. He was one of them. She was still the daughter of a wrongfully convicted felon. The dream she'd been living and the reality she'd forgotten fused together, at war. The pieces didn't fit.

Leo said something to John and they both laughed. Then he put his hand to her lower back, nudging her forward. Tommy chatted about something, but she didn't process his words. The world was a blur. McKenzie went through the motions as her mind fought for clarity, walking where she was led, numb and robotic.

"McKenzie!" Leo's voice broke through the haze.

She looked up. "Huh?"

They were standing next to the helicopter, and her whisper was immediately lost to the wind as the blades spun overhead, thunderously loud. A warm jacket rested over her shoulders, though she wasn't entirely sure how it had gotten there.

"Ma'am?" another voice called.

McKenzie turned her face toward the sound, realizing a man was offering his hand. She took it, then let him pull her up and through the door. A pair of headphones slid over her ears, blanketing the world in an eerie calm. Leo jumped inside and buckled himself into the seat by her side. His hand came to her knee and squeezed once in a reassuring fashion, but she didn't meet his eyes.

"Is Ryder secure?" Leo's voice crackled through the headphones.

"He's in transit to Washington."

Leo nodded. She could feel his gaze trace the line of her jaw, but she continued to stare out the window, watching the helicopter blades spin faster and faster.

"Is he talking?"

"Not yet," another man answered. "We're working on a deal."

"It's only a matter of time."

"He's got nowhere left to run."

"We caught the bastard."

Is this how the men who arrested my father spoke? McKenzie couldn't help but wonder as she hugged her arms around her waist, pulling the jacket close. It was the middle of the summer, but she felt cold. *So cocky and so casual as they ruin a man's life?*

Leo wasn't like that. She knew she wasn't being fair, but it was easier to group them together, to push him away. Turned out bravery, at least the emotional kind, wasn't quite her forte. Instead, she shrank into her seat, trying her best to melt away. The blades spun faster and faster, until just like that, they were airborne. McKenzie watched the ground retreat, growing smaller and smaller, until the wedding was nothing more than a bright spot amid a sea of darkness. From up here, the woods that had loomed so large were nothing more than an indistinct carpet of shadow. The fire that had seemed so menacing flickered like a simple tea light. She willed her memories to do the same, to shrink and wither and fade away, until the grip they held on her heart stopped hurting so much.

"Are you okay?" Leo's voice drew her gaze from the window.

"Yeah." McKenzie finally met his eyes, wondering if he could see the silent goodbye hidden within her own. "I'm fine. I'm just excited to go home."

Then she crossed her legs, so he had no choice but to pull his hand away, and shifted toward the window. Returning her focus to the dark night outside, she tried her best to leave everything that had happened there behind her.

- 25 -

Leo

Leo reached for the phone on his desk, but halfway there, he let his hand drop with a thud against the heavy wood surface. A moment later, he lifted it...then put it down. He tapped his fingers and forced some air through his gritted teeth, then grabbed the bright red stress ball sitting behind the keyboard. Pushing off the ground with his feet, he swiveled toward the wall and threw the ball. He caught the rebound, then threw it again, then caught, then threw, repeating the motion for he didn't know how long, until someone finally told him to politely shut the F up. He jerked in his seat and promptly returned the ball to its spot, then stared at the phone some more.

I should call her. I should definitely call her.

I should—

What am I saying? I can't call her.

Of course I can't call her.

I—

Leo growled under his breath and leaned back in his chair, pushing off with his toes so it bounced back and forth as he ran over the list one more time.

Reasons to call her?

There's only one—I want to.

Reasons not to call her?

She never actually gave me her number—I stole it from a federal database. We've only been back in New York for two days, so I'll definitely come off like a desperate stalker. Oh, and there's the fact that even though I gave her my number, she hasn't tried to call me. Not once, at least since the last time I checked five minutes ago. So, yeah. That's a pretty clear sign she doesn't want to see me.

Leo sighed and tapped his fingers on the desk again.

What to do? What to do?

He reached for the phone and dialed before he could stop himself.

"Leo!" Manny's voice was frustratingly cheerful as he answered the phone. "What's up, big bro?"

"How's Hawaii?"

"Oh, terrible. Just terrible. Worst place in the world."

"How's Mom?"

"Absolutely heartbroken that you couldn't come on our brothers' trip and she was forced to take the spot instead."

"So she's having the time of her life?"

"Pretty much."

Leo rolled his eyes even as a grin came to his lips. He sighed dramatically for effect. "I'm glad someone is benefiting from my misfortune."

A deep chuckle transferred through the line, and something else too, a gentle, repetitive crashing sound.

Leo sat up. "Are you on the beach right now?"

"With a Mai Tai."

"Isn't it like"—he paused to glance at the clock, doing the math—"9 a.m. your time?"

"It's five o'clock somewhere, bro. And I only have another twenty-four hours before I fly to Hong Kong. I'm milking this vacation for all its worth."

"Where's Mom?"

"Taking a walk." He could practically hear the shrug in his brother's voice. "Last I saw, she was holding her phone about two inches from a flower, snapping a photo. I'm teaching her how to use Instagram."

"Good Lord."

"Want me to go find her?"

"No, no." Leo waved his hand through the air, as though his brother would somehow see. "I'll talk to her later."

"So, how's that work thing going? You find that girl?"

Leo pursed his lips—this, right here, was why he'd waited two days before calling his family. He never knew what to tell them, about his job or his life. He didn't want his mother to worry. He didn't want his brother to think he didn't have all the answers. He didn't want either of them to know how dangerous the path he'd chosen could be, not when it would only stress them out. But he didn't want to lie either. "Oh, I found her all right."

"What was that?"

Leo scrunched his brows. "What?"

"That voice," Manny continued, an edge of excitement infiltrating his tone. "I know that voice. That's the voice you used when Missy DaLuca shot you down for prom, when that girl who lived in the apartment down the hall—oh, what was her name? Lucia! When Lucia said she didn't think it would be a good idea to date her neighbor."

"No, it's not—"

"Wait!" Manny interrupted. The giddiness in his tone brought a frown to Leo's face. "Are *you* calling *me* for dating advice?"

"Absolutely not."

"You are! Has hell frozen over? Is the apocalypse upon us? Have I been flung into an alternate universe, or something?"

"You watch too many science-fiction movies."

"And *you* must seriously be desperate to be calling me for help."

"I wasn't calling you for help," Leo retorted, trying and failing to keep the growl from his voice. "I was calling to make sure you and Mom were okay."

"Because Hawaii is such a dangerous place."

"Hey!" His nostrils flared. "Those islands are teeming with active volcanoes."

"So, who is she?"

"I'm hanging up."

"Can I tell Mom? You know how she's always harping on one of us to give her *bebés pequeños*. Last night at dinner, all I heard was, *Nietos, Manuel. Quiero nietos.*"

"If you value your life, you'll shut your mouth."

"Ooh, I'm scared."

"Manny."

"Oh, wait. I think I see her. Mom!"

"Manny. Manny!"

With a chuckle, the line went dead.

Little shit. Leo stared at the phone in his hands with a snarl across his lips. *Oh how quickly he forgets who protected his ass throughout all of grade school. And helped him pay for college. And—* Leo released a breath and rolled his eyes. *Who am I kidding? If I were him, I would've done the exact same thing.*

Apparently, being a smart-ass ran in the family.

Leo dialed another number, stalling yet again. His partner answered on the second ring.

"So, have you called her yet?"

Jesus. Can't I catch a freaking break? "I don't know who you're referring to."

"Jo wants me to tell you to stop being a stubborn asshole."

"Jo said that?" Leo arched a brow. "Or you?"

Nate paused on the line. "Both."

"That's what I thought." Leo rolled his eyes. At this point, they were practically spinning on a nonstop basis. "What else did Jo say?"

"That she doesn't want to get involved. She's meddled too much already."

Really? Jo was a professional hacker. She'd practically made a career out of involving herself in other people's business, and yet, she chose now to stay out of it? His hour of need? "Do I need to remind her I saved her life not too long ago?"

"*I* saved her life."

"With my invaluable assistance."

"You both saved my life," a feminine voice interrupted. *Not getting involved, my ass.* "And I'm eternally grateful, Leo. Really, I am. But you and McKenzie need to figure this, whatever this is, out on your own."

Leo perked up. He'd talked Nate's ear off about the days he'd spent with McKenzie—mostly to get his help deciding what, if anything, needed to be included in the official report. In case anyone was wondering, shower sex? Not necessary. Until this conversation, Leo hadn't said a word to Jo and gossip wasn't his partner's thing.

"So… McKenzie told you about us?"

Jo sighed. "Goodbye, Leo."

A soft click came through the line. *People have* got *to stop hanging up on me at pivotal moments in the conversation.*

"That wasn't a no," he murmured.

"I thought you weren't calling about McKenzie," Nate muttered, undeniable mocking in his tone.

"I wasn't," Leo answered immediately. His partner scoffed. "No, really. I was calling to ask if you'd seen the report on the address I gave you, the house where I found McKenzie."

"Yeah, I read it."

"And?"

"Seems odd she'd be taken to a house in the Catskills that just happens to be owned by a corporation the FBI has never heard of before."

Thank you! Leo leaned toward his desk, opening the document on his computer. The fire that had spooked McKenzie had in fact been electrical, and the burning house had been two doors down from the one they'd spent the night in. Yet, even still, an annoying tingle pricked at the back of his mind, whispering that something wasn't right. "That's what I told the boss. He agreed—the whole situation doesn't smell right. He's getting the tech team to dig deeper, but I have no idea how long that'll take or if they'll need to get warrants."

"What's your gut telling you?"

That I should call McKenzie... "That I'm missing something."

"We've never seen the Russians use a shell corp with that name before. Maybe it's a new alias?"

"Maybe..." Leo frowned.

"Do you think we're looking in the wrong place?" Nate asked, tone shifting. "What if everything that happened to her is unrelated to our investigation? It's not likely, but it's possible. Worse coincidences have happened."

"But if it's not the Russians, who else would it be?"

They both paused to sigh.

"I might have an idea." Jo slipped softly back into the conversation.

Leo couldn't help but snicker. He dropped his head into his hand, trying to muffle his laughter. Of course she hadn't hung up.

"Jo!" Nate snapped.

"What?" She didn't sound the least bit apologetic.

"How do you even know about this? It's confidential government information."

"I thought you wanted me to see," she retorted, sounding shocked. "You left the document wide open on your laptop, which you left sitting out on the kitchen counter, in the middle of my domain. I mean, I only have so much self-control, especially when it concerns my friends."

"Good to know you take FBI security precautions to heart, Parker," Leo interjected.

He could perfectly envision his buttoned-up partner pinching the bridge of his nose with an exasperated expression written across his face. But Jo was Jo, reformed criminal or not. Hacking was in her blood.

You can take the girl out of the life, but you can't take the life out of the girl. Leo, for one, wasn't complaining. "What'd you find, Jo?"

"Don't encourage her, Leo."

"I found a name. Not sure who he is, you called before I could dig any deeper."

"What is it?"

"Henry Waineright."

Leo hastily jotted it down and double-checked the spelling.

"I'm going to pretend I didn't hear any of that," Nate murmured as soon as Jo was done rattling off letters. "Jo, please get off the phone—for real this time."

"Okay, I will."

"We're going to have a conversation about professional boundaries later."

"Can't wait," she murmured wryly.

"Do I need to remind you of the terms of your plea deal?"

"No…" She sighed. "I love you."

"Love you too."

The phone *click*ed.

Leo tried to wipe the silly grin from his face, then remembered that Nate couldn't see it, and left it alone. "That was adorable, Parker."

"Shut it, Leo."

"No, I mean it. I get all warm and fuzzy thinking about you two crazy kids."

"Would you like me to call McKenzie and tell her you've been moping around for two days like a preteen with a crush, agonizing about whether or not to call her?"

Leo sighed. *Leave it to Nate to suck the fun out of things.* "Point taken."

"Good. Now, is there something else you want to talk to me about?"

"Actually, yes." Leo took a deep breath, licking his lip as his stomach made a little leap up into his throat. He'd been delaying the conversation for two days, but this morning, he'd woken up on the floor of his hotel room with the sheets twisted like a snake around his limbs, and he'd decided he'd finally had enough. If his time with McKenzie had taught him anything, it was that maybe it wasn't the worst thing in the world to ask for help. "I know you're on medical leave right now, or well, you're supposed to be, but did you mean it when you said you wanted to take a step back for a few months? Take a desk job? Focus on paperwork?"

Nate waited a moment to speak. "You want a new partner?"

"No!" Leo quickly interjected. "Hell no, Parker. You're stuck with me."

"It's okay, Leo. I get it. Just because I want to take a little break doesn't mean you do too. I understand."

"No, that's not— I didn't mean—" He sighed. "I was thinking a little downtime might come in handy. I— I— " *Just spit it out.* "I was thinking I'd maybe go talk to that counselor, the one the boss made you go see after everything in the Bahamas."

"Oh," Nate chirped, taken aback. "Yeah? I think that's a great idea."

"Yeah?"

"Yeah."

It was the closest they'd ever come to talking about Leo's night terrors, and it hardly counted as a conversation. But he knew his partner. They didn't need to say a lot to mean a lot—sometimes it was all about what went unsaid—and he'd be forever grateful for the acceptance and understanding in Nate's tone.

"You want me to make a referral for when you're back in DC?"

"I'd appreciate it. I'll be back next week."

"Consider it done."

"Thanks, Parker."

"No problem." His partner coughed, clearing his throat. "Call me if that name comes up with a hit, okay? And don't tell Jo I said that."

Leo shook his head. "Bye, Parker."

They hung up and his gaze immediately dropped to the name he'd scrawled across a piece of paper. Before he knew what he was doing, he'd typed it into the federal database and run a search. Using Jo's information wasn't technically legal, per se, but he found when it came to McKenzie's safety, he was willing to blur the lines.

Okay, Henry Waineright. Who the hell are you?

- 26 -

McKenzie

McKenzie stared at the business card burning a hole through her coffee table and read the words again. *U.S. Department of Justice. Federal Bureau of Investigation. Emilio T. Alvarez. Special Agent. Cell—*

She cut off there, same as always.

If she didn't read the number, she wouldn't know the number. If she didn't know the number, she couldn't call the number. If she couldn't call the number, she wouldn't make a total ass out of herself calling a guy who'd probably only given her his number out of professional courtesy. He'd said, *in case of emergency.*

Well, no.

His exact words had been, *Here's my number, in case of emergency. Or anything really. I'll be in New York for another week or so before I head back to DC. So, yeah…here.*

But still, she doubted the fact that she couldn't for the life of her stop thinking about him would be considered an emergency. A pain in the ass, sure. An emergency? Not likely.

Gah!

McKenzie dropped a magazine over the damn thing, but it was like a sixth sense she couldn't shake. The back of her neck tingled with the knowledge of that stupid business card and all the possibilities it entailed.

What would I even say? Oh, hi, Leo. How are you? Yeah, I'm good. No one tried to kidnap me today, so, you know… McKenzie dropped her head against the back of the couch, cringing. *Just shoot me now.*

What she really wanted to say—what she was terrified she would say if she actually spoke to him—was, *Hey, Leo. I know you're going back to DC in a week, and we'll probably never see each other again after that, but, well, the sex was good. The sex was great. And I just thought, while you're in town, it'd be a damn shame to let so much chemistry go to waste. I have a shower in my apartment that's never been christened, so…*

She winced and sat up. *No. Clean break. We had a clean break. Don't muddy the waters any more than they already are. We said goodbye. He's leaving. I should flush that stupid card down the toilet.*

But she didn't.

And she knew she wouldn't.

McKenzie sighed and reached for the remote. The television sparked to life, a perfect distraction. She only needed to make it another hour or two before she left for work, and then the kitchen would be so busy she wouldn't have time to think. Just one more hour—

Her phone buzzed. McKenzie practically fell off her couch as she dove for the device and slid her thumb across the screen to read her message.

@Sprinkle-Ella: Is there a safe laxative I could slip into some cookies to give the paparazzi stationed outside my apartment? Not anything that would inflict permanent damage… Just enough for a few hours of peace?

@TheBakingBandit: OMG you're diabolical…I love it!

@Sprinkle-Ella: Let's just say it's been a long couple of days ;)

Ain't that the truth, McKenzie thought as she stared at the screen. *And I didn't even have it as bad as Addy.*

Her friend's story had gained nationwide popularity and was being covered by all the major media outlets. Compared to that experience, McKenzie's welcome home had been relatively tame. Since Leo had gone missing as well, the Feds tried to keep the story under wraps. A local New York City news station covered her kidnapping, but without the FBI revealing the flashy headline-making details—like Russian mobsters, and her possible connection to the missing Degas, and her friendship with Jo and Addy, who'd both been all over the news—no national stations had bothered to pick it up. There were no paparazzi hunting her down, no reporters chasing her outside her home, no grainy photos of her posted online—*thank God!*

The most unusual thing that had happened since she'd come home was the big movie-style hug she and her mom had shared as soon as the helicopter landed in New York City. McKenzie had audibly gasped when she'd spotted her mother standing uncomfortably beside a row of agents, staring up at the helicopter as it made its descent. One of the Feds noticed her reaction and told her the whole story—how her mother had shown up at the office immediately after being told McKenzie had gone missing, how she'd demanded a spot to sit so she could get updates in real time, how she'd stayed in a hotel across the street for days, how she thought they were all miserable displays of human intelligence for not locating McKenzie sooner, and how she was happy there was at least one agent in the entire FBI who wasn't a useless lout. Leo had smiled at that last part. Apparently, Elizabeth Harper had come to be known as the bane of their existence. The very idea had warmed McKenzie's heart. For the first time in her life, she had that wonderful, elusive awareness of her mother's love. She'd come into the city—she *hated* the city. She'd spent days around federal agents—she *hated* federal agents. She'd slept in a hotel all the way downtown—she *loathed* downtown. It all boiled down to one thing—she loved her daughter, and she'd been terrified of losing her.

As soon as McKenzie had set foot on land, she'd run for her mom, who flung open her arms, and they'd collided. About thirty seconds later, they remembered who they were. McKenzie pulled back and swallowed. Her mother told her she looked a fright and should come home with her to take a hot shower. But the love remained—the awareness that even if they didn't always know how to show it, they felt it, and maybe in the end, that was more important.

@TheGourmetGoddess: I've got a better idea. Does your apartment building have a front lawn or garden?

@Sprinkle-Ella: Yes...

@TheGourmetGoddess: Ask the manager to turn all the sprinklers on next time they're outside :) Goodbye cameras, hello privacy.

@TheBakingBandit: I don't think I've ever been so proud!

@TheBakingBandit: Oh, I've got it. If you give me some time, I might be able to hack into the town mainframe and override the system to turn all the sprinklers in town on, so they'd have nowhere to run. There's a public park across from your bakery, right? There's got to be a central database with a timed watering schedule... One sec.

@TheGourmetGoddess: Jo?

@TheBakingBandit: Yeah?

@TheGourmetGoddess: Dial it back.

@TheBakingBandit: Right.

@Sprinkle-Ella: Wow. I'm really happy I'm not on either of your bad sides. You might have something with that sprinkler idea though!

@Sprinkle-Ella: McKenzie's sprinkler-thing, not Jo's…

@Sprinkle-Ella: I've had enough run-ins with the law to last me a lifetime.

@TheGourmetGoddess: By that you mean none?

@Sprinkle-Ella: Exactly.

@TheBakingBandit: Good job, team!

McKenzie shook her head as she stared at the screen, remembering the realization she'd had back at the wedding—that the three of them worked well together, and could maybe *work* well together. Of course, at the time she'd been thinking of baking and not subterfuge, but same thing. They balanced each other out. Addy was a little too safe, Jo was a little too wild, and McKenzie sat right in the middle. Jo was all creativity, McKenzie was all precision, and Addy had a little bit of both. McKenzie was tough, Addy was sweet, and Jo was that little bit of spice every good recipe required. They fit. McKenzie picked up her phone and let her thumbs hover over the keyboard.

Guys. I had this wild, crazy, totally ridiculous idea while I was stuck in the middle of nowhere baking a wedding cake with a gaggle of drunk bridesmaids—we should go into business together.

She put her phone down without typing anything, the same way she had yesterday and the day before, the same way she probably would continue to do tomorrow and the day after. Because it was crazy—right?

McKenzie had just been promoted to head pastry chef. Why would she give that up to run a bakery, especially after the head chef had been so understanding? When he found out she'd been kidnapped, he didn't give the job to someone else. The restaurant brought in a temp and held the position for her until she came home. He was a great boss who wanted her to succeed. Besides, Addy lived down in South Carolina. Why would she ever want to move up north? And Jo…well, Jo would love it. And Addy too. Working with her two best friends would be so much more entertaining, so much more rewarding, than the cutthroat restaurant world could ever be. The kitchen would come alive again. Maybe she would too— which was precisely why McKenzie was so afraid to say the words out loud, to put them into the world.

They might actually come true.

Even after facing mobsters and being kidnapped and getting lost in the woods, breaking down her walls still seemed like the most terrifying prospect of all.

She felt too safe inside of them. Her loneliness had become a crutch she was too afraid to let go.

The phone rang.

Saved by the bell. McKenzie smiled with relief at the easy out and answered the call. "Hey, Mom."

"Your father's lawyer just called. He wants to have a meeting with us as soon as possible. Can you come out to the house tomorrow morning?"

McKenzie rolled her eyes. There were no pleasantries, just straight to the point. But in a way, she also appreciated it. "Is this about what happened to me? I thought you didn't say anything to Dad."

"I didn't," her mother quipped. Even though she'd only referred to him as *your father* for the past decade, McKenzie knew her mother still loved him. Why else had she stayed married to him? Why else did she speak to him on the phone once a week? Why else did she still pay for lawyers when the past two appeals hadn't even made it to court? Deep down, despite the embarrassment and the shame, her mother still had faith in her father, same as McKenzie. They were both praying for the day he got out, so he could come put their family back together. "I'm not sure what this is about. Your father and the lawyer have been meeting without my knowledge because your father didn't want to get our hopes up, but apparently, they think they've found some sort of new evidence that might bring the case back to trial."

McKenzie perked up on the couch, a fire sparking to life in her chest. "Really?"

"Something to do with new handwriting analysis something or other. It's the same theory they used before, but they think they have proof of the forgeries this time instead of just theories, enough to make a motion for a new trial."

"How?" Her heart thudded, a deep, booming pounding against her ribs. "After so much time?"

"I don't know, McKenzie," her mother said in a tired voice. "That's why the lawyer asked to meet with us tomorrow—to explain."

Right. "I'll be there."

"Does 10 a.m. work for you?"

"Yes."

"Do you want a car?"

"Public transport isn't the devil, you know."

Silence was her only answer—well, that, and the vision of the sneer she knew must've been written across her mother's face.

"Mom?"

"Let me send a car."

"I'll catch a train, don't worry."

"Just let me send the car."

"Mom—"

"Don't be so stubborn, McKenzie. I'm trying to do something nice."

"Thanks, Mom. Really. But—"

"Oh, for heaven's sake. I just spent the better part of a week wondering if you were alive. I don't need any more stress in my life. Do you know the kind of people who use public transport? No. Well, I do. And I'm sending a car—that's final."

She's worried, McKenzie realized, biting her tongue. It wasn't about appearances or wealth or society—her mother was worried. Maybe she always had been, and she'd just never known how to show it. "Okay, Mom. I'll take the car."

She left it at that, figuring that now really wasn't the time to politely inform her mother that something like eighty percent of commuters in New York City used public transport, and that it was a perfectly acceptable— neigh, preferable—way to travel. Or that she—gasp!— used the subway multiple times per day, sometimes even the bus. That was a battle for another time.

They said goodbye and McKenzie gently placed her phone on the table.

Ignoring her friends and ignoring that damn business card, she stood up and walked to her bedroom, then reached deep beneath her mattress for the shoebox stuffed all the way in the back corner. It had been years since she'd looked inside, but the conversation with her mom stirred up old hopes, as well as old fears. She pulled out the first newspaper clipping—*Connecticut Hedge*

Fund Manager Arrested for Fraud Staunchly Denies Accusations. She reached for another—*Jury Finds Charles Harper Guilty on All Charges.*

Her mother had never let her go to the courtroom—she said it was no place for a little girl. Oh, they'd had a good old-fashioned screaming battle about that, but her mother had won, as she usually did. McKenzie had sat at her window every day, watching as her mother's car pulled down the driveway and disappeared. Then she'd waited for it to return so she could pester her with incessant questions that went unanswered more often than not. The newspaper and the internet had been her prime sources of information, but she'd been too young to understand half of what she'd read. By the time she was old enough to grasp the intricacies of the case, she'd stopped wanting to. Her father was in jail, so what did it matter? At least that was what she told herself. The truth was she'd been too afraid. What if her father was lying? What if reading all the facts just convinced her of his guilt? What then? She didn't want to know. Ignorance was better, a twisted sort of bliss. So she'd boxed up all the articles and saved them for another time—a time which had, apparently, finally come.

McKenzie carefully unfolded and scanned the newspaper clipping. The prosecutor had presented a ton of evidence, most of which required a knowledge of the financial markets to understand, but the reporter believed the conviction had come down to one thing—signatures. Her father alleged his business partner had orchestrated the embezzlement without his knowledge. His business partner alleged the same thing. In the end, it had come down to whose name was on the papers—and that name had been her father's. His partner had gotten off scot free, while her father was sent to jail. She didn't need the article to remember the man's name.

Henry Waineright.

She'd seen him in their office maybe once or twice during the annual *Take Your Daughter to Work* day. He'd never come around the house and she'd never been invited to business events—they weren't for kids. When her father was arrested, she'd stolen a picture that had been sitting on the desk in his study, a photo of the two of them when they'd first opened their business. They'd been young—it was from before she was born. But she'd wanted to remember the face of the man her father believed had betrayed him.

What new evidence could there possibly be?

McKenzie dug through the box in search of that old photo, as though somehow it held all the answers the attorneys and the reporters had never had the chance to uncover.

The moment she saw it, she gasped.

It can't be.

It's not possible.

And yet, she knew it in her gut. His brown hair had been white. His pale skin had been tan. His muscles had long since wilted. But his eyes were the same—a brown so deep they were almost black. She'd never forget those eyes.

McKenzie dropped the photo.

Oh my God. He's the man who kidnapped me.

He's the man from the garage.

He's—

A knock pounded against her door, loud and demanding.

"Delivery!"

The voice was muffled and gruff.

I'm not expecting anything.

Panic zipped down her spine. McKenzie ran to the living room and grabbed her phone, no longer caring about her apprehensions.

It was already ringing.

Somehow, she knew exactly who it was. "Leo?"

"McKenzie! Listen to me—"

"Leo, someone's here."

That fist slammed against her door again.

"What? What do you mean?"

The banging intensified.

"Someone's trying to—"

The door crashed in and she screamed.

- 27 -

Leo

"McKenzie!" he shouted into the phone. No one answered. He heard thudding boots and a scream, then heavy breathing. "McKenzie!"

Nothing.

Leo turned toward Tommy, keeping the phone balanced between his shoulder and his cheek as he gripped the steering wheel tighter. "Call the boss, tell him to send backup. Someone just broke into her apartment. Call the NYPD and get local law enforcement on the scene as soon as you can. Tell them to wait for our lead. And for the love of God, turn on the damn sirens."

Done. Done. And done.

Leo pressed the phone to his ear, listening to more breathing, more steps, then the slam of a door.

"McKenzie?"

He pushed his foot on the gas, tearing down Park Avenue. There was something deeply satisfying about zipping over the speed limit and swerving between traffic as the siren wailed. They were twenty blocks away, and all the lights ahead were, for the moment, green.

"Leo?" Her voice was nothing more than a scratchy whisper. "It's not— It wasn't— It—"

"I know," he cut her off. It wasn't the Russians—it never had been. It was Henry Waineright the entire time, and he'd been too blinded to see it. Leo would never forgive himself if she lost her life because of his failure. "Where are you? Are you hiding?"

"I'm in the master bathroom. They're—" She broke off in a stilted cry as a pounding noise carried over the line. The sound made his blood boil. She was too strong to be so terrified.

"It's okay, McKenzie. It's okay. Breathe, okay? Listen to my voice and breathe. I'm on my way." He kept his voice as soothing as possible, even as fury burned beneath his skin.

"They're banging on the door."

"Is it locked?"

"I have my back pressed against it, and I'm using the tub as leverage to hold it shut. But I'm not sure..." She was amazingly composed. Pride warmed his chest. "What if they break it down?"

"Listen to me, McKenzie. I need you to turn sideways so your back isn't up against the door, okay? Can you still hold it shut that way? Use the walls for leverage? I'm almost there."

He honked the horn and let the sound linger until the cars in front of him merged left, leaving the right lane open. *Ten more blocks to go...*

"I think so—"

Pop! Pop!

Two bullets were fired, cutting her off.

There was no accompanying scream, only silence.

"McKenzie!" Leo shouted into the phone. *Fuck!* This was what he'd been worried about—keeping her back to the door left her too exposed. Wood was no match for a gun. "McKenzie!"

"I'm okay," she whispered, breathless. "It was—it was above my head. I'm wedged beneath the sink, and I'm using my legs and my hamper to help brace the door shut."

That wouldn't last very long. They'd broken her front door down to get inside, so it was only a matter of time before they broke this one down too, especially since he had a feeling they'd just blasted through the lock.

Five blocks.

Four.

"I'm almost there. Do you have any sort of weapon? Anything at all?"

"I broke the mirror over the sink when I ran inside." *That's my girl. Smart and shrewd in the face of danger.* "I'm holding two of the pieces in my hands, but I'm not sure— I've never stabbed anyone before."

"Go for the belly or the throat if you get an opening. Or stay low and slice the Achilles tendon—it'll make it impossible for them to chase after you. Do you have any idea how many there are?"

"Three, same as before. I'm not sure if they're the same guys."

Hired hands. He should've known—they hadn't acted like the mobsters he'd been trailing for years. It had been too easy to break into that house, too easy to get her out, too easy to get away. They'd been biding their time.

Two blocks.

One.

"I'm almost there. I'm turning onto your street."

"Leo," she whispered. "I—I'm scared."

The vulnerability in her voice broke his heart. "I'll sav—"

He was cut off by a round of bullets, then the crash of what he knew was the door caving in. A man shouted as though in pain—maybe McKenzie had managed to get him. There was grunting, breathing, the sound of her scream, then another deep groan.

As soon as he reached her building, Leo slammed on the brakes so hard the air burned. He tore out the door and shouted orders to the six NYPD officers gathered outside. "We have an active shooter, possible hostage situation. I want two on the front entrance to the building, two on the fire escape—I don't know where it is. Find it. And I want two with my partner and me. We're going in now."

Everyone fell in line.

It felt wrong to run headfirst into danger without Nate by his side, but Tommy was a good backup. Former military, like Leo, so there was an ease between them he might not have had with someone else. They understood each other the way only two vets could. As they waited for the elevator, Tommy tossed Leo a bulletproof vest he'd brought from the car. No one said anything—they didn't need to. They were all trained professionals, and to act otherwise would be a disservice to them. When the doors opened, they stepped inside.

Leo pressed the button for her floor and watched the numbers slowly tick up. Funny how the last time he'd stood in this very spot, he'd been tired and annoyed, unable to see past the expensive fittings and the pretentious doorman, ready to get it over with. Now, he felt as if his entire life waited on the other side of those metal doors.

They opened.

Leo's eyes immediately focused on the door hanging off its hinges at the end of the hall, but he didn't run—

he kept his composure. He wasn't alone this time. Using hand signals to communicate, he and Tommy went in first, leaving the two officers to follow as cover.

Leo heard her before he saw her.

A feminine grunt slipped around the corner, the sound of her struggling. Leo pressed his back to the wall and craned his neck to get a view down the hall, quickly analyzing the scene. A man stood by her bedroom door, attempting to guard it, but he was looking over his shoulder, mumbling something. Inside the room, McKenzie was splayed chest-down across her bed, struggling. A man leaned over her, pressing his knee to her spine to hold her down while he tied her wrists. His handgun rested on the edge of the bed next to McKenzie. A black sack covered her head. The third man wasn't within eyesight, but he was presumably still in the master bathroom where McKenzie had been hiding. Leo couldn't see that far into the room, but it was possible she'd gotten a slice in with that broken piece of mirror.

He slipped back behind the wall before any of the men had a chance to spot him. The element of surprise was all he had.

Two men in sight, he signaled. *I'll take the first. Follow behind with cover. No eyes on possible third target.*

Leo spared a moment to take a deep breath, steeling his nerves.

Then he charged.

"Drop your weapons!"

Obviously, they didn't listen. The lead man lifted his gun—it was the only thing Leo needed to see before he fired. One shot to the head. The man was down by the time Leo reached the door and ran through. The second man was too slow—his fingers fought with the rope he'd been tying around McKenzie's wrists. Leo dove, catching him around the midsection before his palm found its weapon. They slammed into a tangled heap on the floor, struggling for dominance. Shots were fired, but Leo let his training take over, focusing on his own fight, not letting anything distract him. He slammed the butt of his gun into the man's head, trying to knock him out rather than shoot him. He wanted one alive—he wanted answers. The man shook off the blow, but he was stunned long enough for Leo to roll over and secure him facedown beneath him. He grabbed the cuffs in his waistband. The man struggled, but Leo had already won. Cinching the cuffs around the jerk's wrists was just the final, satisfying blow.

"I have one target down and one target secure," he shouted to the room, not lifting off the second man's back until he spotted the gun that had fallen off the bed. Leo emptied the clip and threw the now-useless weapon onto the ground.

"Third target down."

It was done.

The uneasy knot that had been coiling tighter and tighter these past few days unraveled in an instant. She was safe. She'd be safe.

It was finally done.

Leo jumped up so fast it was a wonder he didn't get a head rush and untied the knots around McKenzie's wrists. He tugged the bag off her head, and before he knew it, she was in his arms, burying her head in his chest as she trembled and held him with all the strength she had left. One of his hands gripped her waist. The other dug into her hair.

"Shh," he whispered, pressing his lips to her forehead, because he couldn't keep from touching her. She didn't seem to mind. McKenzie melted against him as he ran his fingers through her hair. "Shh. It's okay. I'm here. It's over. It's over."

He didn't know how long they sat in the middle of that bed, separate from the rest of the world, before McKenzie finally found the strength to lift her head and meet his eyes. She sniffled, trying to stifle her tears. "You want to know something crazy, Leo?"

He drew his brows in. *Crazier than this? Two dead bodies, and hitmen, and bullets flying all over?* "What?"

McKenzie swallowed. Her eyes narrowed, as though she was trying to make sense of her own thoughts. "I knew you'd come."

"Of course I came."

"No," she said with a slight shake of her head, her voice laced with yearning. There was something important she wanted—no, *needed*—him to understand. They were back in that dark house, surrounded by candlelight, the only two people in the world, baring their souls—except this time, the bright light of day reflected off her irises. "Before you called, before we spoke, before you got here, I just knew. The second I realized who was after me, I knew you'd stop them. I knew it like I know the sky is blue, like I know the grass is green, like it was an undeniable truth. I knew you wouldn't abandon me. And I don't think I've ever felt that way before, Leo. Not with anyone in my entire life."

He didn't know what to say—his throat was too clogged to speak. Instead, he brought his hand to her cheek and ran his thumb along her skin.

"Isn't that crazy, Leo?" she whispered, uncertain.

"No," he murmured back, a simple response, but it was the only one she needed to hear. All the doubt fled from her gaze, replaced with something so pure and so brilliant, he was sure he'd been ruined for all other eyes. None would measure up to those blue pools staring up at him, wide open for the first time, so deep he feared he'd drown within their depths. "I don't think it's crazy at all."

And then he kissed her.

The second their lips touched, he knew his world would never be the same. It was as if every kiss he'd previously experienced had been in black and white, like Dorothy before she got to Oz, barren of the essence of what made life worth living. He'd shut himself off from the world for so long, he'd forgotten what he'd been missing. Here, now, with McKenzie, he was seeing in color. She reached up, he leaned down, and they met in the middle, colliding in perfect harmony, the most wonderful sort of chaos. He realized in that moment that he didn't need to keep proving to the world that he was a hero, someone good, someone different from his father. One person's faith, if it was the right person, was enough.

A gentle cough interrupted their kiss.

He ignored it.

The cough grew a little louder.

He didn't want this moment to end.

"Alvarez!"

At the sound of the boss's voice, Leo jumped about five feet in the air and probably lost about five years of his life in the process. He spun so fast he feared he might have whiplash. At the sight of Tommy standing along in the door with a phone in his hand and a wide grin across his lips, Leo deflated.

Behind him, McKenzie snickered.

"Jesus," he muttered. "I thought he was actually here."

"I heard that," the boss said, voice booming from the phone. "What exactly were you so worried I'd see?"

He gulped. "Nothing, sir."

"Good. Get your ass down to the field office immediately. I've got Elizabeth Harper on the other line, biting my ear off about her daughter. Apparently, the doorman tipped her off, and she wants answers. I'd like to give them to her before she rips my balls off and feeds them to me on a silver fucking platter. Understand?"

That's an image I really didn't need put in my head. Leo glanced over his shoulder toward McKenzie, who pursed her lips to keep from laughing. "Understand, sir."

"And drop Miss Harper off at the Four Seasons on Fifty-Seventh Street on your way downtown. Her mother bought her a hotel room for the night and told me to tell you to tell her that she's sending a car tomorrow to bring her home to Greenwich because she doesn't want her spending another day in that godforsaken hellhole of a city. Can't say I disagree."

Leo couldn't help but grin as the smile vanished from McKenzie's face and she muttered, "Good Lord."

How do you like it?

"Will do, sir."

The boss hung up.

Tommy shrugged with an apologetic expression and slipped the phone back into his pocket. "Crime-scene investigators are on their way. The coroner too. I'll stay here to wait them out. The cops took the third guy to the local precinct for questioning."

Leo's gaze dropped to the floor and landed on the lumpy white sheet by the door that was splotched with a big red spot of blood. He knew there was a body beneath it, a body he'd shot, and a second one somewhere else. They'd need to take pictures and prints, eyewitness reports. McKenzie's apartment was about to become a zoo, and he needed to get her out of there before that happened. He turned around to offer her a hand, noticing her cheeks had gone pale. Her eyes were pointed toward the ground. Leo grasped her limp fingers and pulled her to her feet, then gently guided her from the room. He tried to block the wall with his body as best he could, but the blood spatter was unmistakable. So was her shiver. He put his arm around her shoulders and held her close, wishing there were more he could do. But the second those men broke in, they'd ruined her home for her, her safe space. It would never be the same again.

He decided right then and there that her silence truly was the worst sound in the world, and this time was even worse than before. The absence haunted him as he led her down the hall, into the elevator, and out the front door. All he wanted to hear was her laugh. All he wanted to see was her smile.

"You know," he said when he couldn't take it anymore. They were in the car, easing from the curb.

"Next time you want to see me, you can just ask. I'm flattered you keep finding these really over-the-top ways to get my attention—thrown in the back of a van, locked in a basement dungeon, broken ankle in a storm, second attempted kidnapping—but a simple phone call would suffice. I didn't grow up like you did. I'm not that fancy."

McKenzie turned toward him with a sly smile as her cheeks flushed with newfound life. "Now that you mention it, how exactly did you get my number?"

Shit. He stiffened. He'd forgotten that part. *Play dumb.* "What do you mean?"

"You called me?"

"Did I?"

She tossed a sidelong glance in his direction.

Leo shrugged. "It's standard FBI procedure to get contact information for recent kidnapping victims. Must've been in your file."

"Mm-hmm, sure."

Abort, he thought with a swallow. *Denial isn't working. Time to go on the offensive.* He knew just what to say. "Hey. Now that *you* mention it, why didn't you call me?"

McKenzie snapped her face forward and lifted her fingers to scratch at the back of her neck. "You said in case of emergency."

"No," he countered. "I said in case of emergency, *or anything really.*"

"Right, like in case I saw anything suspicious, in case I thought I was in danger—"

"In case you were bored and wanted to go out for dinner. I heard from the guys there's a great Thai restaurant around the corner from your building."

McKenzie stared at him blankly, then scrunched her entire face in frustration. "Well, why the hell didn't you just say that before?"

"Why didn't you call and ask?"

"Well—" She broke off with a sharp exhale and glanced out the window. Leo flicked his gaze to the side, watching her intently. She sighed and turned to find his eyes. "Well, maybe I was scared."

He reached across the seat and cautiously laced his fingers through hers. "Well, maybe I was too."

"Praise the Lord," she muttered as she tightened her hold and pulled their clasped palms onto her lap. "We actually agree on something."

"It's about damn time."

They grinned.

The celebration was short lived as he pulled up outside the hotel where McKenzie would be spending the night. Through the glass doors, he could make out glossy marble floors and a massive flower arrangement that probably cost more on its own than his entire stay at the hotel he'd been assigned downtown. *Gotta love that government budget.*

He knew it didn't make sense—that he had a great job, and solid savings, and a position in society that demanded respect—but still, he didn't feel as though he belonged here. Not the same way McKenzie did as she slipped out of the car without a moment's hesitation, without even a goodbye.

She glanced over her shoulder. "Aren't you coming?"

"Didn't you hear my boss? I need to get my ass to the field office."

She rolled her eyes. "Well, I know that. But don't you want a key to the room?"

He froze, tilting his head as he eyed her and arched a brow. "Do you want me to have a key to the room?"

"I thought we just went over this?"

"Did we?" *I feel like I would've remembered that conversation.*

"Didn't we?" She shook her head. "Leo, in the name of being brave, I'm going to say this one time and one time only. I like you. And you're leaving at the end of the week, so I feel like it would be advantageous to us both to make good use of the time we have left before you do. So…" She dipped her chin, staring at him hard, as though silently adding, *Do you understand what I'm trying to tell you?*

Do I? He wanted to be sure, because he had a feeling that once they started down this road, there'd be no turning back. At least for him, and he had to know if she was ready to take that leap too. He'd been a marine, and now a Fed, but asking this question still for some reason felt like the bravest thing he'd ever done. "And what about after this week?"

"After…" McKenzie trailed off, glancing up toward the sky. His chest clenched. He didn't breathe until she looked back at him, eyes glittering with humor. "After, we do what everyone else in the world does. We figure it out as it comes."

That was good enough for him.

Leo shifted the car into park and got out. McKenzie took his hand as the butler opened the front door of the hotel. They walked in side by side. By the time he left, he had a key burning a hole in his suit pants and a mind full of all the things he planned to do to her later.

Later.

He sneered as he eased the car from the curb, heading downtown. Was there a more frustrating word in the English language? All he wanted to do was turn the car around, race up to that hotel room, and give the word *now* a new meaning. Or maybe the word *yes*. Or maybe—

The phone in his pocket buzzed.

Thank God for a distraction. He needed to cool his jets, get to the office, and interrogate the suspect to make sure no one came after McKenzie again. Then he needed to find this bastard Henry Waineright and give him a piece of his mind. After that, they could have all the *later*s they'd ever need.

He pulled his phone out of his pocket and stared at the screen. It was a message from an unknown number—well, unknown to his phone, but after staring at that same number for the past two days, he had it memorized.

There's a nice big bed… McKenzie texted.

He growled under his breath. *This is what I get for telling her to call me.*

The phone buzzed again. He didn't want to look down, but he couldn't help himself.

…there's an even bigger shower.

Pain. He was in physical pain.

Good Lord, that woman is going to be the death of me, he thought as he honked the horn, silently thankful for New York City and all its horrible drivers. There was no better way to vent frustration. Still though, his lip quirked even as his body burned. Leo ruefully shook his head and sighed. *Oh, but what a fun demise it'll be.*

- 28 -

McKenzie

One Year Later

McKenzie leaned back in her lounge chair and crossed her ankles as she took a sip of her Piña Colada. *This is the life.* The sun beat down on her skin, turning it a nice golden tan. Waves pounded against the shore, creating a soft, soothing rhythm. She might have been unemployed and homeless, but she'd never been so relaxed in her entire life.

@TheBakingBandit: Guys...GUYS! I think I found the perfect spot.

@Sprinkle-Ella: Oooh, where?

@TheGourmetGoddess: Again?

@TheBakingBandit: I mean it this time!!

@TheGourmetGoddess: Is it in our budget?

@TheBakingBandit: Yes!

@TheGourmetGoddess: Is it in one of our preselected locations?

@TheBakingBandit: Duh...

@TheGourmetGoddess: Is it a total shithole?

@TheBakingBandit: I prefer the term "fixer upper"...

@Sprinkle-Ella: Send pictures! I'm sure it's nothing a little TLC can't fix!

It had taken McKenzie about a month to finally build up the courage to pitch the idea of going into business together, just as something hypothetical. Addy and Jo had immediately loved it. But McKenzie had just started her job as head pastry chef, something she felt she owed it to herself to give a chance. Addy was still a media phenomenon, and she'd fled the country to do some traveling while her celebrity died down. Jo was still dealing with the ramifications of her past. So they'd agreed to take six months before they even spoke about the idea again, to let it sink in, percolate, and process.

Six months later, to the day, Jo had messaged them three words—*Let's do it.* And it was done. They spent the next five months putting together a business plan. Jo would be the face of the business and would run the front of house. McKenzie would hang back in the kitchen, doing more of the daily grind. And Addy would be in charge of custom orders, specializing in cakes. They'd come up with all their recipes together, playing off their strengths, and they'd use their stories—the good, the bad, and the ugly—to gain some early publicity. At least, that was the theory. In a few days' time, they'd finally be living in the same city, ready to put it to the test. They'd be soft launching the new bakery with a food truck so they could make a little money and get the brand going before hard launching when the storefront was done…assuming they could ever agree on a spot.

McKenzie flipped through the photos of the real-estate listing Jo had sent and took another sip of her drink.

@TheGourmetGoddess: Actually, this isn't half bad.

@Sprinkle-Ella: It's GREAT!

@TheBakingBandit: Told ya :)

@TheGourmetGoddess: Let's all go take a look next week. Can you make an appointment with the broker?

@TheBakingBandit: Already on it!

"What are you so smiley about?"

McKenzie looked up to find Leo standing over her, bronze skin gleaming in the sun as water dripped down those perfectly lickable washboard abs. It was a sight she didn't think she'd ever grow tired of seeing. Then again,

Leo in a suit, Leo in sweatpants, Leo in absolutely nothing at all… She really couldn't go wrong.

Her grin widened, but he didn't seem to notice. "Jo thinks she found a place."

"Again?"

She couldn't help but chuckle. "That's what I said."

Leo rolled his eyes and tossed his towel around his neck as he sank into the lounge chair by her side. After stealing a quick sip of her drink, he reached over and laced their fingers together, letting their hands dangle between the seats. "Are you going to go see it next week?"

"After I get settled in."

Leo turned to look at her, a soft smile on his lips, a bright look in his eyes. She recognized the expression because she saw it in the mirror every morning she woke up beside him. It was a look of contented disbelief, a look that silently wondered how the hell they'd found themselves here, and at the same time thanked all the gods in the world that they had. Not on this beach per say, but together. Happy and healing and in love.

Ever since that first night at the Four Seasons in midtown, they'd been inseparable. They'd spent three blissful days holed up in that hotel room together before Leo had needed to travel back home to DC. Only he didn't. Because when he brought McKenzie back to her apartment and saw her visibly tremble at the sight of her bedroom—a place she couldn't even enter without remembering the warm blood that rushed over her hands as she stabbed a man or the pain of a sharp knee against her back while beefy fingers tied a rope around her wrists—he'd said *screw this* and stayed, calling in on some overdue vacation. They spent another ten days at the Four Seasons while she listed her apartment for sale, found a temporary rental, packed up her things, and moved. By then, after practically two weeks of living together, McKenzie was hooked—hooked on the way he looked at her, the way he touched her, the way her entire day was so much better because she knew it would end wrapped in his arms. And Leo had been too. They'd been dating long distance for the past year, but as soon as they got back from the Caribbean (they'd made a pact to save Hawaii for a future honeymoon), McKenzie would be *settling in* to his apartment.

Oh, it wasn't perfect, not by a long shot, but McKenzie was surprised to find she preferred it that way. Leo still snored like some sort of dying beast, but he promised he'd give nasal strips a try when she moved in. McKenzie was still a neat freak, though she promised she'd try not to take her own anxieties out on him. On a good night, they made love and he fell asleep curved against her back with his arm around her hip. On a bad night, she'd wake to his thrashing, or sometimes, she'd just wake alone. Since he'd started seeing a therapist, the good nights came more and more, the bad less and less.

McKenzie went with him a few times, to talk about her father, being bullied as a kid, her memories of the kidnapping. Between the two of them, they still had their fair share of demons, but they were figuring it out together. They didn't need to be perfect people, because all those sharp edges they'd been hiding from the world were what made them fit together. They were perfect for each other, and that mattered a hell of a lot more.

"Excuse me, sir?" McKenzie looked up at the sound of an unfamiliar voice. A man with the logo of the hotel embroidered onto his shirt stood over Leo. "Your tour guide is here."

McKenzie scrunched her brows. "We didn't sign up for a tour."

"Yeah, we did," Leo said quickly.

McKenzie stared at him. "No. We didn't."

"Emilio Alvarez and McKenzie Harper?" the man interrupted. "Noon island jet ski tour?"

"That's us!" Leo jumped to his feet, still holding her hand. She was pulled to a seated position, but she didn't stand.

"Leo."

"McKenzie." He had the audacity to smile.

"Leo," she said again, through gritted teeth.

The poor hotel guy started backing away. "Um, he's just down by the cabana waiting for you, whenever you're ready. Take your time."

"Come on," Leo urged and gently tugged on her hand. She didn't budge. "Don't you trust me?"

"Of course I trust you." She paused to cast a sidelong glance at the jet skis resting on the sand at the other end of the beach, the ones she'd had no idea were intended for her. McKenzie met Leo's eyes and smiled sweetly. "I just don't trust you with motor vehicles, not even the kind that are driven on water."

"It's been a year since I drove that motorcycle off the road." He rolled his eyes. "Intentionally, I might add. In order to save your life—"

"Yet, shockingly, the memory hasn't dulled with time."

He frowned at her. "You're going to have to get over this aversion eventually, you know."

"Yeah?" she countered, yanking her hand out of his so she could cross her arms. "Why's that?"

"Because your boyfriend has a need…" A wicked little gleam lit his eye, one she'd seen enough times to know she wouldn't like what was coming next. McKenzie tried to roll off her lounger, but Leo's arms came around her waist before her feet even touched the ground. Before she knew it, he'd thrown her over his shoulder as he shouted, "A need for speed!"

"Leo!"

"What?"

"Put me down."

"Why?"

"Because your girlfriend has a need to keep all of her limbs in one piece."

"McKenzie, just try," he said, not letting go, but instead marching confidently across the sand. "If you don't like it, I'll bring you back. I promise. But you at least have to try. No more running from things we're afraid of, remember?"

"I knew you'd throw that back in my face eventually," McKenzie muttered under her breath as she rolled her eyes. It was a promise they'd made each other during that first week in New York, to never let the other be ruled by fear again. Though, she didn't quite anticipate it playing out this way.

McKenzie sighed.

Leo must've sensed his victory, because he sped up as if to capitalize on her hesitation. Before she knew it, they'd reached the cabana and he set her down. The tour guided waited patiently, then started to review the safety instructions.

McKenzie tuned him out as her thoughts went back to that promise, back to Leo, back to the many ways her life had changed since he'd forced her to open herself up to the possibilities the world had to offer. There was her relationship with him, a blessing in and of itself. There was her budding business with her friends, something she never would've imagined before those fateful few days in the woods. There was her family, which was slowly piecing itself back together now that her father had a great chance of being released from jail.

It turned out the new evidence her father and the lawyer found had been significant after all—significant enough for his old business partner to shit his pants as soon as he heard the news. Thirteen years ago, before the arrests, back when Henry Waineright had learned from an inside source that the Feds were sniffing around his business, he'd hired a well-known forger from the northeastern part of the US to falsify documents in order to frame his partner for the crimes he himself committed. That forger's name was Robert Carter, a professional art thief living in Pennsylvania with his family at the time. The man had been a genius at what he did. The forgeries were undetectable, and they would've remained that way forever if his daughter, Jolene, hadn't handed herself over to the Feds over a decade later. As part of Jo's plea deal, she'd given the FBI unrestricted access to her father's files—detailed accounts of the many illegal activities he'd partaken in over the course of his life. Buried within those files, so insignificant to the rest of the world yet everything to McKenzie, were scans of the original documents from her father's company—signed by a Mr. Henry Waineright, not by Charles Harper. When Henry Waineright learned of the update, he'd tried to kidnap her as a bargaining chip to secure her father's silence. If not for Leo, it might've worked. Instead, Henry Waineright was already behind bars for extortion, kidnapping, and attempted murder, in addition to embezzlement and fraud, and a judge had granted her father's motion for a new trial. The DA were dragging their heels—they hated being wrong—but the lawyer said he was confident her father would be out before the new year.

The coincidence was almost impossible to believe. In fact, McKenzie didn't believe it, not at first, not until Leo had bent a few rules and let her read the FBI reports with her own two eyes. There'd been anger—lots of anger—and grief, too, that her best friend's father had been the one to indirectly send her own father to jail. Jo had apologized a million different ways—even now, months later, guilt still flickered every so often in her gaze—but it hadn't been necessary. McKenzie, of all people, understood. She'd spent her entire adolescence wishing people wouldn't judge her for the supposed sins of her father, so there was no way she'd force her friend to endure the same fate, especially when Jo was the only reason the truth had ever come to light, the only reason hope had found its way back into the Harper household.

McKenzie and her mother were still too similar to not fight, but they were getting better and they were trying to be more open about their feelings. Her father's voice had more life in it than she'd heard in years, an honest joy instead of the feigned positivity he'd projected for so long. McKenzie was different too, lighter, happier, freer. She could feel it.

It was like a snowball effect, in a way. One good thing happened, then another, then another, and with each roll down the hill, her walls had thinned, her heart had opened, and her life had grown, so empty and then suddenly so full she didn't know what to do with herself.

And none of it would've happened if Leo hadn't chased after her the day she'd been thrown in that van—if he hadn't decided, right then and there, that she was someone worth saving.

"You ready?" Leo asked, bringing McKenzie back to the present.

She stared at the jet ski, took a deep breath, and shrugged. "Ready as I'll ever be."

"Excellent."

Leo took her hand and helped her onto the seat. Then he hopped on, taking the spot in front of her. The jet ski revved to life. McKenzie immediately wrapped her arms around his waist and held tight.

"Admit it," she muttered into his ear as they bobbed in the water, waiting for the instructor to take the lead. "This was all just an elaborate ruse to get my breasts pressed up against you, wasn't it?"

"We both know I don't need to resort to cheap tricks to make that happen," he whispered back, looking over his shoulder to toss her a wink. "Now, hold on."

"I hate it when you say tha— Ahhh!"

Laughter rang in her ears as they took off and slammed into the crest of a wave, going airborne. She squeezed her eyes shut and hugged him closer. Leo hollered loudly, uncaring as his joyous scream got swallowed by the wind.

"Give in to the thrill, Harper!"

McKenzie shook her head against his back.

"Just once. For me."

She opened her mouth and screamed.

Wow. That actually did make me feel better.

She did it again. Leo joined in. Soon, it became a challenge—who could be louder, who could be more ridiculous, who would break first. As they raced across the surface of the ocean, McKenzie kept her arms wrapped around his waist and pressed her cheek to the angel wings inked onto his back. With her eyes closed, it almost felt as if they were flying.

My guardian angel.

He'd saved her life in more ways than she ever could've imagined—but that still didn't mean she'd let him win. McKenzie slid her hands across his chest until they were in just the right spot, then dug her fingers in deep, wriggling them against his skin.

Leo barked out a laugh, losing control of the jet ski. They went flying and careened into the water with a splash.

"Not fair," he sputtered, spitting the ocean from his lips. "That was a clear violation of the rules."

"What rules?" she countered.

"Weren't you listening to the safety instructions?"

"And..."

"And the guide clearly stated that thou shalt not tickle the driver just because *thou* was close to breaking first."

"Was not."

"Was too."

McKenzie swam over and put her hands on his shoulders, then used all of her body weight to push him under the water so she reached the jet ski before him. Leo let her, smoothly dropping down beneath the surface and disappearing. Suddenly, two hands cupped her butt cheeks from below, giving her a boost up. He took a little squeeze before letting go. McKenzie finished climbing onto the jet ski and turned around, meeting his face grin for grin.

"Couldn't help myself." He shrugged as he treaded water. McKenzie scooted forward on the seat and patted the spot behind her. Leo arched a brow. "You want to drive?"

"What? Don't think I can handle it?"

"On the contrary, this might be the sexiest thing you've ever done."

Leo climbed up in one fluid movement, like Poseidon emerging from the sea, all muscle and skin and glistening water. *That might be the sexiest thing you've ever done.* McKenzie swallowed. How long was this tour, exactly? Because her thoughts were quickly shifting in another direction. Leo mistook the pause for hesitation.

"Aren't you going to show me how it's done?" he goaded, dangling the key before her eyes.

McKenzie straightened her shoulders, grabbed the safety lanyard, and slid it around her wrist. Trying to ignore the fact that she had no idea what she was doing, she put the key in the ignition. *You've got this. You've got this.* Taking a deep breath, she squeezed the throttle. They burst forward, completely out of control, and Leo nearly went flying. McKenzie let go, alarmed. They stopped cold.

"You know," he quipped, "if you're trying to kill me, I can think of easier, less painful options."

"Leo, I—" She spun with an apology on her lips, but he was smiling.

"Come on. I'll show you how."

Leo reached forward and wrapped his arms around her as he placed his palms to either side of hers. McKenzie settled back against his chest, wondering why she hadn't suggested this before.

He whispered instructions into her ear as she slowly tested out the throttle again, more cautiously this time. After a while, they figured it out, the same way they'd figured everything else out—together.

* * *

Thank you for reading!

I hope Leo and McKenzie stole your heart, the way they did mine. If you have a moment, please consider leaving a review. Even a few words can make a huge difference in someone deciding to give my book a chance.

While this love story is complete, there are more *To Catch a Thief* adventures to enjoy!

Don't miss the other two books in the series—*Hot Pursuit*, following the love story of sexy thief-turned-baker Jo and uptight federal agent Nate, and *Stolen Goods*, following the love story of devilish thief-on-the-run Thad and daydreaming cake designer Addison.

Both are available now!

About The Author

Bestselling author Kaitlyn Davis writes young adult fantasy novels under the name Kaitlyn Davis and contemporary romance novels under the name Kay Marie.

While she's been writing ever since she picked up her first crayon, she spends more time these days with her "mom" hat on than her "writer" hat - and she wouldn't have it any other way! But she does squeeze in as much writing (and reading!) as she can. Storytelling is a vital part of who she is, and she can't thank her readers enough for keeping this beautiful dream of hers alive.

Connect with Kay online:

Website: www.KayMarieBooks.com
Instagram: @KayMarieBooks
TikTok: @KayMarieBooks
Facebook: Facebook.com/KaitlynDavisBooks
Goodreads: Goodreads.com/Kay_Marie
Bookbub: @KayMarie1